SKYWARD

Sometimes love
is the best
resistance

SUSAN WHITE

ACORNPRESS

Skyward
Text © 2021 by Susan White
ISBN 978-1-77366-078-3

Designed by Cassandra Aragonez
Edited by Penelope Jackson
Printed in Canada by Marquis

Library and Archives Canada Cataloguing in Publication

Title: Skyward: sometimes love is the best resistance / Susan White.
Names: White, Susan, 1956- author.

Identifiers: Canadiana (print) 20210243805 | Canadiana (ebook)
20210243813 | ISBN 9781773660783
(softcover) | ISBN 9781773660790 (HTML)

Subjects: LCGFT: Novels. | LCGFT: Dystopian fiction.
Classification: LCC PS8645.H5467 S59 2021 | DDC jC813/.6—dc23

The publisher acknowledges the support of the Government of
Canada, the Canada Council for the Arts and the Province of Prince
Edward Island for our publishing program.

P.O. Box 22024
Charlottetown, Prince Edward Island
C1A 9J2
Acornpress.ca

ACORNPRESS

To Burton (our Augustus)

Once you have tasted flight, you will forever walk the earth
with your eyes skyward, for there you have been,
and there you will always long to return.

Leonardo da Vinci

CHAPTER 1

EMERY LOOKED AROUND THE ROOM, moving only her eyes while keeping her head still, as a Keeper led her into the grand hall. She had never been in the Elite dining hall. She'd heard accounts from some of the others. It was usually the Olders, in the last division, who were put at the table to be tested, and as far as she could calculate, she was not yet considered an Older. But perhaps she had lost count of her years, or been too young to keep track, the fall of the first snow her only way of calculating the beginning of a new year. She also knew that sometimes the cover kept the first snow out.

Emery wasn't sure where the word *year* even came from. Some of the others used it, and those who did seemed to give age a great importance. She also knew there was a certain point when Olders were released. Where they went, Emery wasn't sure, but it always seemed they were excited about Release Day.

Emery remembered with embarrassment a time when she thought the Olders were the same as the Old Ones. Dixon had laughed at her confusion.

"The Old Ones don't live in this compound, Emery. Everyone knows that much."

"Where do they live, then, if you know so much?"

Dixon said the Old Ones lived just outside the main gate somewhere. He had never been there, but Olders sometimes got sent to look after them. Before his release, Terrance was sent there for a while, and he told Dixon a little bit about the place that housed the Old Ones. The Old Ones were kept in a building where they were fed and kept comfortable until they died. Dixon told Emery everything he knew, and since that day she had picked up more details and had a genuine interest in knowing more.

One detail intrigued Emery the most. The Old Ones in the compound outside the wall grew up in a time before the wall existed. That fact had piqued Emery's curiosity about the Before time. Emery questioned anyone she thought might have any knowledge of that time; before the walls were built. The walls contained the Establishing Compound, which was divided in two parts, one side housing the Elites the other the Less Thans from infancy to Older. The Less Than side of the Establishing Compound was all Emery knew besides the shards of rumour regarding the other side and the Old Ones' Compound.

Audrey, who cooked in the Less Than eating house, said there used to be families before the wall was built. The families had their own houses where they raised their children instead of bringing them to the Establishing Compound. Thompson, who was at least a first snowfall younger than Emery, seemed to take such pleasure in telling what he knew. Before the wall was built there had been towns, cities, even countries. Emery wasn't sure what those things were, but Thompson said they had names, boundaries, and laws, and had no real wall separating them.

The most confusing thing Thompson told her was that outside the wall there might still be families, countries, and another life entirely. There might not be Establishing Compounds, with one side holding Elites and one side holding Less Thans, everywhere.

For weeks afterwards, Emery had paid close attention to the way things were in the compound, even once walking right up to the part of the wall closest to her sleeping house. She could not reach up to the top of the wall but touched the brick and mortar, wondering what was on the other side.

Emery had been careful not to ask questions or talk about any of the facts she was learning when a Keeper was nearby. She knew instinctively that talking about outside the wall around a Keeper or an Enforcer was dangerous. And Less Thans had no business talking to the Keepers or Enforcers, except to answer obediently.

Emery had definitely not spoken to the Keeper now leading her through the Elite dining hall. She'd been finishing her morning chores and was looking forward to joining Dixon and Sadie on the walk to the eating house. After four days of heavy rain, Emery was anxious to feel the warm sun as she walked across the compound. The weather didn't often matter as the Keepers just closed the cover when it rained after letting enough rainfall in to fill the water cisterns. Sometimes it would be days before they peeled back the cover. Those days left Emery craving a glimpse of the sky above. As long as she could remember, that gaze toward the sky had filled her with a happiness like no other.

But as Emery finished her task, absorbed in the anticipation of getting outside and being able to look up, Rigley grabbed her arm, startling her, and abruptly commanded she come with him through the tunnel separating the Less Than side from the Elite side. It wasn't until they entered the Elite dining hall that Emery realized it might be her testing time.

Testing was something a Less Than learned about early on. The truth was, every day of a Less Than's life was a test of some kind. They learned early how they were to behave, when they could speak, and what was expected of them. Failure to respond in the appropriate manner resulted in adjustments that trained them for future tests. Keepers carried out the management duties, but it was the Enforcers who conducted the training and adjustments. A Less Than learned early on it was best to avoid the wrath of an Enforcer.

"Sit here," Rigley announced as he pushed Emery toward the solid wooden chair.

In the Less Than eating house, long benches were pulled up to the large tables where trays were set before each diner. The trays held sections filled with lumps of food, distinctive only by colour and a slight variation of taste. Each meal was a replica of the meal before and each portion carefully measured to provide the exact nourishment required for the weight of each recipient. Morning, noon, and evening meals were exactly the same.

Rigley pushed in Emery's chair and stepped back. Emery was overwhelmed with the plethora of sights before her. The round table at which she sat held eight other diners and one empty chair. The table was covered with a satiny white cloth and round discs set at each place. Sparkling silver tools of some type flanked the discs and glass vessels holding a sparkling liquid that reflected the overhead light.

Emery raised her eyes slightly and could see a large opening in the ceiling above. Sunlight streamed down onto the table. A colourful arrangement of flowers in a fancy glass receptacle sat in the middle of the table. She turned to see a long line of uniformed Olders each carrying a large tray. She recognized the second Older in line as Henderson. He had been in Dixon's sleeping house before being released some time ago.

Emery made no effort to acknowledge Henderson but scanned the line wondering if there were others she would recognize. She would offer no greeting, of course, but felt a twinge of excitement knowing she could tell Dixon the whereabouts of a released Older.

Smells quickly filled Emery's senses, interrupting her thoughts. She did not know what she was smelling but felt pleasure as she took in the aromas.

The diners around Emery began talking, the cacophony rising steadily. Emery could understand the words but heard them as if in a vacuum, knowing the conversation did not include her. She knew if she were to speak, Rigley would quickly remove her. There had been simulations establishing that very basic truth. Was this the test, she wondered? Would she pass the test if she just sat and said nothing for long enough?

The Olders set their trays on stands and began removing individual dishes. The aromas became stronger and words were spoken by the Olders announcing each dish as it was set on the table. Emery was trying to remember each word so she could tell Dixon and Sadie, but her concentration was broken by the booming voice of Tonka.

Tonka was the meanest of the Enforcers and Emery wasn't surprised to see he was dragging a Less Than toward the table.

"You were to wait for me, Rigley. There are two Less Thans scheduled for testing today. What were you thinking, bringing one by yourself? What if she were to fail with no Enforcer around? And you have no jurisdiction to remove an Elite if one of them fails. Tennyson must always be in attendance. The dining test is among the most important and cannot be conducted in such a shoddy manner."

A tall man approached the table and stood an arm's length away, legs apart and hands behind his back. This man was unfamiliar to Emery, but each diner turned to him with a respectful nod and a chorus of greeting.

"Good morning, Master Tennyson."

"Let the test begin," the man said, motioning toward Tonka.

Emery looked across the table at the girl Tonka had brought in. Her blond hair was tightly wound into a bun at the back of her head. She was wearing the typical garb of the Olders, the outfit they received when they entered the last division. After a few seconds Emery retrieved her name: Daisy.

Emery could not remember ever hearing Daisy speak. Less Thans remained silent in the company of Keepers and Enforcers but usually friendships and relationships flourished when they were with the others who shared their sleeping house or task assignments. Daisy completely kept to herself. She seemed at times to be invisible. It was rumoured that Daisy had failed several tests and remained in the Establishing Compound far beyond her release age.

Diners began picking up the dishes, spooning the contents onto their discs before passing each dish along to the next diner. Their exclamations of delight and anticipation for the bounty of the table were clear. She trembled with the realization that exposure to the bounty was the essence of the test. The smells, the sights, and the pleasure the Elites obviously got from the foods being served were a temptation she was expected to ignore. As with all tests, there had been no instruction, just the entrenched truth, that as a Less Than she was not entitled to any pleasure or reward.

Emery bit her lip and tried to find the place within that gave her the ability to shut herself off from the shame and humiliation of her status. Her resolve and determination would see her through. She would put the smells and thoughts of the delicious-looking food completely out of her mind. She looked quickly across to Daisy, wondering if she too had that inner place. If she did, why had she not yet been released from the Establishing Compound?

Emery was startled by the gaze of the diner sitting beside Daisy. The girl had piercing blue eyes, and as Emery looked across the table, those eyes made direct contact with her own. What Emery saw made her tear up. Kindness was in the message the gaze delivered. Emery gave the girl a quick smile hoping Tonka or Rigley would not notice the interaction.

Daisy's eyes were not visible. Her head was bowed and Emery could see she was shaking. She felt pity for this girl, who appeared to be overwhelmed by the test. How long would they require them to sit at this table before taking them back to their own side? Emery wished she had not seen the splendour of this grand hall. It was better not knowing. Emery trained her gaze downward, trying to return to the concentration that could take her from this place.

A sudden movement by the large man caused Emery to look up and take notice of the activity across the table. The blue-eyed girl was speaking directly to Daisy. Her words were muted by the noise around the table, but Emery could detect what was happening. The blue-eyed girl was offering Daisy a helping of the food on the dish she was holding. With one hand, she scooped a portion up and was waiting for Daisy's reply.

The large man was looming over the blue-eyed girl's shoulder, his face showing his severe displeasure. Tonka arrived behind Daisy. The diners became silent. Emery held her breath, wishing to freeze the moment or rewind it. Her heart beat rapidly.

Daisy looked up and spoke. "How very kind of you. I would love some."

A dollop of food dropped onto the disc in front of Daisy, but the quick movement of both men knocked the dish and spoon from the blue-eyed girl's grip and spilled the liquid from the glass in front of her. Both chairs were pulled out violently. Tonka jerked Daisy to her feet. The blue-eyed girl was removed in a gentler fashion, but the seriousness of her action was clear. Tears were streaming down her cheeks as the attendant began his barrage.

"It is unacceptable to offer food to a Less Than. You have not only shamed yourself, Victoria, but also dishonoured every Elite in the compound. The notion that pleasures enjoyed by Elites can be shared with a Less Than is an abomination counter to all you have been carefully bred to believe. Your training and indoctrination were almost complete, and your careless disregard for this basic precept undermines all your instruction. You will be removed and retraining will begin immediately."

Minutes later, Rigley pulled Emery to her feet and led her from the grand hall behind Tonka, who had thrown Daisy over his shoulder. After being removed from her chair, Daisy had forcefully seated herself again and picked up the silver tool, taking some food and cramming it into her mouth. She reached for the second bite as Tonka grabbed her arm and threw her to the floor. From her crumpled position, Daisy raised her head and stared fearlessly into the face of the angry Enforcer.

§

"She glared right at him," Emery repeated, having told the story several times to Sadie as they were preparing for lights out at the sleeping house, hours after her return from the dining hall.

Sadie hung off every word and kept asking questions about the Elite dining hall.

"White cloths, flowers, discs instead of sectioned trays? Smells with words? Round tables and individual chairs?"

"Yes," Emery had answered again and again. "Do you think I am making it all up? The dining hall was a place of sights and sounds and wonderful smells like nothing I have experienced before. But it is Daisy's courage that I can't stop thinking about. She glared right at him, at Tonka. It scares me still to think of the look she gave him. I was afraid he would strike her with a viciousness that might have brought her end. How could she have been so brave?"

"The talking will now end." The booming announcement echoed from the speaker above. *"Lights will be extinguished in two minutes. And to the Less Than number 38; tomorrow your task assignment will be replacing Less Than number 57. The incarceration of number 57 leaves a tasking vacancy. Number 38 will report to the east gate after first meal and be escorted to the compound for the Old Ones. This is a thirty-day tasking and is not to be discussed."*

The sleeping house darkened and Emery felt her way to her bunk. Emery had heard rumours of what incarceration meant and where one was taken to be punished. Emery felt fear and sympathy for Daisy. She thought of the blue-eyed girl and wondered if she too had been incarcerated. Somehow, she was sure it would not be in the same place as Daisy and no doubt would not be as severe. The large man had said retraining would occur. Was Daisy being retrained too, or simply punished? Punished, no doubt, for refusing to show fear.

Emery pulled the scratchy wool blanket up to her chin. Her mind was racing with thoughts of the day. The brief look into the extreme difference between the Less Than side and the Elite side was overpowering. Emery's curiosity after picking up snippets of truth seemed to be magnified by her brief exposure to the place where the Elites ate. Was the elaborate room she'd seen typical of the rooms and buildings in which Elites lived their daily lives?

She imagined the Elites who were bedding down for the night on the other side of the compound had not been herded into large windowless rooms to lie on narrow, uncomfortable bunks. She imagined too that whatever covered them and kept them warm was not as scratchy and unforgiving. Perhaps the pillows beneath their heads were fluffy and welcoming.

Emery turned over. Often when sleep refused to come quickly she would attempt to whisper to the others, low enough so that the monitor would not pick up the sound. There had been nights when Sadie and the other girls would squeeze in under the cots and spend hours talking and laughing, quietly of course, and those times had been such fun.

Tonight, however, Emery felt anxious and nervous and needed quiet solitude to figure out the tangle of feelings the dining test had left her with. Daisy had been tempted by the delicious-smelling food. She had allowed herself to imagine the pleasure of eating it. But even more than that, Daisy had allowed the thought that she might be entitled to enjoy it. She crossed that solid line. But there had of course been no physical barrier. Emery and Daisy had been placed at the table with the lure of smell and sight, and only training and indoctrination armed them with the tools to resist the temptation. Establishing Compound, it was called, and on the Less Than side everything came together to establish the deep belief that as Less Thans they had no right or entitlement to any pleasure whatsoever.

And what about the blue-eyed girl? She had looked right at Emery and had seen her. Was that her most serious indiscretion? None of the other Elite diners had paid any mind to them. With the simple act of a brief gaze, the blue-eyed girl had offered kindness. She may have gotten away with that, as Tennyson, Tonka, and Rigley had not witnessed the look that spoke so loudly of thoughtfulness and compassion; the fleeting look that acknowledged the very existence of a single person, a Less Than.

But the blue-eyed girl had gone further. She had moved to include and welcome a Less Than. She had offered a Less Than a pleasure. She had made a choice to share the bounty she as an Elite was simply entitled to. That action was deliberate, and in lifting the spoon and allowing herself to actually enter the space that should have been out of bounds to her, the blue-eyed girl took her compassion to another level. The action was immediately detected by the large man and once carried out could not be undone.

Daisy had calmly accepted the gesture. Emery could still hear the echo of Daisy's response.

"How very kind of you. I would love some."

Daisy's simple response said so much. She acknowledged the blue-eyed girl's kindness in a sincere manner, showing no surprise in the offering. She accepted the kindness with no trace of guilt or shame and no proclamation of her unworthiness. Daisy had accepted the food as an equal, and the blue-eyed girl had offered it as such.

These thoughts caused Emery much tossing and turning. The interaction in the dining hall had happened so quickly. The act itself seemed so small, so harmless, but the magnitude of the fury Tennyson, Tonka, and Rigley had displayed gave it an enormity that still shook Emery to the core. And the courage Daisy displayed kept coming back to the forefront of Emery's thoughts. Daisy had slid back into the chair and without fear of reprisal had taken a bite of what the blue-eyed girl had offered her. Was it the lure of taste and smell, or was it something bigger that propelled Daisy to take such a bold risk?

Was Daisy regretting her actions in these dark hours, wherever she was being held? Was she wishing she had kept her head down and ignored the gesture? Or was she filled with pride and a sense of victory, however small and inconsequential the act? She hadn't gotten away with her action, but she had made a stand nevertheless. She had definitely left an impression on Emery, and Emery's thoughts of Daisy at this hour were filled with esteem and even a bit of envy.

I am going to the Old Ones' Compound tomorrow was Emery's last thought as she finally drifted off to sleep.

CHAPTER 2

EMERY HAD WALKED BY the east gate before but had never seen it opened or had the occasion to walk through it. She now stood beside it nervously. She had hurried though her prep time and rushed to the eating house, emptying the sections of her breakfast tray in record time. As she ate the lumps of food, she wondered for a second what the trays being brought to the Elite tables might contain this morning.

After placing her tray in the tray window, she'd left the eating house, not having spoken a word to anyone. The announcement had said her tasking was not to be discussed. Emery wasn't sure if she would have been disciplined if she'd mentioned her tasking to Sadie or Dixon. She would have lots to tell them when she returned tonight, and despite the instruction, she would be bursting to whisper details about her day.

Rigley approached Emery and interrupted her thoughts. "You will follow me through the gate. Keep your eyes straight ahead. Ask no questions. We will walk along a path for approximately four minutes. When we get to the compound you will be given specific instructions. Such an annoyance for them to have to train a new person. Obviously not a consideration number 57 gave any thought to. A consideration she is rethinking, no doubt, given her consequence⸱"

Emery could feel the warm breeze as soon as she walked out through the gate. Even without daring to look up, she could tell that the sun was shining brightly. Green grass edged the cement squares that created the path they were following. She would have loved to step off the path and feel the earth from which the grass was growing. Any earth inside the wall was contained in pots or raised garden beds. She'd never been tasked to gardening so had no experience with the feel of dirt.

It was more than just the breeze and the sun that filled Emery's senses. There was a range of sounds unlike anything she'd heard inside the wall. She tried to single out the sounds to identify each one, but they were unfamiliar. She wanted to stop and take in each sound, to widen her gaze or even ask Rigley what she was hearing, but she knew that was not wise, so she concentrated on putting the sounds to memory. Maybe an Old One would know such things.

Her tasking at the Old Ones' Compound was for thirty days. Thirty days could offer her many opportunities to learn from an Old One. She would be patient and wait for the answers she craved so badly.

Emery heard a loud sound, an animal of some kind. The sound came closer and her careful concentration was broken as a brown hairy thing crossed her path, almost causing her to trip.

Rigley grabbed Emery's arm to steady her. "Get that thing off the path. Dogs are to be leashed this close to the wall. If I were to call in a report, that mangy beast would be taken from you. The bylaws cannot be ignored."

"I am so sorry." A woman stepped onto the path and grabbed the dog by the collar fastening the leash she was holding to a silver clip. "He ran when I opened my door and I just caught up to him. Bad boy, Disco."

"Get that creature out of our way and I'll not report you this time."

Emery felt the brush of the dog's wagging tail before Rigley jerked her arm to start her moving along the path again.

"Ridiculous name for a dog and a ridiculous kind of music," Rigley grunted to himself. "We're here."

Rigley pushed some buttons on a pad of numbers. Each push made a small beep; four beeps and the metal door opened.

"You will be inside for the day. I will return for you one hour before lights out. You will have your noon and supper meals here, as well as two short break periods. The rest of the time you will be expected to ensure the Old Ones are adequately cared for. Ronda, the compound manager, will conduct your training. Listen to her carefully. She does not appreciate having to repeat herself. There are strict rules about interaction with the Old Ones. Most are compliant and do not try to communicate with the workers, but occasionally a lucid one oversteps their bounds. Do not get caught up in that. Conversation and interaction of any kind are prohibited. Sit on this bench and wait to be received."

Emery watched Rigley push buttons on a pad similar to the one outside. Perhaps if she watched him carefully she would figure out the four-number code that opened the metal door. Trying not to be too obvious with her stare, she watched Rigley's fingertip.

The metal door closed with a loud click. Emery looked out from the small foyer to the room beyond. The walls were painted the colour of the sky. She could see no windows, but a stream of sunlight fell across the floor from the far corner of the large room.

"You must be number 38? Stand up and follow me. All the Old Ones are still in their sleeping quarters. I will begin by instructing you on the morning protocol. It is a straightforward procedure carried out with each resident. Particular details regarding toileting and transporting are written on the card beside each bed. Don't be distracted or put off by those who attempt to interact with you. The best method is to totally disregard the Old One and allow no resistance to the task at hand. Your goal is to get the Old One from their bed to their feeding place quickly and then immediately attend to another."

Ronda led Emery into the large room, taking her up to one of the feeding stations. "Do you see the numbers at each place?" Ronda asked. "You will see a number on a wristband of each Old One. It corresponds with the numbers at their feeding station. You bring the resident into this room and sit them at their place, making sure to match the numbers. Be very mindful of this, as the nutritional allotment is streamlined to supply the needs of each resident. After seating the Old One, press this button before leaving to retrieve the next resident and the food will be dispersed. If high efficiency is reached, all feeding places can be filled before the gong rings. However, this timing allows for no deviation from routine. I will take you to number 2217 first, as he is probably the one who tries the hardest to distract the workers."

Emery followed the woman back out into the main hall and past the large glass door through which the sun was streaming. Beyond the door Emery could see an outdoor area with benches and some greenery. They turned left and began walking down a narrow corridor. Some doors along the corridor were open, and Emery could see workers with residents in various stages of the morning protocol. Some Old Ones were standing, some were being dressed, and some were being placed in automated chairs.

"Pay close attention," the woman instructed as she slid open a door, the name Augustus Davidson hand written above the bold number 2217.

"Top of the morning to you!" came a cheerful voice from the bed.

Emery could not see the Old One who had spoken, only a mound of bedclothes.

"Number 2217 will try to get us to talk to him, but I will show you what is expected."

"It's pretty Ronda this morning, is it? To what do I owe such an honour? My good looks, no doubt, and my wit. And you have another lass with you. Where's my girl Daisy?"

"Number 2217 is able to relieve himself without assistance. He walks to the feeding station. His day attire is hanging on that hook."

Ronda pulled back the bedcovers and lifted the man's shoulders, raising him to a sitting position.

"Oh, I can relieve myself with no assistance all right. My claim to fame, apparently."

"Swing your feet onto the floor and don't even bother putting an act on for the new worker. Daisy will not be here for many days. Don't think I don't know she broke protocol. You won't be distracting me with your chatter. And you'll not be the last one in place this morning. Now stand up and get yourself into the lavatory."

"I believe you just spoke to me, Ronda. A friendly word or a smile might not hurt."

"Number 2217 thinks I will respond to his endless prattle. It would be best he stop his foolishness or I will put a request in for meds that will put an end to his resistance. I would just as soon sedate him and transport him to his feeding in an automated chair. I wouldn't even be opposed to feeding him intravenously. Daisy thought I didn't know what was going on. She just might have a rude awakening when or if she returns, to find her old friend Augustus meek and mild and as a chatty as a rock."

Augustus shuffled across the room and entered the small lavatory. Before closing the door he flashed a look toward Ronda, who had turned her back to him.

The look was meant to be one of defiance, but Emery could see fear in the Old One's eyes.

"This is day attire for a male resident. When number 2217 comes out, you will pull off his sleeping attire and slip on this jumpsuit. You will place these rubber-soled shoes on his feet and lead him to the feeding station. He is probably the most mobile and easiest to move in the entire compound, but he has repeatedly been the latest one to arrive at his feeding station. Daisy began her mornings attending to several others but always finished with Augustus, taking much more time than necessary with him. I began to have my suspicions, and after making inquiries and then setting up a monitor, I realized the delay was due to Daisy allowing herself to be caught up in conversation and interaction with number 2217, which, I repeat, is forbidden and will not be tolerated. I hope I have made myself clear on that, and make no mistake, if you follow the path number 57 chose, I will come good on the threats I just made to number 2217 and you will also suffer consequences.

"I have also implemented random assignments with no repeats," Ronda continued. "Allowing a worker to have continual interaction with the same Old One is just asking for trouble. I suppose I should thank number 57 for showing me that error in my management of things. You are here to perform necessary tasks, not to interact with the Old Ones."

Ronda stood in the doorway watching Emery as she began to dress Augustus when he came out of the lavatory. Emery tried to conduct her task quickly and efficiently but also to convey some compassion for this Old One, who hadn't uttered a word since coming out. She of course said nothing either.

After slipping the rubber-soled shoes onto the man's feet, Emery pulled Augustus to a standing position and took his arm. Ronda had left the room and was nowhere to be seen in the long hallway. Just steps before reaching the feeding station door, Augustus stopped and leaned his head close to Emery, whispering three words.

"Hello to you."

The next three Old Ones offered no resistance at all and didn't make a sound as Emery took them from bed and got them to their feeding station. Number 2002 wore protection and Emery changed her diaper before her day attire was put on. Emery helped her into an automated chair and wheeled her to her station. She then assisted 1999 to the lavatory. After 1999 relieved herself, she was dressed and put on a scooter-type contraption that transported her to her station. Number 2112 was already dressed when Emery entered her room. She smiled at Emery but stayed silent. She reluctantly accepted Emery's arm as she walked quite ably to her station.

Emery seated number 2112 at her place beside Augustus.

"Good morning, lovely Doris," Augustus said. A loud gong drowned out the rest of his greeting.

Ronda stood beside the speaker, waiting for the gong to stop echoing before speaking.

"Timing has been met this morning. Workers, check the board for each resident's day plan. We have a new worker, number 38. Number 48 will shadow her, assist her, and report any problems to me. The two-gong bell will signal removal from the feeding stations."

A tall girl crossed the room toward Emery. She motioned to a bench and the two girls sat down.

"I'm number 48. You can call me Meredith. The two-gong bell will ring in about five minutes. Some of the Old Ones will not have finished feeding. Go to the ones who are done first, and that will give the others a bit more time. Whichever residents you were assigned are the residents you stay with all day. We used to have the same residents every day, but now we receive a card in the morning with the random selection listed. We only have a few minutes to clear them all out before the cleaners come and scour the place. You're here because of what happened with Daisy, right?"

"Are we allowed to talk to each other?"

"They won't stop us during the down minutes or during our two breaks as long as we don't speak too loudly or look like we're having too much fun. Smiles and laughter are definitely not tolerated. Daisy used to say the funniest things in the most inexpressive ways. The hard part was not laughing. You get really good at it though. It's the same when you interact with the Old Ones. If you can keep all expression from your voice and your face blank, the administration doesn't catch on. I see that Ronda took you to Augustus first. He's the one they target the most. It doesn't stop him, though."

"Ronda said she would put him on something to stop his foolishness."

"She says that all the time. Empty threats, though, unless she gets the doctor to go along with her. And the doctor we have right now really cares about the Old Ones and doesn't listen to Ronda unless an Old One hurts someone or themselves. Dr. Dickinson wouldn't just sedate Augustus for talking too much."

"So do you talk to the Old Ones sometimes?"

"Yes, most of us do. Norman and Tabitha are about the only ones who don't. They go along with the rules and seem to enjoy it. Not the rest of us, though. We have perfected a method, and if you're really careful you won't get you caught. It's kind of a knack. Have you ever heard of ventriloquism? It's talking without moving your mouth. There's projection to ventriloquism, but that's not the important part of what we've learned to do. It's talking low enough without moving your lips too much so the admin staff doesn't notice, but loud enough so the Old Ones can hear you. And it's always being aware of when to take the opportunity to talk. Usually you can talk freely in their rooms, although Ronda has been known to stick monitors in trying to catch offenders."

"She said she did that to figure out why Daisy took so long getting Augustus to his feeding station."

"That's what we figured. I thought Daisy would be banned from the compound as soon as Ronda had the tribunal against her. But then Daisy was taken for her dining test and didn't return."

"I was there."

"Where?"

"The Elite dining hall, I saw what happened."

Two loud gongs rang, startling Emery and putting an end to the conversation.

"I'm shadowing you all day. I'll show you what I mean by choosing the time to talk. Follow me to the Day Plan board."

§

It was just getting dark when Rigley arrived to escort Emery and several others back to the compound. As he dropped Emery off at the door of her sleeping house she could barely contain her excitement. She had glimpsed the moon overhead before entering the gate. Looking up she could no longer see the sky, but she knew that above that cover a bright, round moon shone down on her.

"The Old Ones have numbers—names too, but their names are hardly used. They move them about, slotting them in places, matching their numbers like it's a game on a large playing board. The Day Plan board shows where each Old One goes and for how long," Emery said, sitting down across from Sadie. "Do you know a girl named Meredith?" Emery continued. "She is in Audrey's sleeping house, I think. She works at the Old Ones' Compound. She was with me all day, shadowing me, the manager called it. She was very helpful and kind. She talks to the Old Ones even though it is forbidden. When we took number 1999, named Vera, to her second placement, we were well out of earshot from any of the administrators and the three of us talked. I actually did more listening than talking. Vera is many first snows old; eighty-nine, she told me. She remembers when the wall was built. A terrible, shameful time, she kept saying. I hope I am assigned to her again soon. I have so much to ask her."

"Are the Old Ones scary?" Sadie asked. "Are they wrinkled and old?"

"Their bodies look old, I suppose, but their eyes twinkle, especially when they smile. Augustus is old but seems young in so many ways. He is funny and friendly. I feel so sorry for him."

"Why?" Sadie asked.

"He seems trapped. Even though he smiles and offers friendly words, it's as if he longs to be somewhere else. Ronda is cruel to him. It is as if he is not seen. He is kept locked up and they try to force his silence and cooperation. He fights them, though. When I look at him it reminds me of what I saw in Daisy."

"I don't know why you care so much about the Before Time. How can knowing about what things were like before help with how they are now? The way I see it, it's better to mind our own business and hope for a job we like once we are released. This Daisy you seem so impressed with isn't getting anywhere with her actions. I can't think being incarcerated would be any fun."

"Do you think it's fun being released and told what job you will do or what Older you will have babies with? And how about leaving your baby at the Establishing Compound and never seeing it again?"

"That's what I mean. Why get yourself all worked up about something you can't change? Even knowing how the Elites live seems like something I would rather not think about."

"But what if it doesn't have to be that way? From what I can tell, not everyone grows up within the wall. Somehow we got brought here, but what if we could get away and live a different life than what our status has shaped for us?"

"That kind of talk is going to get you in trouble. And I'll tell you this: if they hear you talking about such things, I'm not going to get in trouble for encouraging you."

Emery sat down on her bunk and pulled a notebook out from under her mattress. "Fine. I won't talk to you about anything important anymore. You can think Daisy is stupid to fight the way things are, but I think she is courageous."

Emery took a writing tool from the pages of the notebook and began to write.

I will get to know Augustus and Vera better. They have knowledge and wisdom. I hope I will get to attend to them again soon. There are lots of other Old Ones I want to get to know too. Yesterday I saw on the Day Plan board that number 2000 was put in the courtyard for one hour. I hope I get assigned to an Old One that gets placed in the courtyard. I wouldn't be surprised if Ronda forbids Augustus from going there, because it seems like it would be a place he would enjoy.

"The talking will now end."

Emery closed the notebook, stuck the writing tool in its pages, and slipped it back under the mattress. She would be very careful to whom she spoke about all this. For now, she would concentrate on the twenty-nine days she had left at the Old Ones' Compound, where each moment held the possibility of learning more.

CHAPTER 3

EMERY WAS DETERMINED TO take in more details on this morning's walk to the compound. The sun was not as strong as yesterday and the breeze seemed cooler. Rigley was a few steps ahead, so Emery allowed her gaze to move from side to side while walking along the path. The green grass spread out and round areas of flowers edged the path as well. Emery could even see a tree or two. She didn't know until yesterday that what she was seeing was even called a tree.

"I used to cut trees," Augustus told her while she was helping him into his sleeping attire.

"What is a tree?" Emery had asked, and he went on to explain. It was surprising just how much he was able to tell her before she had to leave to attend to the next resident.

The tree Emery could see now just off the path was one that had leaves for some of the year. The leaves were still green, so Emery guessed the outside season was summer. That was something else Augustus had mentioned: seasons.

Something fluttered and Emery saw a black-winged animal rise from the tree and swoop across the sky. She stopped and looked upward.

"Head down and follow me. Must I watch you at all times?" Rigley fell back and grabbed Emery's arm.

Rigley pushed three and possibly seven but shifted his body to block the placement of his finger on the last two buttons. *Three and seven,* Emery thought. Perhaps she could stand closer when he used the pad to let himself out.

Ronda was standing inside the door when they entered. "Here are your assigned residents," she said, passing Emery a slip of paper. "Get right to it."

Emery scanned the sheet, quickly looking for numbers 2217 and 1999. Neither was on the list. None of the Old Ones she'd attended to yesterday were on the list.

"You will see you're with different residents today. You will be working with every resident before you repeat one, but you will soon see that one is the same as the other. Some are diapered and transported in the chairs. Some can relieve themselves and walk to their places. Others are basically bedridden and only require a cleaning once a day and some checking of their connections. By the time you have gone through the rotation, you will be trained in all cases."

Emery hated the way Ronda spoke of the Old Ones as if they were just numbers. As disappointed as she was that she wouldn't get more time with Augustus and Vera today, she was anxious to meet others. She was sure each Old One had something to teach or share with her. She would get to know them all in the time she had here. Emery walked away, realizing that getting close enough to watch Rigley leave this morning was not happening. She would have to try harder tomorrow when they entered.

Number 1899. Emery opened the door bearing that number. She could see a shock of snow-white hair sticking out from the blanket.

"Good morning," Emery whispered. "What is your name?"

"Oh, I have a talker this morning, do I? You be careful, little lady. They'll whisk you right out if they hear you being kind. My name is Vivian, but you can call me Vivie. My daddy never called me anything but that. 'You've given her an old lady's name,' he told my mother. But I'm an old lady now. An old lady and nobody even bothers to use my name. Number 1899. How ridiculous is that? What does that even mean?"

"Are you able to get up on your own, Vivie?"

"Yes I can, dear. Just put the pillow over my head and hold it till I stop breathing, the day you see that I can't. It's bad enough in this terrible place, but when I can't even get myself around, I don't want to be here. You're new, aren't you?"

"Yes. Do you know Daisy? I am filling in for her."

"What have they done to her? I kept telling her she had to be more careful. What a sweetheart, that dear Daisy."

"She failed her dining test," Emery answered. "You probably don't know what that is, but it's something they make the Less Thans do before they get released."

"A Less Than? What kind of a stupid title is that?"

"That's what they call us. All the workers here are Less Thans. I don't think Elites work, although maybe the administration staff were raised as Elites. I don't know."

"You know, dear, I'd love to tell you everything I know about the terrible system you are a part of, but we have talked long enough. Admin roam these halls and if they think a worker is taking too long getting one of us to our feeding station they will come in to make sure we are not speaking to one another. Let me hop up and get myself to the bathroom. We will talk again. Thank you for your kindness, dear."

After getting Vivie to her feeding station, Emery entered the next room and saw the resident was bedridden. She spoke softly to number 1000 but got no response. She read the instruction card and began preparing for the resident's sponge bath.

"You have a name, you are not a number. I don't know if you can hear me, but I will speak to you as I wash you. I am going to lift your leg first and remove the pad beneath you. How about I call you Jane?"

Emery didn't know where the name Jane came from, but as she looked at this feeble woman, the name surfaced and with it a feeling of sadness. Had she ever known a Jane?

It took Emery about eight minutes to carry out the care of number 1000 and move on to the next room. She quickly got her next four residents to their feeding stations just as the gong sounded. She sat down beside Meredith on the bench.

"Did you care for Augustus or Vera this morning?" Emery asked.

"I started with Augustus today. He is in top form. He even walked right up to Ronda and tried to hug her before sitting down. He is such a character, but I fear his boldness is going to be his undoing. Who did you tend to this morning?"

"I met a woman named Vivie. Do you know her?"

"Yes. Vivie has a wealth of knowledge. It's as if she's not forgotten anything from the almost one hundred years she's been alive."

"She is almost a hundred? Wow."

"Two of my residents are being placed in the courtyard after noon feeding," Meredith said. "Go check the board and see if any of yours are."

Emery walked across the room toward the Day Plan board. She looked over to where Augustus was seated. She could hear his voice as he chattered away to those around him. Ronda stood a few feet away, glaring at him.

Her third resident, number 1112, was to be seated in the courtyard for one hour after breakfast feeding. Emery wondered if she could place her other residents and transport number 1112 last so she could sit awhile outside with him. Yesterday's placements had not included the courtyard, but when she took Vera to the craft room she'd been told to stay with her.

§

Emery wheeled number 1112 into the courtyard. "I'm going to put you under this tree, Thomas. It will be cooler in the shade." The day had become warmer since her walk to the compound.

Emery looked around the courtyard. She did not recognize any of the other residents, but a couple of them were seated on the bench across the courtyard, talking to each other. A worker stood a little apart from them and didn't appear to be paying the least bit of attention to their conversation. Emery wished she was closer and could hear them talking. Every bit of conversation was an opportunity to learn more about life outside the wall. Meredith had warned her about Norman and Tabitha, though, and it was Tabitha standing a few feet away from the two on the bench.

Emery would be careful to keep her interaction with Thomas limited and her voice low.

"It is a nice day, isn't it, Thomas?"

"I suppose."

"You like to get outside, don't you?"

"Yes I do, but it makes me wish for home even more. I was a farmer. Days like this would be busy, a good haying day with the breeze and the strong sunshine."

"What is a farmer?"

"Heavens, child. Don't they teach you anything inside that wall?"

Emery moved a bit closer to Thomas, turning away from Tabitha's stare.

"They only teach us to do certain chores and know our place."

"Well, they must feed you inside the wall. Farmers grow that food and raise the animals that give you meat and milk. Of course, the bastards who built those walls forty years ago found a way to strip the farmer of a good living."

"Our food does not look like anyone grows it. It is coloured mush."

"That's what they did, created factories and processed the hell out of good, farm-raised food."

Emery thought back to the sights and smells the trays in the Elite dining hall had offered. Maybe farmers grew the food they were served.

"That's the kind of slop they feed us too. I fed my pigs better than they feed us here."

Emery had so many questions she wanted to ask this man. What were pigs? Where did he used to live and be a farmer? What was milk? She was ten first snows old and knew so little about the world outside the wall. But perhaps the most important question and the most troubling was the nagging thought that even if she learned all she could about that world, would she ever have the chance to live a life anywhere but within the restrictive existence growing up inside the wall had groomed her for?

"You are not supposed to talk to the Old Ones."

Tabitha's voice startled Emery. She stood up, realizing the girl was standing right behind her.

"I could report you and Ronda would make sure you didn't get back in."

Emery did not know how to reply to the threat, but something in the girl's eyes gave a different message. She looked back at her, trying to hide any fear from her stare.

"Which sleeping house are you in?" Tabitha asked.

"Number five. Which one are you in?"

"I am in number seven. I saw you on the walk over last night. Do you know the girl you are replacing? They say number 57 will not be back."

"We are not really supposed to talk to each other either, are we?"

"No, but the admin staff rarely come out to the courtyard. Daisy used to say they were afraid they would like the outdoors too much. It's how Ronda keeps them and us under her thumb; not giving us the chance to like anything too much."

"Do you like the Old Ones?"

"Yes, I do. I have worked here for quite a long time and I hope when I'm released I will be assigned here. That is why I'm so careful not to get caught talking. I know some of the others think Norman and I are Ronda's pets and real sticklers for the rules, but really we are just biding our time waiting and hoping. Norman was released a few months ago and this is his two-year tasking. We are hoping I get the same assignment so we stay together and can eventually get married. Following all the rules seems the best way to have the future we dream about. Daisy chose to take a different approach. Unfortunately it didn't work very well for her."

"Have you had the dining test yet?"

"Yes, I have. I passed it. Norman prepared me for it, afraid the food would be my undoing. What about you?"

"I passed it, but I was there when Daisy failed. It was awful."

"I figured that was what happened. Some said she was incarcerated because she tried to break Augustus out of here, but I thought if that was true Augustus would be gone too, or at least Ronda would have made sure he was drugged and kept bedridden. Half the bedridden Old Ones don't need to be, you know. They don't dare kill the residents outright but they speed up the process."

A flash of light caught the corner of Emery's eye, and she turned quickly to see the large glass doors opening. Ronda was heading toward them. Emery's heart was almost beating out of her chest. Had she seen Tabitha and her talking? Was the courtyard monitored and had she heard their conversation?

"Tabitha. I need you to take number 2222 back to her room and then take number 2456 to the medical station. Dr. Dickinson is here to see her again. We have to put an end to her annoying outbursts. Emery, I believe it is almost time to relocate your resident. Number 1112 would stay out here all day if we let him. Pretends he's driving a tractor or some foolish thing. Honestly, the smooth running of this place would come to a screeching halt if I didn't look out for things."

Ronda turned, leaving the courtyard as abruptly as she had entered.

"I hate that woman," Thomas grumbled. "If I *was* sitting on my tractor, I'd run her down. Flatten her right out and plough her under. Good fertilizer for sure."

Emery looked over, nodding at Tabitha who was helping number 2456 across the courtyard. The Old One was shuffling along vacantly. Emery could not imagine her having outbursts of any kind. Meredith had been wrong about Tabitha. She was not what she appeared to be, and Emery was quite sure she had just made a new friend; a new friend and a new ambition to work toward. Maybe she too could be assigned to the Old Ones when her release day came.

§

People work outside planting crops and tending to them. Food is grown or raised. Vegetables grow just like the greenery in the courtyard. Thomas owned a large farm. Once you are released you are assigned a job and you get to live somewhere outside the wall. Olders can get married. Norman and Tabitha want to get the same assignment so they can be together. They want to get married someday.

Emery wrote frantically in her notebook. Lights out would come soon, and she had so much she wanted to put down. It might help to make sense of everything. It was all so confusing. She had so many questions and felt anxious and excited at the same time. A dream of a different future was beginning to form.

She and Tabitha had had a chance to talk again for a few seconds at supper feeding time when they were the last two in the room removing their residents. Number 3301 had upended her food dish, sending a disgusting mess halfway across the room.

"If you ever do that again, number 3301, your food will come through a tube stuck in your arm and your arms will be strapped down. Don't think for one minute your little outburst will get you anywhere." Ronda had left, gagging and hollering for Emery and Tabitha to clean the mess up.

They were kneeling on the floor beside a bucket with scrub brushes in hand when Tabitha had whispered the words that were now echoing in Emery's head as she looked up from the notebook.

Not everyone has to turn their babies in to be raised inside the wall. Some Olders live in houses after they get married and they keep their children.

Sadie walked over to Emery's bunk and sat down. Emery closed the pages of her notebook.

"Have you stopped talking to me? Just because you leave every day doesn't mean you're not one of us."

"No, of course not. I don't think that at all. I only get a few minutes now before lights out."

"We used to talk after lights out. Now every night you come back and start writing in your stupid book."

"I'm sorry, Sadie. I am tired after working all day. How about tomorrow night we plan an after-lights-out party under my cot?"

"Don't do me any favours, Emery. All of us know you think you're better than the rest of us. We're not getting out every day and seeing all the sights outside the wall. Pretty soon you'll be released anyway. Dixon says once you pass the dining test you are on the list for release."

Emery hadn't considered that. She'd been so caught up with thoughts of her thirty-day tasking at the Old Ones' Compound she hadn't considered that her release might be soon. What if her release didn't include an assignment to the Old Ones? What if she were placed somewhere she knew no one? What if she were kept within the wall doing jobs, like the Olders she'd seen serving food to the Elites?

Outside the wall you could gaze at the sky. You could feel the warmth of the sun and the drops of rain. The wind blew your hair.

"What do you know about the dining test, Sadie?"

"I know what you told me. I know they take us to the Elite dining hall. I know that girl named Daisy failed it."

"She chose to fail it. We have a choice, you know. They try to convince us we don't, but we do."

"So you think being incarcerated is a good choice? We don't even know what happens if we're taken away for punishment."

"No, but we do know the rules they make are wrong."

"Dixon said you would start talking like that. He says you are asking too many questions and if they find out they'll take you to wherever they've taken number 57."

"We don't have to use the numbers they give us, Sadie. We have names and *we* should always use them. They take away who we are when they call us by number. They do the same thing to the Old Ones, but each Old One has a name and a past that matters."

"What are you talking about?"

"They give the Old Ones a number and don't talk to them. They don't listen to them either, and they act like what the Old Ones remember and know isn't important. They take the past away from the Old Ones and they take away *our* future. They teach us that we don't matter, but we do matter. What they are doing inside this wall is wrong."

"I'm going to my bunk. The lights will be out soon. I'm not going to get caught talking, and for sure they won't hear me saying things like you are saying. Maybe you should just write your crazy thoughts in that book of yours and stop saying them out loud."

Emery pulled her blanket up and stared up at the dark ceiling. Her thoughts were dangerous. The words she was writing would be forbidden and if her notebook was found she would be punished. But what was she to do with all the information she was getting? She could not ignore the things she was discovering and she could not quiet her deep desire to be free.

CHAPTER 4

THREE, SEVEN, ONE. Emery was pretty sure those were the first three digits Rigley had pressed to open the door. It had been pouring rain, so the walk from east gate to the compound had been hurried. Emery would not have minded going slower and letting the rain soak through her clothing. It was an amazing feeling as the drops fell on her skin. Rigley apparently didn't share that feeling, and he spoke harshly, instructing her to keep up with his sprint along the path. But she had seen his fingers on the pad. The last number might have been four.

"Ronda will be out this morning. I am in charge. Go quickly to your first assignment."

Emery did not recognize the woman who had just passed her the assignment sheet with the list of residents she would be caring for today. Emery quickly went to the room of the first Old One on the list.

Number 1135 rolled over to face Emery as she approached the bed.

"Good morning, dear. You look like a drowned rat."

"It is raining. A lovely warm rain though. What is your name?"

"My name is Evelyn. What is your name, dear?"

"I am Emery. Do you know where your name came from, Evelyn? Do you know who named you?"

This question seemed pressing and brought a wave of emotion as Emery asked it. She'd stayed awake for a long time last night thinking about what she had said to Sadie about names and numbers. What was a name? Why did it seem so important to call the residents by their names, not their numbers? When she talked to friends within the wall, she never referred to their numbers but always called them by name. The Keepers and the Enforcers seldom used names but seemed to take great pleasure in reducing the Less Thans to a number. It was the same pleasure Ronda took when addressing the Old Ones by their numbers.

"Well, dear, I was named after my grandmother; my father's mother but, my own dear mother never really liked the name. She called me Maude, which is my middle name. Funny, I haven't thought about that in a very long time. I never knew my paternal grandmother, so I don't know why my mother wasn't partial to her. What about you, dear? Where did your lovely name come from?"

"I don't know. I just have the one name, no middle or last name. I have no idea who named me. I usually get called number 37."

"It's just a name, dear. A name or a number doesn't make you who you are. I was the same little girl whether I went by Maude or Evelyn. And whether they like it or not, I'm the same woman even if they call me number 1135."

"But you knew the people who named you."

"That is true, and I'm thankful for that."

Emery cut the conversation short at that point, telling herself it was so that she could efficiently attend to this resident and move on to the next one.

A while later, just as the gong sounded, Emery sat down beside Meredith on the bench. "Where is Ronda this morning?"

"There is a tribunal, I think. Apparently, someone took Augustus off the grounds yesterday. I feel sorry for whoever it was."

"How do you take a resident off the grounds?"

"They took him right out through the front door, apparently."

"Who is the woman in charge this morning?"

"We call her Stoneface, but her name is Lois. She is second in command and really wants Ronda's job. Butter wouldn't melt in her mouth when Ronda's around, but she tries to undermine her every chance she gets."

"What does 'butter wouldn't melt in her mouth' mean?"

"I have no idea. I think butter comes from milk or something. I've just heard some of the Old Ones say it about someone who acts like they wouldn't do anything wrong. Who do you have today?"

"Evelyn, Stanley, George, Mary, Vincent, and Winona."

"Wow, you are good with names. I've been here for seven months and I still don't know all the residents' names. I don't know their numbers off by heart either. I always remember number 1999 and number 2217 though. Vera and Augustus are hard to forget. I hope Augustus doesn't get punished for yesterday."

"Do you know where your name came from, Meredith?"

"No. I figure whoever received me the day I got dropped off just opened a book of names and picked one. They opened to the M names, I guess. I don't know why they even bother to name us."

"Maybe our parents name us before they drop us off."

"Maybe. Have you checked the Day Plan board yet? Let's look and see if any of our placements line up."

§

Ronda arrived back just as Emery was taking Winona from her feeding station at lunchtime. She was shifting Winona from her seat to her wheelchair when Ronda spoke from across the room.

"Number 38, I need you to take number 2245 back to her room. The Day Plan board has her placed in the entertainment room, but that room is closed today. The worker who operated the movie machine is no longer with us. Once you deliver your resident to her room, go get number 2217 and bring him to my office."

"She's as mad as a wet hen, isn't she?" Winona whispered.

Augustus was sitting in the common room, his head bowed, eyes closed, nodding off in the heat of the afternoon sun streaming in through the window. Emery sat down in the chair beside him, startling him awake.

"You're not my girl today, missy."

"No I'm not, but Ronda told me to bring you to her office."

"Oh boy. I'm in trouble now," he laughed. "Take me to the principal."

Ronda was pacing back and forth when Emery and Augustus entered the room. "Sit him down in that chair in the corner and pull up a chair beside him."

"You interrupted my nap, Ronda. Or maybe I'm dreaming."

"You're awake, all right, and you better listen to what I have to say. It seems to me every time there's a problem these days you're right in the middle of it. I can't get anyone to go along with me or I'd make sure you wouldn't be causing any more trouble. Dr. Dickinson for some reason takes your side every time. He even tried to tell the tribunal this morning that it would be a good idea to let you go off the grounds for outings on a regular basis. He almost has some of those other dimwits convinced that outings are a good idea for all the able-bodied residents. They have no idea the trouble they're asking for if we start that foolishness. And that miserable number 51 took all the blame for yesterday. He said he took you outside so he could meet some girl at the park. He said you had no part in it and that you kept telling him he was breaking the rules."

"That wouldn't sit well with you, now would it, Ronda? That poor boy didn't have to take the fall for me. Donald took me outside because I asked him to. We wouldn't have gotten caught, either, if that old battle-axe Lois hadn't been in the park too. Bet she didn't tell you the whole story when she told you we were outside. If you're looking for someone to blame for all the trouble around here you should start by looking at her."

"I don't need you telling me how to run this compound, old man. I have enough trouble with all those bleeding hearts on the board of directors. And that Dr. Dickinson. Elite training fell short in his case."

Ronda walked to her desk and picked up a folder, leafing through it. She threw the folder down and stomped back toward Augustus.

"This is how it's going to go. I'm still in charge, and until that changes, this compound will be run by my rules. I am going to assign number 38 to you every day, all day long, for two weeks. You will be confined to your room even during mealtime. A tray will be brought to you. Maybe your confinement will make you appreciate what you had and regret your rebellious behaviour. And I hope you feel bad enough about number 51 to think long and hard about doing anything that might ruin number 38's future."

The walk back to Augustus' room seemed long. His usual jaunty step had slowed, and his face was downcast. He did not speak until Emery had settled him in the chair in the corner of his small room.

"Damn her," Augustus sputtered. "It makes me so angry that she can condemn a nice young man like Donald and punish him for something as harmless as taking an old man outside to feel the fresh air. And now I've caused you to be held prisoner in this wretched room for two weeks."

"Don't worry about that part, Augustus. I know she's punishing you, but I'm quite happy I get to be here. I expect we can come up with some ways to make the two weeks not seem so bad. I can't think of a resident I'd rather spend fourteen days with."

"Oh, you're sweet, Emery. The first thing you should do is search this room for her spying contraption. Daisy found it the last day she was here, but that nasty Ronda probably snuck another one in. Look under all the furniture. Daisy found the little black spying box stuck to the back of the dresser."

Emery spent the next few minutes carefully scouring the underside of the chair, table, bed, and lamp and examining every inch of the dresser. She searched anywhere that might make a good hiding place for a device that would monitor the conversation in the room. Emery knew the monitors in the sleeping house were stuck several places on the ceiling. They were out in plain sight and everyone knew they were activated once lights went out.

"I can't find anything," Emery said, sitting down on the edge of the bed.

"Well, let's take our chances then. I expect if you've missed it we'll know soon enough, as I'm sure Ronda will burst in here in a rage if she thinks we're having too much fun. First thing I think I'll do is teach you how to play checkers. I miss that Daisy. She got so she could beat me hands down."

"Checkers?"

"Pull that table up closer to me and bring the other chair over. See that board with the black-and-white squares? That's a checker board. The box of checkers is in my top dresser drawer. I'm surprised Ronda hasn't confiscated my game. But she probably thought once Daisy left it wasn't any good to me."

§

Checkers is a game of skill and strategy. Two players move the round checkers one square at a time diagonally. You can jump an opponent's checker and capture it. Once you get your checker to the last row, it is crowned king and can move forwards and backwards.

As Emery put her writing tool down and reread her description of the game Augustus had taught her to play, she thought how alike kings and Elites were. A checker that wasn't crowned king could only move in one direction. They had to go exactly where the rules stated. But once crowned, they chose their direction. They could move back and forth to get the win. It was as if the Elites wore a crown of some type and lived a life of freedom.

Augustus had been so patient teaching her the game. He had won several times before she finally was able to block his final checker and take the win. It had been so much fun and Emery looked forward to playing again the next day. She looked forward to the conversation continuing as well. Augustus had told her quite a bit about himself.

When Emery entered the sleeping house a few minutes ago, a female Keeper had been waiting for her. What she held out to Emery would no doubt add to Sadie's mounting resentment. Florence had brought Emery the set of garments issued to females in the last division: a grey and a navy tunic, two sets of heavy leotards, and two pairs of lace-up shoes. The undergarment was a pull-on, one-piece thing with adjustable straps.

Sadie hadn't spoken since the Keeper left and had not let on she'd even noticed Emery's new garments. She was already in her bunk, her back to Emery, and Emery did not try to break the silence, instead choosing to spend the last minutes of light writing in her notebook.

Augustus Randall Davidson was born eighty-one years ago in a small village called Ravenville. He was one of thirteen children and his father owned a small hardware store. They lived in a big sprawling house near a lake.

The room filled with the inky darkness of the night; another stretch to lie awake, allowing Emery's mind to process the truths the last few days had presented. She felt such excitement at the prospect of spending more time with Augustus. In her time assigned to only him, she could ask questions about life outside the wall. He may even know about the building of the wall and the history behind the system that created Less Thans and Elites.

CHAPTER 5

EMERY WAS QUITE SURE three-seven-one-four opened the door, and she'd even been close enough to see that the same code opened the door again to let Rigley out of the compound. She remembered Meredith telling her that Donald had taken Augustus right out the front door. She wondered how they had walked out with none of the administrators seeing them. Looking into the large room off of the foyer, she saw several staff members. Was there any time of day when the room might be empty?

Emery realized she wouldn't be able to investigate that while she was spending her days in Augustus's room. Maybe she could ask Meredith to find out for her. But she probably wouldn't even get a chance to talk to Meredith in the next thirteen days.

"Why are you standing there staring off into space?" Ronda barked, breaking Emery's concentration. "You know where you're assigned. Be on your way."

Augustus was coming out of the lavatory when Emery entered his room.

"That woman might think she's trapped me in this small room, but what she doesn't know is just how far I travel during the night."

"What do you mean?" Emery asked. "You don't sneak out at night, do you?"

"Not literally, my dear, but my dreams take me all sorts of places. I was back in my childhood bedroom last night. Terrance and I shared the attic bedroom, which had a narrow door leading out to a small balcony. Last night I jumped from that balcony railing, and before hitting the ground I soared skyward."

Emery did not want to appear stupid or rude, but she had no idea what Augustus was going on about. What did he mean? She considered ignoring his story but instead decided to ask him to clarify. How was she to broaden her knowledge during this opportunity if she chose to stay quiet?

"What is a dream?"

"A dream? Surely you dream at night when you sleep. They haven't been able to control your sleeping hours too, have they? A dream, my dear, is a vivid story that plays out in your head while you sleep. Anything is possible in a dream. Flying, for instance. I stopped having flying dreams for a long time after I got in this wretched place, but they have been returning."

"I don't know what flying is either."

"Oh, my dear child. We have a lot of work to do. What a terrible thing they did to you young people when they put you behind a wall and decided to limit your experiences. Criminal, it was, but no one fought them. Have you seen a bird before?"

"I don't know. On my walk here a few days ago I saw a black thing in the sky. Was it a bird?"

"Yes, I'm sure that is exactly what it was; a raven or a crow, probably. In the natural world it is mainly birds that fly, besides bats and insects. Some creatures glide or hover a bit, like so-called flying fish and flying squirrels, but birds can take flight and soar great distances."

Augustus continued. "And man has invented flying objects like balloons, helicopters, planes, and rocket ships, of course. These inventions have enabled man to take to the sky."

"Is that how you fly in your dreams, in a manmade invention?"

"Oh no. When I take to the sky in my imagination or in my dreams, I fly like a bird. I soar overhead. That flying allows me to go wherever I want to go."

"How did Donald get you out the front door the other day?"

"It wasn't the first time. He had me out several days in a row before we got caught. Lois was meeting three of the administration staff in the park. She saw us about the same time we saw her, unfortunately, but we heard some of what she was saying. A few of them have a plan to get rid of Ronda. That should make me happy, but I'm afraid what Lois has in mind for this place if she gets rid of Ronda is even worse than how things are now."

"What do you mean?"

"Well, from what I can figure, Lois wants to double the number of Old Ones currently in the compound. She wants to have them all medicated and bedridden so she can cut back the staff of Less Thans they need and use all the rooms to house the residents. She plans to get rid of Dr. Dickinson too and bring in a doctor that will go along with her plan and ultimately allow the termination of the weakest residents."

"Why didn't you tell Ronda that?"

"Do you really think she would listen to me?"

"Are there others going along with Lois?"

"At least the three who were at the park: the tall man, Richard I think his name is, and Thelma and Roberta."

"How would they get rid of Ronda?"

"I think part of their plan was letting Donald get me out the door so many times and then being the ones to catch us. Her discovering my *escape* was probably used as evidence that Ronda is not on top of things and is not keeping track of the residents. This place makes a lot of money for the owners, you know."

"I don't know what money is."

"Well, that's something you haven't missed out on knowing about. Money and greed are behind just about everything. Financial gain was certainly behind the walled compounds being built. Forty years ago, a few powerful men implemented the self-serving system as a solution to some of the social and economic problems of the day and people bought into the lie. Then as part of the plan every walled compound took over an already existing senior care home and began running it for profit. The compounds provided cheap labour and compliant workers. The transition happened so gradually no one put up much of a fuss. In those days I didn't even imagine myself an old man, let alone one who would end up in a place like this."

A knock came on the door and Meredith walked in with Augustus's breakfast on a tray.

"Good morning, you two."

"Good morning, Meredith. I see the food they deliver is just as disgusting as the food that comes down the tube," Augustus said. "Set it down on the table and I'll pick away at it. Can you sit with us a spell?"

"I can stay for a short time, I guess. All my residents are at the feeding station, so I have about five minutes. How are you two doing stuck away in here?"

"We're doing fine," Emery answered. "Apparently the room isn't being monitored or we would have heard about it by now, I'm sure. Augustus taught me to play checkers yesterday."

"Hopefully you're right about the monitor, unless they're just setting you up and waiting for some serious breach before they pounce on you. They listened in on Augustus and Daisy for at least a week, I think."

"Well, I'm not going to let them scare me," Augustus replied. "And until they stop me, I'm going to just keep on doing what I do and saying what I say. Keep your ears open, though, Meredith. I don't want Emery getting sent back, or even worse being incarcerated. Poor Daisy, I think about her day and night."

The afternoon checker game was a long one. Emery was cautious and finally was able to take Augustus's last checker off the board.

"I think I'll have a nap," Augustus stated.

"I tired you out with my skill, did I?"

"You have caught on quickly, that's for sure. You're a smart girl, Emery."

"Why do just a few of us question life inside the wall?"

"I'm not sure why. It's a choice, I think. Sometimes it seems easier to just accept the way things are and not get yourself in a state about it. I must admit there are times I look at the heavily medicated folks around me and envy the peace they have."

"Daisy doesn't accept the way things are, does she?"

"No. She's a fighter, but look where it got her."

"I know, but even when Tonka was striking her, she did not falter. She glared at him and I felt even in her fear she was strong. I want to be like that. I want something different than the life being a Less Than offers."

"Then you'll get it. Whether it's a wall or a prison that contains you, what goes on inside your head, your heart, and your spirit is something you can control."

Emery sat across the room and watched as Augustus gave in to the comfort of sleep. She watched his chest move up and down with the steady heartbeat and his relaxed breathing. In such a short time, she had developed feelings for this elderly man, and in her mind claimed him as the family she never had. She wasn't even sure how she knew family was something she was missing. She reached into her pocket and took out a piece of paper.

Augustus used to live in a place called Ravenville. The code to get out of the building is three-seven-one-four. Lois allowed Donald and Augustus to leave several times. Maybe she would turn a blind eye to us if we left. Maybe if we leave we will not come back. Maybe Augustus and I can go to Ravenville.

Emery closed the door quietly and stepped out into the corridor. She could see Tabitha leading Vera slowly down the hall. Neither one turned to look at Emery as she walked behind them and out into the common room. Several Old Ones were seated around the room. Emery nodded toward them and moved into the foyer.

Three-seven-one-four. The heavy metal door sprung open. Emery looked around quickly. There was no one in sight. She stood frozen as the door shut again and relatched. As she walked back into the large room, the metal clang of the closing door echoed in her ears and the flutter of possibility beat in her chest.

Augustus took a leather-bound book out of his bottom dresser drawer. Passing it to Emery, he said, "This album holds the memory of my beloved home and family. It was all they allowed me to bring the day they came for me."

Emery opened to the first page and her eyes fell on a photograph of a large white house. Taking in every detail, she felt a familiarity and affection for the structure.

"Is that the balcony you flew from?"

"Yes. The balcony was built as an afterthought when my grandfather built the house. It was narrow and tight and no one ever sat out on it. The large front veranda on the other hand was a gathering place for many during all seasons of the year. Father kept the snow shovelled off of it and we would sit out there on moonlit nights even in the dead of winter. The moon was always a main attraction in our house. A full moon never went unnoticed."

"The moon is what you see in the sky at night, right? I saw the moon for the first time when I walked back the other night. We are usually in our sleeping house before dark. One night a while ago we had a drill and were filed outside after midnight, but the cover was closed. I was disappointed because I thought I'd finally get to see what the sky looks like at night. Dixon told me about the moon and the stars."

"Well, that's the first thing we'll do when we get out of here. We will make sure you get a really good look at the night sky."

"I opened the front door while you were napping. No one was around and I stepped into the foyer and pushed the code. The door opened."

"Good girl. Donald didn't tell me the code. How did you figure it out?"

"I kept watching the Keeper who brings me in the morning, and when he opens the door at the end of the day. Do you think we really will be able to get out someday? And do you think we could stay out if we wanted to?"

"We can do whatever we put our minds to. I probably couldn't get home by myself. But I think with your help I could get there."

"Is your home still standing?"

"As far as I know. No reason to think it's not. It was well built and I made sure it was well kept. It should still be standing, unless some bastard ploughed it down for profit. Someone may have moved into it though."

Emery flipped the page, completely caught up in imagining the adventure it would be to leave the compound and travel to Ravenville, wherever Ravenville was.

"Does the lake have a name?" Emery asked.

"The maps call it North Lake, but as kids we always called it Flossie's Pond after an old dog we had. She was just a pup when she swam the width of it, came out on the other side, shook herself off and ran back in, swimming back to where we stood on shore. She swam that water every day until it froze over and was always the first in when it thawed. All winter long she'd run across the frozen surface, yipping as if to scold the ice for being there."

"Is this a picture of Flossie?"

"No, that was her pup, Duke. Had lots of dogs since old Duke, but he was one of the great ones. Ranger was my last dog. He kicked up quite a fuss the day they came for me. God knows if the poor old guy is still living."

"I saw a dog the first day I came here. It almost knocked me over. His tail was moving back and forth. Is that a good thing?"

"A dog's tail speaks louder than anything else. A wagging tale is their way of telling you they trust you, they're pleased to meet you and ready to be your friend."

"Rigley hollered at the woman who owned the dog, telling her it needed to be on a leash."

"Of course he did. They want everything on a leash, in its proper place and under their thumb."

"I would like to have a dog someday."

"Then someday you will."

§

"There's trouble brewing," Meredith stated, setting the supper tray down on the table and seating herself on the chair. "Dr. Dickinson is gone. I took one of my residents for her checkup this afternoon and it was a different doctor. A very different doctor, from what I can tell. He was not one bit nice. Ronda is gone too."

"Are you sure?" Emery asked.

"Oh, she's gone, all right. At noon feeding Lois announced that she was now the compound manager."

Augustus ate his food quietly while Meredith began describing some of the changes Lois was already making.

"There are no more courtyard placements or any activities. Residents are to be taken right back to their rooms after each feeding. She wants them put right back into their beds, even the ones who are mobile and normally stay quite active all day."

Emery remained silent too, letting Meredith talk without showing any alarm or any knowledge of what motives Lois might have. Meredith was gone from the room before Augustus spoke.

"You know what this means, Emery. We have to get out of here before it's too late. If we are going to escape this place, we need to leave tomorrow."

Emery let what Augustus said about escaping settle in her head as she walked briskly back to the east gate. Rigley seemed especially chatty, but Emery had not responded to any of his questions.

"I hear the compound has a new manager. What happened to Ronda?

I don't know Lois, but rumour has it she has big plans to make the owners more money. Were there many changes today?"

"Not that I saw," Emery answered quickly, surprised Rigley was even asking her anything.

"Well, what good are you if you can't give me the lowdown on what's going on inside the compound? Maybe tomorrow night you'll be more informative. I might even be convinced to let you stroll over to the compound on your own one of these days if your information is worth anything to me. I know you'd like to spend some time gawking around. You're one of those that like the outdoors, aren't you? I don't see the attraction. Just bugs and bother as far I can see."

Emery walked through the gate, but not before looking quickly up at the sky. It was just coming on dark and she could see the moon, not quite as round and full as it had been the other night. A waning moon, Augustus had told her.

This time tomorrow night I will sleep under the moon and my gaze will not be hurried, Emery thought as she opened the sleeping-house door. *And I will see the moon in all its phases.*

Bugs and bother and so much more. Trees, grass, flowers, birds, and other animals. Sunshine, rain, wind, and snow. The moon and stars and the wide-open sky. Lakes and streams, rivers and oceans. Homes, family, and dogs.

Emery looked at the words she'd written and tried to stop her shaking. Her tremors were from excitement, but with that excitement came a fear stronger than she'd felt before. Life up to a few days ago had been predictable. Even when her curiosity had surfaced, she'd never entertained the idea of truly escaping. She'd begun to think about a different future, but leaving the compound with Augustus and taking a journey to find a new life was more than she had imagined. And they were leaving tomorrow.

Wear my second change of clothes under my garments in the morning. Carry my notebook and my grooming things in my small satchel. Tell Rigley I was told to bring it to the compound. I will think of a reason for that later. I will have to leave my second pair of shoes behind. I cannot say any goodbyes. Even with Sadie's anger of late, she has been a good friend. I hope she someday begins to see a life beside the one she's being forced to live. And Dixon, I will miss him. I must dismiss this and concentrate on what lies ahead.

"Dixon went for his dining test today and he has not returned yet. His place was empty at supper meal."

Emery quickly shut her notebook, hoping Sadie had not been able to read any of the words from where she stood just inches behind her. "What?"

"His dining test. Dixon was taken this afternoon. He's not back yet."

Emery tucked the notebook under her blanket and stood to face Sadie. "Maybe his testing was at supper meal. He will be in the eating house in the morning. Dixon will pass the test, I have no doubts about that. If anyone can remain unflustered and not give in to temptation, it's Dixon. He's stubborn, you know that."

"Yes, but I also know he's been weaker of late. He has not been the same since you were tasked to the Old Ones. You may not know it, but his wit and spark are due to you."

"That's foolishness. We have known Dixon all our lives and have never known him to be without his humour and his tenacity."

"Nevertheless, what I say is true. He has been pining for you."

"He'll be fine. I wish I'd been able to tell him more about the test. I did describe the food and told him how powerful the smells were. Surely that armed him a bit for what he found himself up against. He will be fine, I tell you."

"I suppose you don't think he'll take a bold stand like your precious Daisy did? All I've heard from you is how brave and special Daisy was in her failing of the test. Would you not hope the same thing for Dixon? Wouldn't passing the test mean he was weak in your eyes?"

"I did not say such a thing. I passed it, didn't I?"

"You may have passed it, but you've not been the same since. The mutterings of your discontent have been very obvious, even to Dixon. You may have in your questioning set him up to fail, and then what?"

"I refuse to even think of that right now. Lights will be out in a couple of minutes. We'll sleep, and in the morning Dixon will be right beside us on the bench just like always."

"Fine. You can believe that, but I'll not sleep so soundly."

Emery climbed into her cot knowing sleep would be a long way off for her as well. Now worry mixed with the anxiety and anticipation of tomorrow. Would she be able to leave with Augustus if Dixon was not in the eating house in the morning? And if she waited one more day to hear word of Dixon's fate, would one more day be too late? Augustus was convinced their escape had to be tomorrow.

CHAPTER 6

AT LEAST DIXON WAS AT BREAKFAST. He hadn't come to sit beside her, but he had come in, escorted by a Keeper, and sat alone in the far corner. He must have passed, but something had happened to give him such a compliant demeanour. He hadn't even tried to make eye contact with her.

Last night in her sleeplessness she found herself wishing Dixon would not return. She imagined him taking the stand Daisy had taken. Even if it meant incarceration, a defiant attitude would arm him for the day when he might try to escape. If he escaped, it was possible they might meet again somewhere outside the wall. If what Sadie said was true, maybe Dixon had thoughts of her someday, years from now, being the one he'd share his life with.

Was Dixon's defeated look because he had passed the test, but felt shame? She wished she could get closer and exchange a few words. But she already felt conspicuous moving stiffly with her double set of clothes. She'd told Sadie she needed her satchel to perform some barbering and shaving duties on an Old One.

"Since when do you trim hair and shave old men? Don't they have a facility for that in the compound? And why are you wearing both of your new tunics? I can see your grey one under the navy one. New fashion trends outside the wall, are there?"

Emery ignored Sadie's remarks and kept eating, trying to settle the rumblings in her stomach.

§

"I hear some Less Thans are being reassigned this morning," Rigley said. He had started talking as soon as they'd passed through the gate, seemingly bursting with the news. Emery was relieved his chatter was keeping him from paying close attention to her.

"Tonka was told to have several Keepers at the door of the compound an hour after noon meal to escort the Less Thans who are being reassigned. I knew that new one was going to stir things up, but this is fast. Talk is she is going to fill every possible space in the compound with Old Ones. More money to be made by doing that. And there's a big roundup coming. All Old Ones not being cared for by family are going to be taken and brought to the compound."

Emery was trying desperately not to show any reaction to Rigley's words. She wasn't sure why he was even telling her these things. It was not a Less Than's place to know the workings of things within the wall or outside of it. Decisions were made by someone much higher than Rigley or even Tonka. They just carried out orders.

"I helped with a roundup once and it wasn't easy, I'll tell you," Rigley said. "Some of those Old Ones are surprisingly strong. Good thing we had the medicine with us. One shot of that and they were like old rag dolls."

Tabitha's crying was the first thing Emery heard when she stepped into the foyer.

"Stop that blubbering right now," Lois barked. "I'll get this Keeper to take you immediately if you don't pull yourself together. The reassignment ceremony will take place in the feeding station after noon meal and you will accept your tasking gracefully and without protest. If you don't think you can do that, I will send you out now and there will be consequences."

Tabitha straightened up and wiped her eyes with her sleeve. "I am fine, Mrs. Lois. I will attend to my residents and report for reassignment at the proper time." Before leaving she flashed a look toward Emery, the brief gaze holding a huge amount of emotion.

Was Norman being re-assigned too, Emery wondered? Was Meredith? Was she? If she was, where would the window of opportunity be for Augustus and her to escape?

Emery slid open Augustus's door and saw he was already dressed.

"I barely slept a wink. I've been pacing the floor since daybreak."

"Has anyone been in this morning?"

"No, I expect someone will bring my breakfast tray soon. I will eat every scrap of the gruel they give me at breakfast and at lunch and so should you. Who knows when we will eat again? What's wrong, Emery?"

"Lois is making changes very quickly. Today may be our only chance to get away, and if we mess it up..."

"We are not going to talk of failure. This means too much to both of us. We will get out those front doors and get as far away as possible, as quickly as possible."

"There are reassignments being given today. Lois is having a big ceremony, gathering everyone together in the feeding station right after lunch. We won't be expected to be there as you are confined, but if I'm on the list someone will probably come for me. If I'm not, then that is probably when we should get out."

"Okay. Slow down a bit and come sit beside me. From the look of you, you slept as well as I did last night. We have to be smart and think this out. Tell me everything you know."

"The Keeper told me on the walk over that today there are going to be several reassignments. Keepers are to report after noon meal to escort them to their new tasking. He also said a big roundup was coming. Lois is filling up the compound just like you said she would, and she's getting rid of some Less Thans."

"She's probably looking to get rid of the ones who have been here the longest and the ones who have shown the most loyalty to Ronda. You are probably not on the list."

"Tabitha was crying when I came in. She's being reassigned. She had hoped that after her release she would work here permanently. Norman hoped to stay here too. From her state I bet he is also being reassigned."

"That makes sense. I know you're upset, but there is nothing you can do. Right now, the best thing you can do is take a deep breath and concentrate on the resolve to carry out our escape. If Meredith brings my breakfast, maybe she can tell us more."

Meredith had the reassignment list in her pocket, and the only numbers Emery recognized were Tabitha's and Norman's. Ten Less Thans were being reassigned. Their reassignment was not on the sheet, just the ten numbers.

"Maybe at least Tabitha and Norman will be given the same tasking," Emery said.

"Maybe, but I'm sure that's the last thing Lois cares about," Meredith said. "I doubt she even knows that Tabitha and Norman are a couple. If she does, that would be more of a reason for not giving them the same task. Don't think for a minute she cares about any of us."

"So will everyone be at the reassignment ceremony?" Emery asked.

"Yes. We've been told to return our residents quickly to their rooms after lunch and come back for the ceremony. All the admin staff, if they care about their jobs, will be there to show their support for Lois. The owners and directors are going to be there and I'm sure Lois hopes to impress them with her leadership qualities. We have been told to say nothing but to put on a big show of admiration and loyalty. Big smiles and dumb obedience, I guess."

"Emery and I are leaving today, Meredith. While you're all gathered in the feeding station we plan on getting ourselves out the front door. Would you flush my supper meal down the toilet and take my tray back as if nothing was amiss? Hopefully we won't be missed until the Keeper comes for Emery tonight. That should give us a good amount of time to get away."

"I wish I could go with you, but of course that would just complicate things. I'll do my part for sure." Meredith crossed the room and hugged Augustus. "If anyone can do this, you can, Augustus. Daisy would be so proud of you. And Emery, I am pleased to have gotten to know you. Maybe someday I will show the courage you have and make a better future for myself."

"I don't feel much courage right now," Emery replied.

§

Emery squeezed the photograph album into her satchel. She had removed everything but her notebook and stuffed in a warm sweater for Augustus, despite his insistence he didn't need it. He too was wearing two outfits, and he had dry socks in his pockets.

Emery slid open the door and looked down the corridor. Residents were returning to their rooms. She watched for the last door to close and the last Less Than to disappear around the corner.

Emery moved slowly down the corridor, Augustus close behind her. If they were confronted, she would act surprised, claiming she understood that everyone was to come to the ceremony. It was very quiet, but Emery could hear the noise of the crowd gathering off to the left. The feeding-station door was wide open. They would have to move quickly by that door and hope most of the crowd was facing the front of the room, where Lois would no doubt be standing close to the speaker and out of the sightlines of the door they were passing.

"Here goes," Emery whispered as they picked up the pace and scurried by the open door. They rounded the corner and stepped into the foyer. No one was in sight. Emery could hear Richard's booming voice from the feeding station quieting the crowd before introducing Lois.

Three, seven, one, four. The door sprung open. Emery took Augustus by the hand and led him through the opening. They stepped away quickly, the door clanging shut behind them.

"We should stay off the pathway that leads from the wall. Keepers will be arriving soon and we don't want to be anywhere around. Which direction is the park where Donald took you? We probably shouldn't go that way, either. If they notice us missing or heard us leave, that is probably where they will look first."

Augustus had stepped into the middle of a clump of birch trees and appeared to be frozen. Tears were streaming down his cheeks. "I will find my stand of trees. I will again stand under the canopy and gaze up into the sky. I will hear the rustling leaves and feel the rough bark on my fingertips. I will walk the roadway where for years I hauled out logs to make my living and provide for my wife and son. I will return to my woods and there I will die."

"We will not talk of dying right now, Augustus, and you will get where you long to go. But we'll not get there standing still. There will be time for tears, a time for talking, and a time for looking up at the sky. Right now, this is the time for moving. We will take this street and walk until we tire."

For the first few minutes Emery was consumed with the possibility of someone coming up from behind, stopping them, and taking them back. After a while, though, the danger of that seemed to lessen. Apparently no one had seen them leave, and now even if their absence had been noticed, they had come far enough for it not to be an easy find.

Eventually the street they walked along turned into a wider, busier highway, and they walked for quite a while before either suggested stopping.

"It looks like a diner up ahead," Augustus said. "We could stop there and rest. I have no money, but hopefully they'll allow us to sit a spell."

"I hadn't even thought we would need money. Is there a way to get it?" Emery asked.

"Well yes, jobs make money, but getting a job means living somewhere, and we will need to get to Ravenville for that. I pray my home is still there and available to us."

"Do you know how far away it is?"

"No. I was brought here in a van and was not in any state to notice the travel."

Emery opened the door of the Roadside Diner and was immediately hit with the smell of food. She was instantly taken to thoughts of her dining test. The smells and the sight of food heaped high on the plates the woman was carrying completely overwhelmed her.

"Do Elites live here?"

"No, this is called a diner or a restaurant. People come here to buy meals instead of cooking them in their own homes. The life you are going to see is nothing like what you have known inside the wall. Less Thans and Elites live out here but in a much freer, uncontrolled way. Less Thans have been trained to work outside, and Elites have been raised to own the businesses and profit from that work. Some are able to escape the system, but the economy and the laws in this region have been manipulated to support that structure. It is complicated, and you cannot know it all today. I myself spent years trying to live my life as if the system did not exist. That is easier when you live in a place like Ravenville."

"You will have to guide me and help me along the way. But one thing I need to know. Are there Keepers and Enforcers I need to fear and be on the lookout for?"

"No, not really. The system does have recruiters, and sometimes Keepers and Enforcers are sent out for a specific task like the roundup of Old Ones. But if you are careful, you can pick them out and stay clear of them. One thing we should try to do is get you a change of clothing. I am thinking the garments you wear may speak loudly of your status as a Less

Than not yet released."

Emery walked up to the counter and boldly spoke to the woman standing behind it. "My grandfather and I are travelling and somehow he has lost the money from his pocket. Is there a task I could do to earn some moneys?"

The awkwardness of Emery's words and her appearance did not go unnoticed by the woman behind the counter. Tanya no longer went by number 12, but it took several years before she had been able to completely put the feelings of that designation behind her. Her release had come nearly ten years ago, and her first tasking had been in the large kitchen of the local hospital. After two years of service her supervisor had given the employees the opportunity to find employment elsewhere.

Tanya had started washing dishes at the diner, and her outgoing personality and pleasing appearance had caught the eye of the owner's son. She and Robert now owned the place, and because of marriage to an Elite, she hadn't had to worry about the possibility of her two young children being taken as babies and raised inside the wall.

"Your *grandfather* looks tired," Tanya said. "I don't suppose you want to tell me exactly where you're travelling from. I won't ask any questions, but what I will do is give you both a good hot meal. I'll pay you to clear tables and fill the dishwasher while your grandfather rests, and while you're doing that I'm going to make a quick trip home and get you a change of clothes. I haven't seen those tunics sold in any stores around here, and believe me, if they were I wouldn't be buying one. I wore my last drab tunic, I'll tell you. Now have a seat and I'll send Ruth over to take your orders."

§

"My wife made the best fried chicken," Augustus stated as he picked up a crispy chicken leg from his heaping plate of fried chicken, mashed potatoes, and gravy. "I have not eaten anything as delicious since, and certainly not after getting to the compound. This is nearly as good as my wife's chicken; nearly as good, and I'm not complaining. What did you say to that young lady, Emery? They are treating us like visiting royalty."

"I told her you lost your money. I told her you were my grandfather. I wasn't even sure if it was the right word but I told her we were *travelling*. She's gone home to get me clothes. I think she might have grown up as a Less Than."

"Well, isn't that nice of her. There are good people out there, Emery, and you will learn to tell the difference. Maybe you already know how. You took to me, didn't you?"

"Pretty hard not to take to you, Augustus."

"How about you call me Grandpa? It fits your story, and I'd be pleased to have the honour."

Later, Emery stood at the sink rinsing the stack of plates. She had been tasked in the eating house kitchen briefly once, but the sectioned trays and traces of the lumpy food looked much different than what she was seeing left on the dirty dishes Ruth was bringing her. Even the food left behind on these plates looked better than what she had eaten all her life. This new life she'd chosen by walking out of the compound held the possibility of the kind of food she'd seen in the Elite dining hall. The meal she'd just eaten was already proof of that.

The fish had been flaky and white, covered with a crisp golden coating, and the french-fried potatoes were hot and crispy. She had taken in the smell, the feel, and the look of her heaped plate before enjoying the tastes. And Augustus had relished each bite of his meal.

Emery wished she'd gotten a chance to talk to Dixon about the food he'd seen. He would have given great descriptions of the smells, the way it looked, and the greedy diners consuming it. What would Dixon think when she didn't return? He wouldn't know until morning. Sadie would probably tell him that she hadn't come back to the sleeping house, when they sat together at breakfast tomorrow.

"I'll show you how the dishes are placed in the dishwasher," Ruth said, interrupting Emery's thoughts. "I'll put the soap in and you can just push this button once you've filled it up. After that, take this stack of clean plates to the trolley in the dining room. Then set the empty tables."

Emery did not want to ask any questions. She remembered how the tables had looked in the Elite dining room. Discs were called plates, and the tools were forks and knives and spoons. She recalled how they were laid out. She would set them up like that and also look at the tables already set to make sure she was doing it correctly.

Emery was setting the last table when Tanya walked in though the diner door. She was carrying a large bag. She motioned to Emery to come to the back office with her.

"I brought you a few things," Tanya said, pulling some clothing out of the bag. "I thought you could use several outfits, and some sleepwear. Do they still issue you those ghastly one-piece things to wear under your tunic? If so I suggest you throw that ugly thing away as soon as you can. I must admit, when I first got out I developed a real clothes-shopping addiction. I couldn't believe the colours, the fabric, and the feel of the pretty clothes available. I've tamed my addiction somewhat, although Robert might not agree. Anyway, with the clothes in my closet I could outfit half the Establishing Compound if they came to me. But I only brought you a few items, thinking you wouldn't want to lug too much on your *travels*. Try this on."

Emery slipped the tunics up over her head and threw them onto the back of the chair, leaving her one-piece underwear on as she pulled up the stretchy patterned pants Tanya had passed her. She then pulled the orange shirt over her head. It was soft and smooth and felt so good as it billowed and fell almost to her knees. The sleeves were puffy with an edge of black.

"That is lace around the cuffs. It fits you perfectly. I knew it would. The pants are called leggings, and they are the most comfortable things to wear. I brought you several pairs of leggings, some tops, and two pairs of jeans. I brought you two dresses, too. You can have a look at them and try them all on when you get to wherever you're going. Where are you going?"

"Ravenville. My grandfather comes from Ravenville. I don't know where it is."

"It is about an hour's drive from here, I think. Too far for your grandfather and you to walk, I know that. I can probably get you a drive there. Do you have anywhere to go once you get to Ravenville?"

"My grandfather's house is there. We are hoping to be able to stay there."

"They won't spend much time looking for you, if they look at all. One Less Than and one Old One are not worth much to them. If you get to Ravenville and stay below the radar, they won't bother trying to bring you back. You're almost due for release anyway, aren't you? They will have lost a worker, but unless you were groomed for a special job they won't care."

"It was very kind of you to feed us and give me these clothes."

"Your grandfather must be tired. How old is he?"

"Eighty-one. He was pretty worn out from our walk here. He's tough, though."

"Well, I can give you a place to sleep tonight, and in the morning I'll get you a ride to Ravenville. The guy who delivers our produce drives right past there."

Emery began folding her discarded garments, trying not to give in to the emotion caused by this woman's kindness.

"I would just throw those hideous clothes in the garbage can if I were you, Emery. You have shown courage and gotten away from the life that called you to wear the uniform of conformity. Throw the clothes and the future they tied you to in the garbage and move toward the life you chose when you and your grandfather got away."

CHAPTER 7

EMERY ROLLED OVER ON the narrow couch. A sliver of light was peeking in through the gap in the window blind. She had slept so soundly and could see that Augustus was still asleep on the single bed across the room. She could hear footsteps on the floor above.

"The diner opens at seven in the morning," Tanya had said when she passed Emery some bedding the night before. "I'll lock the place up when I leave, but don't be alarmed when you hear noise upstairs in the morning. Ruth comes in at six o'clock for breakfast prep. If you wake up that early, I'm sure she'd appreciate your help if you want to go up and help her. I will add that to the pay you earned cleaning up earlier."

Emery jumped up and made her way into the small bathroom. Last night she had hung her clothes on the hook on the back of the door, wearing a comfortable soft pair of what Tanya called pajamas that had been in the bag of clothes. Deciding to wear the leggings and orange shirt again, she dressed quickly. If she got out quietly, Augustus could sleep a while longer while she went up to help Ruth.

"Good morning, Emery," Ruth said, looking up from the vegetables she was chopping. "How was your sleep? I'll get you to fill up the jam racks first. How's your printing? The breakfast specials need to be put up on the board. The chalk is on the ledge and the list of specials is beside the cash register."

Emery started replacing the small packets of jam and peanut butter. She was tempted to open one of the packages labelled *Strawberry Jam*, to taste the red substance she could see through the clear plastic. It looked interesting, as did the brown peanut butter.

Emery walked to the counter for the list, then picked up the white chalk and began writing the items on the specials board. She had no idea what any of them were.

Eggs Benedict $8.95
Lumberjack Omelet $6.95
Breakfast Burrito $4.95

Emery thought about the money she'd made last night. She would buy Augustus a lumberjack omelet. Whatever it was, he would like the name.

"The specials board looks great, Emery. Set a coffee mug at each place, would you please? We open in ten minutes. You'll be surprised how quickly this place fills up once I light up the open sign. Do you think you could take orders? Tanya called and said she's going to be a few minutes late. She has to drive her daughter to school."

Emery had taken several orders and was just bringing the first order out of the kitchen when Augustus entered the dining room.

"You snuck out without waking me, Emery. I was a bit confused. Didn't know where I was at first."

"Good morning, Augustus," Ruth called from the kitchen window. "Your girl is a natural. It's like she's worked in a diner all her life. Find a seat and she'll take your order."

"Do you want a cup of coffee, Augustus?" Emery asked, walking toward the booth where he'd seated himself.

"I thought you were calling me Grandpa now."

"Right. Coffee, Grandpa?"

"You're happy right I want coffee. I have not had a cup of coffee in the morning since the day they locked me up. Janey and I would always sit with our morning coffee and relish the gift of another day. I'd get to the woods most mornings by eight o'clock, but never before I'd had a cup of coffee with my sweetheart."

"Your wife's name was Janey?"

"Yes, have I never told you that? Janey Louise Davidson. She was Janey Walsh when I met her, but for fifty-five years she carried my last name. Marrying that girl was the smartest thing I ever did."

"They have something called the lumberjack omelet. Thought you might want to try it. I think I have enough money to pay for it."

"Then the lumberjack omelet it is. A good hearty breakfast seems in order, though I don't expect to get to the woods today. What time did Tanya think that chap might be heading toward Ravenville?"

"She said he usually makes his delivery around two in the afternoon.

The Roadside is his last stop, so we should be in Ravenville by four o'clock at the latest."

"Imagine that. In Ravenville before I sleep tonight. It's a miracle is what it is, a bloody miracle."

"I think the miracle is that we headed in this direction and that you got tired just as we came to this diner. Stopping here and meeting Tanya is the real miracle. What are the chances we'd have found such kindness anywhere else? We might have found just the opposite. We might have been turned in and found ourselves right back at the compound, and things would not have gone well for us, I'm sure."

"I thought that too as I was drifting off last night. Janey always used to say things happen for a reason. She was wise like that and always saw the good side. I never found it that easy."

A few minutes later, Emery was sitting across from Augustus digging into a stack of blueberry pancakes. Tanya had come in and insisted that Emery stop working and order something for her breakfast. She had made it clear that whatever food they ate before leaving with the delivery man would be on the house.

"On the house, she called it." Emery said taking a huge drink of chocolate milk, which was the most amazing drink Emery could imagine. "For the food and beverages alone, escaping was worth the risk."

§

Max Taylor was a big, burly man with a shaggy beard and bushy eyebrows. His face seemed hidden by hair, but his twinkling eyes shone through, and when he spoke, his booming voice carried a melodious, unthreatening tone. Emery held the door open as he began unloading each box of produce from the back of his truck, announcing each one as if the contents were valuable treasures.

"My broccoli is stupendous today. Fresh and green, each floret bursting with broccoli flavour. I just picked it this morning, the dew still in droplets. I've new potatoes that are like golden nuggets. I've a flat of the last few strawberries that I'll get this season and a flat of the raspberries that are just starting. That's the beauty of fruit in season, there's always something coming next. My romaine is lovely, a sight to behold. You'll take some brussels sprouts, won't you?" Max hollered to Ruth. "A good cook can bring a brussels sprout to life, and you are one good cook, Ruth."

"You are a flatterer, Max. I swear you could sell eyeglasses to a blind man," Ruth said. "This young lady is working for us today. Emery and her grandfather are looking for a ride to Ravenville. Would you have room for them?"

"I expect I would. You seem impressed with my produce, miss. Would you like a taste of something? Bite into this tomato and tell me if you've tasted a better one anywhere else."

"I've never tasted a tomato," Emery replied.

"Never tasted a tomato? Where have you been, under a rock?"

"Not exactly under a rock," Tanya answered, coming into the room. "She's been somewhere where real food is withheld."

"Oh, she's come from inside the wall, then. Only a few of those left and thank God for that. Well, young lady. You are in for a treat today."

Max Taylor passed Emery the large red Beefsteak tomato. "Just bite it and let the red juice run down your chin. Close your eyes and take in the heavenly taste. Next you need to sit with a bowl of strawberries with just a hint of sugar and drizzled with clotted cream. And Ruth, you need to caramelize some of my Vidalia onions and fry up some of these mushrooms for her."

"She can't experience all the tastes and smells on her first day," Tanya said.

"No, I suppose not. And she got to eat here, which makes her a pretty lucky kid."

"There you go again with your sweet talk. Ruth told you they need a ride, right? Can you do that?"

"I sure can. I just have a couple more boxes to unload."

Max turned toward Emery who was taking the last bite of the tomato. "I was right, wasn't I? Here, give this one to your grandfather."

A while later Emery and Augustus were seated in the cab of Max Taylor's truck. The bag of clothes was on the floor at Emery's feet and a box of some of Ruth's baked goods was sitting on Emery's lap. The goodbyes were quick, but the connection Tanya's kindness had established was sincere. Emery also had fifty dollars in her pocket. When Tanya put the bills in her hand, tears had streamed down Emery's cheeks.

"Now, you and your grandfather get yourselves settled in Ravenville," Tanya instructed. "Don't venture back here for a good long time. The life you find there will be all you need to erase the damage they've done to you inside that wall. You are so much more than they ever allowed you to believe. You will make your way, and the future you will build is the future you were meant to have."

Emery would have rather taken the seat by the window but had squeezed into the middle. As the truck sped along the highway, it was amazing to see things move by so quickly. The sky was a deep blue and the green of trees and grass blurred by her. Buildings and other vehicles came in and out of her sight and it was overwhelming. There was so much to take in. She had so many questions but kept silent, trying hard to process everything she was seeing and feeling.

Max was taking them farther and farther away from the compound and the wall. They were getting closer to Ravenville and to the house in Augustus's album. When they got there, Emery would finally be able to take the time to look up at the sky. She had looked out the small basement window last night after Augustus fell asleep, trying to see the night sky. She'd thought about going up the stairs and out the door to stand under the moon and stars but was afraid to. Would the door be locked when she tried to come back in? Would there be anyone around that might see her? Was there anyone even looking for them?

She wondered what Rigley had done when he'd come for her and been told she was gone. Would Tonka have sent him to look for her? What had Sadie said when she didn't come back to the sleeping house? By now Dixon would know. Had Lois sent people to look for Augustus? Had Meredith gotten in trouble? Was Ravenville far enough away to be a safe place? The recruiters had come to the house by the lake to get Augustus. What would keep them from coming there again?

"So you lumbered for a living, did you?" Max asked.

"Yes, I lumbered on family land on North Lake Road. Do you know the area?"

"Yeah. My farm is just a few miles from North Lake on the East Branch Road. I bought the old Harrity farm, which was one of the best farms around forty years ago before family farms were outlawed. The ground sat fallow for thirty years before I bought the property and started working the land again. Making a living growing produce isn't easy, but at least they leave us alone now. Hard breaking into the market, though, with so many people oblivious to what good food is. Luckily places like the Roadside appreciate fresh fruits and vegetables. Some stores are starting to as well. My wife and I worked hard at making inroads and there's still plenty to do.

"Is your place the one at the end of that road? Always loved that house. It's not empty, you know. Not sure who's living there, but I've seen people coming and going and I've seen lights on at night."

"Well, I guess we'll see when we get there. I was out in the yard when they came for me. Everything in the house would be just as I left it. Must be squatters living there. I don't suppose I'll get any help from the authorities. It must have been authorities who reported me living there by myself. Such a stupid law that Old Ones with no family to care for them are to be institutionalized even when they are perfectly capable of looking after themselves."

"Well, you have your granddaughter now, so maybe they will leave you alone. If you need my help with the squatters I'm a pretty big guy and can be quite convincing."

"Thanks. I guess we'll just see what we're up against when we get there."

Emery noticed the North Lake Road sign as Max turned off the highway. Mounting excitement and nervousness were making her feel a bit nauseous. She tried to quiet her nerves and enjoy the sights on both sides of the road. And then a wide expanse of a deep blue, a much different blue from the vast sky above it, came in to view. It was spectacular.

"That's North Lake. It's beautiful, isn't it?" Augustus said, reaching for Emery's hand, trying to stop her shaking. Tears streamed down Emery's cheeks.

Max pulled over to the side of the road. "This warrants getting out and taking the time to really appreciate the gift of this lake. I drive by it every day and I can't even imagine never having seen it. You have lived all your life robbed of such beauty, but today it is finally yours. Get out, Emery, and go to it."

Emery bounded down over the steep bank and stopped at the edge of the lake. She bent to dip her hands in the shallow water.

"Kick off your shoes, roll up your pants, and walk in," Augustus called from the side of the road.

Emery pulled off her shoes and walked right in, not concerned about getting her leggings wet. She felt the small rocks under her feet and felt the rippling water as she walked deeper. She closed her eyes and listened to the birds and the rustling branches of the trees, felt the warm sun on her cheek. Her heart beat rapidly in her chest. She felt more alive than she had ever felt before. It was this place and this moment she had longed for all her life. Whatever happened after this moment, she would always know the exhilaration of being in the lake.

Augustus was on the shore when Emery finally opened her eyes. He was smiling broadly, his hand extended, motioning for her to come back to the shore. "You can come out of the water, Emery. This is your lake now. This lake is what you'll see every morning when you gaze out your bedroom window. You will walk along a different shoreline and you will swim in its waters. You will be just like Flossie and feel this lake in all seasons, waiting through the deep freeze for the day you'll return to her waters. Flossie's Pond will be for you what it has been for so many others. Everything has brought you to this place, and you needn't fear it being taken from you."

Emery waded in to shore and allowed Augustus to enfold her in his arms. She wept with joy and with the expulsion of misery and a deep sadness she could not even put words to. She let the tears fall and the sobbing continue until she knew the comfort of their release.

"Let's go home, Grandpa," Emery said, taking Augustus's hand and helping him up the steep bank.

§

A rusted metal mailbox still showed the name Davidson. Max pulled the truck onto the driveway, the rough gravel slowing him down. As the truck bumped along, Emery could see the large white house at the top of the hill. She saw colourful clothes fluttering on a long line stretched from the house to a large tree. The truck came to a stop a few feet away from the stairs leading to the front veranda. The front door opened.

"It's Terrance," Emery stated. "It's Dixon's friend Terrance!"

Augustus squinted his eyes, trying to get a better look at the young man walking toward them. It was impossible for this young man to be the person his mind was telling him it was. The young man he saw would be a man just a few years younger than himself, if the man he thought he was seeing was still alive. "It can't be Terrance. Terrance has been dead for twenty years," Augustus whispered.

Max was the first one out of the truck, walking toward the man, who had been joined by a young woman holding a small child. Augustus slid out of the truck and Emery followed. Emery was the first to speak.

"Terrance. It's Emery. I'm Dixon's friend. You were in his sleeping house, weren't you?"

"Emery? Right. Yes, I was. Is this Augustus?"

"Yes, this is Augustus Davidson. You're living in *his* house," Max said moving closer to back up the force of his statement.

"Augustus, you're my great-uncle. I am John's son, Terrance's grandson."

The colour drained from Augustus' face. He faltered a bit and Emery reached out to steady him. Terrance rushed to help. He led Augustus toward the house.

"Come and sit, Uncle Augustus. Valerie will get you a cold drink. The heat is making you feel faint."

"It's not the heat I'm feeling, young fella. I buried my little brother some twenty years ago and here I stand today looking right at him. My old ticker nearly stopped when I saw you crossing the yard."

Valerie passed her son to her husband. "I will go in and get drinks for us. You all take a seat and get to know one another."

"Thank you," Augustus said. "My father always said a few minutes on this veranda looking out at that lake could make friends of the worst enemies. Not that we are enemies. Just the opposite; we are family, and I must say I'm a happy man to find family living in my house."

"I had no idea who I was or where I'd come from when I was released four years ago," Terrance began. "I was assigned to a job in Rockport, and one day a man came in, walked right up to me, and told me he was my father. I wasn't taken to the Establishing Compound as an infant. I was taken from my father after my mother died in an automobile accident. They said a man could not raise a child by himself and took me from him when I was four years old. I remembered some things—my name and the lake."

"Janey and I went to John's wedding. That was the only time I met your mother. We knew she had died and heard when you were taken. I remember being glad Terrance hadn't lived to see such a thing."

"My father started searching for me around the time he figured I would be released. It took him a few months to find me. The day he came into the shop and introduced himself, he brought me right to this house. He didn't know you were gone, Uncle Augustus. Ranger met us when we got out of the car and he had no intention of letting us anywhere near the place. The poor guy was a mangy, hungry mess. But when Dad called his name, his tail started wagging and he soon became my best friend for the two years he lived after we moved in. I wish he was still here to welcome you home, Uncle Augustus."

"I do too, but I'm glad you were able to make his last years good ones. It's been a heartache not knowing his outcome. Is John still living?"

"Yes. Dad is remarried and lives in Rockport. Wait until he hears you've come home. And it's your home, of course. Valerie and I will start looking for a new place right away."

"Don't be ridiculous, Terrance. This is a big house. At one time there were fifteen of us living under this roof. No reason at all why the five of us can't live here together."

Augustus turned as Valerie came through the screen door and her little boy ran toward her. "What's this little guy's name?"

"This is Zachary. He's almost two, and we're expecting another in four months," Valerie replied.

Max took the tray from Valerie and set it down on the table. "Thanks so much for the lemonade. I hope you don't think me rude if I drink it and run. So, I guess I don't need to kick the squatters out for you Augustus. I had better get going."

"Thank you so much for bringing us home," Augustus said, getting to his feet. "Don't be a stranger."

"Are you kidding? I'll be stopping by. I have to introduce this girl to real food, remember."

"Bye, Max. Thank you," Emery said.

Emery stepped down off the veranda steps. It had been a busy few hours since arriving. After the introductions and saying goodbye to Max, Emery had followed Augustus inside and watched as he absorbed every inch of the house he had missed so deeply. He'd been thrilled with some of the changes Terrance and Valerie had made since moving in. He was also overjoyed to see many of his possessions still in their places, especially the framed photographs covering the walls and on tables and shelves.

"This is my Janey," Augustus called out from the living room. Emery came into the room and took the photograph from Augustus as he stood, not even trying to hide his tears.

Emery was as overwhelmed by the homecoming as Augustus. Although the layout and contents of the house were not familiar to her as they were to Augustus, everything about the house seemed important and meaningful. Each room held a warmth and welcoming as strong as if she herself had lived there. And the photograph of Janey, the beloved wife Augustus held in such esteem, brought a deep feeling of connection, shaking Emery to the core.

As Emery stood holding the photograph, gazing into the eyes of a woman she had never met, she remembered instantly calling the unnamed resident Jane and feeling the tug of that name. She felt that same tug looking at this photograph. Jane Louise Davidson was someone to her. The eyes she looked into were eyes that had once mattered to her. Emery remembered Augustus saying that Janey believed things happened for a reason.

Now as Emery looked up at the night sky, she shook with the truth of everything that had come together in the last few days, from taking the dining test to making it to Ravenville.

A light shooting through the sky caught Emery's eye and she called out in delight. She thought of just a few nights ago when she'd written her confused thoughts in her notebook. There was so much she didn't know, so many things she didn't understand. This vast sky was mysterious and beyond her comprehension, but what she did know as she stood in this beautiful silence was that she was exactly where she was supposed to be.

CHAPTER 8

WHEN EMERY WALKED INTO the kitchen, the morning light was streaming through the window over the sink. Zachary was sitting in his high chair, greedily stuffing food from the tray into his mouth. Valerie was pouring herself a cup of coffee.

"Good morning, Emery. I hope Zachary didn't wake you. He always wakes as soon as the sun rises and announces his eagerness to get up loud and clear. I got to him as quickly as I could. Terrance left for work a few minutes ago and Augustus headed up the wood road about an hour ago. He was just like a kid excited for Christmas morning."

"I don't know what Christmas morning is, but I know how anxious he was to get up to the woods. When we got out of the compound I practically had to drag him out of the trees so we could get walking."

"Terrance figured you guys escaped. He thought you were a bit young for release and wondered how Augustus got away from the Old Ones' Compound. I don't know too much about all that. I grew up in a regular home pretty far away from that system. I learned quickly though when I met Terrance just how damaging that life can be. Especially when you are taken from your family like Terrance was."

"I don't remember any life but life as a Less Than. I think I always knew it was wrong to treat people as we were treated, but I just lately started to really question it."

"What can I make you for breakfast?"

"I have no idea how to answer that question. Food is something we learned very little about. Our food came to us as lumpy mush with no taste. I'll take whatever you have and be very happy to get it. Yesterday I had pancakes at the diner. They were amazing."

"I should have realized that. I remember Terrance saying how wonderful it was to eat real food. His obsession with food has made him into a really good cook. He does most of the cooking, as you saw last night. I'll boil you an egg and make you some toast. Would you like some coffee?"

"No thanks. I tasted coffee yesterday and don't quite see the attraction. I'd take some chocolate milk if you have any."

"I do. It's in the fridge. Help yourself."

Emery opened the fridge and stood mesmerized at the bounty on the shelves. She saw a bowl holding leftovers of the supper they'd eaten last night. Sausage penne, Terrance had called it. She could recall the taste of the creamy sauce and the chunks of meat that had been on her plate last night.

"Would you mind taking that cloth by the sink and wiping Zachary's face and hands for me? Then you can lift him out of his highchair. He's just playing with his food now."

Emery wiped Zachary's little face and hands. She'd never been tasked with caring for the babies and toddlers and had no experience with kids this young.

As she lifted him from his high chair, Zachary wrapped his little arms around her neck. "Emmy," Zachary cooed.

"He likes you," Valerie added. "He doesn't just take to anyone. He knows you're family already."

Emery ate the food Valerie placed in front of her. Zachary had already covered the kitchen floor with the contents of a plastic bin in the corner and was taking great pleasure in throwing things.

"Toys for this guy right now are nothing more than a make-work project for me," Valerie said, leaning over to pick Zachary up from the middle of the mess. "Thank goodness he still naps in the morning. I'll pick this stuff up after I put him down for his sleep."

"I'll pick it all up for you. I'll do the dishes, too. Is there anything else you want me to do?"

"No, not right now anyway. Once you are done the dishes you should get outside and look around. You could walk up the wood road and meet Augustus."

"Yes, I will do that. Do you swim in the lake?"

"Yes. Do you swim? Oh, that's probably a dumb question. You lived inside the wall. We can go to the lake when Zac wakes up. I have an extra bathing suit if you want to wear it."

"I would really like that. Thank you."

§

Emery had walked quite a way up the steep wood road before she caught sight of Augustus. He was sitting with his back to her on a big rock. She stopped, not wanting to startle him. A large bird took flight from the branch of a nearby tree and as Augustus turned his head to watch it he noticed Emery.

"Emery. Come join me."

"It is so quiet and peaceful here," she said, sitting down on the rock beside Augustus.

"It is peaceful indeed, but not as quiet as you might think. The squirrels make their fair share of noise. The chirping of the birds is magnificent, and if you are still enough you can hear the rustle of the leaves in the breeze. I heard the tap-tapping of a woodpecker a while ago. Ranger used to dart in and out of the thicket, and he could get the woodland creatures moving. I miss the sound of my tractor purring in the background. Janey used to step out on the veranda to listen for that sound and the sound of my chainsaw so she would know I was all right.

"She was a worrier, even though she was the most positive person I ever knew. Every day when I'd come in for supper she would say how relieved she was that I'd survived another day in the woods and that today was not my last day. I used to tease her and say I'd be standing at her funeral, proof that her grim predictions had not come true. I never thought I'd actually stand at her funeral, though. I always believed she'd outlive me. Used to tease her about the yard sale I'd have to sell all her knickknacks and such. Never did that though."

"How was your first sleep back in your own bed?"

"It was good for the most part. I was thrilled to be back, but my dreams were a bit troublesome. Funny how the old brain works."

"Since you mentioned dreams to me, I've been paying closer attention to whether or not I dream. I think I do and probably always have, just never knew what they were called. I've noticed the dreams I've had since we decided to escape have been different. I dreamt about the lake last night."

"Were you swimming?"

"No, I don't think so. Valerie said she'd take me swimming when Zac gets up from his nap. I'm happy about that, I guess, but to be honest I haven't got a clue what swimming is."

"I keep forgetting about your limited knowledge and experience. You know how you waded out into the water yesterday? Well, swimming just takes it a little bit farther. You let your body drop into the water. The human body is quite buoyant, meaning it will float. Now, it's not quite that easy, but with practise you learn to move your arms and legs and let the buoyancy of your torso assist with movement through the water. That's called swimming." Augustus paused. "We used to call Tate a little fish. He took to the water as soon as he walked."

"Who is Tate?"

"I've not told you anything about my boy, have I? No reason for that, really, but I don't start my conversations with people I meet telling them about my dead boy. I don't hide the fact, but I keep it close, just as I keep his memory right with me. Tate was our only child. We'd waited a fair spell before the good lord saw fit to send him to us, and we sure as hell didn't have him long enough before the good lord decided to take him back. It's never long enough when a parent buries a child."

"I'm going to stand up and start walking again before I seize up," Augustus continued. "Wait till we get to the top of the hill and you see the place I call the park."

They'd walked a short distance before Emery spoke. "How old was Tate when he died?"

"He was ten. Healthy one day and at death's door the next. Janey blamed herself, but there was nothing she could have done. She got him to the doctor as soon as the fever started, but the virus that attacked his body had taken hold and no treatment changed the outcome. The dream I had last night was one I've had a hundred times. Sometimes it's in a different place, sometimes the hospital, sometimes Janey's mother's house, and sometimes different rooms in our house, even been in our old Chevy half ton a few times, but always it's Janey holding her boy after his life had drained away and always the fight she put up when she had to let him go. Don't suppose that picture will ever leave me until I join them in the Rockport Cemetery."

Emery and Augustus rounded a corner, and what caught Emery's eye was the way the sunlight was streaming though the tall trees. The sunbeams flickered on the forest floor. She looked up to the canopy of mostly evergreen boughs with a few leafy branches mixed in. The overall effect was astounding.

"This is the park. I've only cut a few trees out of this stand over the years. This was Tate's favourite place. He would play in here for hours. He had names for every stump and an entire world imagined out, the park's perimeter being the border of his made-up country. I found treasures he left behind years after he passed. I still hope I'll come across something more in here."

Augustus put his hands on Emery's shoulders and looked into her face. "Emery, meet my boy Tate. There's not another place on this property you will feel his presence any stronger than right here. I am a happy man to be able to bring you to this place and introduce you to my son. You are now a part of my family, and I welcome you to the park. This land and this beauty now belong to you as well. May you never be taken from this place or have this place taken from you."

The walk down the road and back to the house was silent. Augustus seemed a bit winded, but the joy was obvious on his face. Emery had been overwhelmed with the proclamation that she was considered part of Augustus's family and the property belonged to her as well. She wondered how Terrance and Valerie would feel about a stranger with no blood ties laying claim to a place they regarded as theirs.

Just before entering the house, Augustus turned to Emery, offering words as if he could sense her reservations. "Terrance and I spoke last night. We looked at the legal papers, the deed and such that state living relatives of my parents Harold and Ethel Davidson are entitled to this land and its dwellings for all time until such relatives no longer exist. Those documents are the reason they couldn't sell the place to pay for my care in the compound. I asked him to have your name legally included in the relatives listed and he agreed to take the papers to John today and ask him to arrange for a lawyer to have that done. You know, it may sound farfetched but part of me believes you are a relative that was somehow taken and by some miracle returned to us by simply walking into my room a few short days ago."

"Terrance didn't have a problem with that? I wouldn't be surprised if he might think some stranger would have a motive to trick a vulnerable Old One into such an agreement."

"He thought no such thing. He of all people realizes how family lines can be broken by the greed and ulterior motives of the perpetrators of the Less Than and Elite system that came into place under misguided and manipulative forces that took over the government forty years ago. Terrance feels no threat from your presence, only compassion and a willingness to welcome you and give you the home you've never had."

"Thank you, Augustus."

"Don't you mean Grandpa?"

"Right. Thank you, Grandpa."

§

Emery let herself fall into the water. She was only out to her waist, but as she fell she tried to let her body float. She wasn't afraid, only a bit embarrassed by her clumsiness. Valerie had jumped in and was moving through the water in graceful sweeps as she extended her arms and kicked her legs. That is what Emery wanted to be able to do.

"Let yourself move under the water first," Augustus called from the shore. "Get out just a bit deeper and submerse yourself. You'll get the feel of it under water."

"Are you coming in, Grandpa?" Emery called back.

"No, I'll stay on shore and watch this little guy."

Valerie swam back to Emery and stood up. "Just keep trying. No one really taught me to swim. I did exactly what Augustus is telling you to do. You'll be swimming before you know it. I'm going to take Zachary to the house and start getting lunch ready."

A few minutes later Emery was sitting on the dock beside Augustus. "Did Janey swim?"

"No, she never liked the water. It took some convincing for her to even let Tate anywhere near the lake. She was sure he'd go out too deep. She was sure he'd fall out of our old rowboat. She was sure he'd go through the ice in the winter. Funny the things you worry about when you have children. She covered all her bases; was sure he'd fall off his bike, be hit by a car, or get run over by farm machinery. She did calm down a bit over the years, but what actually took our boy she never saw coming. That's the way life is, you know. You can't manage it, fix all the dangers, or control the uncontrollable. Janey learned that hard lesson and it changed her. It changed us both."

"How long has Janey been dead?"

"I lost her almost eight years ago. I'm glad she didn't suffer long. I knew I had to let her go, but if I'd had my way I'd have gone with her. She would have kicked my ass if I'd done anything foolish like that though. She expected me to carry on. She even suggested I court Vera Henderson so I wouldn't be alone."

"Vera, from the compound?"

"Yes, they picked Vera up the same day they got me. If we had gotten together they probably would have left us alone."

"How does the roundup work?"

"From what I can figure, they comb the countryside looking for Old Ones living alone. If there are no descendants they seize the house and property and turn all the assets over to the state. That's where the money is made. But my nephew John was still alive and even though he wasn't living in the house that kept it from being sold."

"How do they get us, the Less Thans and the Elites?"

"That is even more sinister than what they do to the Old Ones. For some of the elderly, being housed in the compound is better than the life they had, although not for many of them in my opinion, especially when people like Lois are running things. But the law that was put into place to fill up the walled communities is criminal, heartless, vile, really, and how society allowed it to happen is beyond me."

Emery realized she was trembling. Augustus's voice had raised and his words held such feeling she wasn't sure she was ready to hear the answer to her question.

"The concept of the walled Establishing Compounds was to adjust society for the sole purpose of creating two distinct classes. The Less Thans were established to ensure a class of compliant workers. They would be slotted into jobs that needed filling, and they would offer no resistance. They would dutifully perform whatever tasks were required of them. The Elites would be raised to intrinsically know their value. They would demand privilege and excess and greedily create the wealth to fuel that desire. Both classes are simply puppets used to attain the 'greater good,' which is government control and ultimately unbelievable wealth for a certain few."

"Where do they get us?"

"This is the vilest aspect of it all. Like with the Old Ones, they look for children, preferably infants, they can say are not being cared for. If babies are born to single mothers, they are taken immediately. They take older children like in Terrance's case who have lost a mother. A law was put in place so fathers would not be legally allowed to raise their children. Then a couple of years after the original Establishing laws, when it seemed they were not attaining the number of children they wanted, they passed the Second Same-Sex Child law."

"What is that?"

"Couples who have a second child that is the same sex as their first child can be required to turn that child into an Establishing Compound. Hospitals must report when such children are born."

"Tanya has two daughters."

"Tanya married an Elite. Now that the system has been in place long enough for a generation of Less Thans and Elites to reach adulthood, a clause was put in place so that Elites are not required to give up their second same-sex child."

"What if Terrance and Valerie have another boy?"

"It could be taken. Hopefully the birth will go unnoticed. During highly populated times they are not as strict about the law. Was your compound full?"

"Pretty full, I guess. Tanya said they would probably let me go and not come looking for me. Maybe that's because they have lots of us right now."

"Well, let's not worry about that today. You know what I said about very little actually being in our control. Let's go in and have some lunch, because right now we can control that."

As Emery opened the back door, Valerie hollered from the kitchen. "Emery, could you please go to the garden and pick enough lettuce for a salad?"

Emery walked back down the steps mulling over the request, trying to make sense of it. The garden? Lettuce? A salad? She remembered Max talking up his romaine lettuce. The romaine was green and crinkly, and she figured it had grown in the earth. She walked around behind the house looking for a place that might have that sort of thing growing. She spotted a patch of brown earth with several long rows of plants growing at different heights, with different leaves and appearances.

The first rows were tall stalks. That wasn't lettuce. The next rows were attached to a long row of some kind of wire. Pods were hanging from the vines. How she knew those terms she wasn't sure. Next came a row of very leafy plants with yellow and green string like things hanging from them.

A salad. Hadn't she taken a plate of something Ruth called salad to a customer at the diner when she had helped serve yesterday's lunch crowd? There had been the crinkly green leaves on the plate. She came to a row she guessed was lettuce. Emery pulled a leaf, realizing in doing so she pulled out part of the plant. She broke the next leaf off leaving the base and not pulling at the root. How much lettuce did Valerie want?

After breaking off about ten leaves of lettuce, she walked back to the house. There was something quite amazing about the garden. Was there work she could do to help with the garden? She hoped so. She really liked the feeling she got standing in the middle of food growing. She thought of Thomas and the happiness and pride in his voice when he talked about farming.

Emery finished the last bite of her salad. Each bite she took had been wonderful because of the taste and the feel and also because of the memory of picking it in that magical place behind the house.

CHAPTER 9

EMERY WOKE UP JUST AS the sun was rising. The house was quiet as she tiptoed down the stairs through the kitchen and out the back door. Her second night had been more restless than the first. She had been so tired when she settled for the night and was surprised when sleep hadn't come. Even after finally falling asleep she had woken several times, one of the times after a very troubling dream.

Last evening had been so amazing. Just as it was coming on dark, Terrance built a bonfire on the shore. Zachary was in bed, so Augustus stayed behind in case he woke up, stating he was too old for such shenanigans anyway. As she and Valerie walked toward the lake the flames rose, embers flickering into the night sky. Emery felt as if she were in a trance. There was something so familiar about the sight, sound, and even smell of the fire. She'd sat on a log staring into the flames, letting the night surround her. It was a few minutes before Terrance broke the silence.

"So how is Dixon doing? I always got a kick out of that kid."

"He's good. He had his dining test so will probably be released soon."

"They're still doing that dining test, are they? I almost didn't pass, would have failed for sure except for the fact that the guy taking it with me made such a scene it took all the attention off of me. By the time they got poor Ronald out of the room and got back to me, I'd snuck a slice of meat and a spear of asparagus. That was my first taste of vegetables, and it sold me on them."

"I picked some lettuce from your garden today."

"Yeah. My garden is pretty good this year. We've had peas and beans, some new potatoes, and the corn will be ready soon."

"Do you think I could help with the garden sometime?"

"Of course. There is always weeding to do."

"Can you tell me more about what happened when you were released?

I keep wondering if Dixon has been released, where he might be and how things are for him if he has been. How does it work?"

"If a two-year tasking is granted on Release Day, you are taken to your job placement and given a place to stay nearby. For the first time, it feels like you have some freedom, but they still control your life. They make you sign a release contract."

"A contract?"

"Yes, a document stating that you will comply with the terms of the employment they have provided for two years. After the two years you can look for other work. The main aspect of the contract is the non-disclosure part."

"What is that?"

"I don't know about Elites, but a Less Than must sign a statement pledging to never divulge anything about the Establishing Compound. It is the consequences of breaking that pledge that deter us from exposing the system."

"What are the consequences?"

"The punishment is the immediate removal from whatever job a person has for re-assignment to a lifelong tasking. The lifelong taskings are not pleasant, and as the name suggests, they are permanent, a prison worse than even the Establishing Compound."

"That's why the system continues to exist and released Olders don't protest it. They control us even after we are released." Emery felt the emotion catching in her throat as the terrifying reality hit her. "If they find me, they will probably give me one of those lifelong taskings."

"The threat certainly exists. But we're safe here, Emery, if we keep to ourselves."

"That's what Tanya at the Roadside Diner told me. I guess all I can do right now is hope for the best for Dixon and be thankful I'm here."

"That's how I look at it. Sometimes I feel guilty enjoying the freedom I have while there are still kids kept behind walls, but I have to put my family first. Dixon will make his way."

Valerie had pulled a bag of white puffy things from the backpack she'd brought to the bonfire. Terrance passed Valerie a tree branch and Emery watched Valerie stick a white thing on the pointy end of the branch and hold it over the fire.

"They're called marshmallows, Emery," Valerie said. "Terrance likes his burnt, but I think toasty brown with a gooey middle is the best way to cook them. You can decide."

After following Valerie's example, Emery watched her marshmallow toast. She was again filled with a sense of familiarity, and even before pulling the marshmallow off the stick she knew how it was going to feel and taste as she brought it to her mouth. It made no sense, but somehow it felt like she had done this before.

§

Emery kicked off her shoes and felt the dew under her toes. Last night her dreams had been filled with turmoil and there had been fires, some looking like the one on the shore last night and others in barrels or under a metal grate. She'd seen a woman in the dream, and this morning she could still clearly picture her. The woman had picked up a small child and run through a field with her. The child was crying.

Emery realized as she walked toward the lake that there were tears streaming down her cheeks. The woman she had seen in her dreams last night was a woman she'd seen in her dreams before. The face had flashed into her mind even in waking moments. Who was that woman and who was the crying child?

"Good morning, Emery," Terrance called from partly down the hill.

Emery tried to pull herself together as she walked toward Terrance but was unable to speak right away.

"Are you okay?" Terrance asked.

"I'm fine. Really, how could I find anything to be upset about here? This is the most amazing place I've ever seen. I am thrilled to be here."

"It is all right for you to be emotional. You have been through a lot in the last few days. It makes sense that transition from life in the compound will be difficult. I remember what it was like for me. It brought up a lot of emotion. I was a long time getting over some of my feelings."

"Did you remember your life before they took you?"

"Yes, I am sure I did at first. I kept crying for my father. I remembered my mother but I knew she was gone. I started to forget, though, and that was the hardest part. I felt so guilty about that, like forgetting was betraying them both."

"I have been remembering things. I can see a woman in my mind and something keeps telling me she was important to me. But you were older. If I was taken as an infant, I wouldn't remember anyone, would I?"

"Maybe you weren't an infant when they took you."

"I should just let it go. What difference does it make, anyway? Augustus has been kind enough to treat me as family and you guys have welcomed me. I have more than I thought possible a few days ago, so I should be content to leave well enough alone."

"That might be easier said than done. Who you are is important. It doesn't change your past, but it can free you and allow you to better accept your future. I know it did that for me. Knowing my father, my family background, and my full name meant a lot to me, especially since becoming a father. I now feel I can give that gift to Zachary. He will always know who he is and where he comes from. You have a right to that as well."

"Well, for now I'm not going to worry about it. Would you show me the garden? I really would like to know what all the plants are."

"Sure. I will give you the tour. We'll have to wait until the dew dries before we start to weed, but by the time I show you the garden, Valerie will have breakfast ready. She said she's making you pancakes this morning. Usually she's not much for cooking, so I'm not sure what's gotten into her, but whatever it is I'm not complaining."

Terrance walked up and down the rows, explaining each plant to Emery.

"These are parsnips. Their seeds take the longest to germinate and have just gotten to the stage where we can weed them. See the crinkly green leaves of the parsnips? After breakfast I'll show you how to pull the weeds around them, and then if you want to I'll let you do the row. That would be a big help. I always dread weeding the carrots and the parsnips, but it feels so good when it's done."

"I can smell each plant. Is that possible, or am I imagining that?" Emery asked.

"No, each plant has its own smell. Most of them have look-alike weeds too that sneak in and try to take root beside the plant. And the dirt smells for sure."

"I like the smells."

Valerie called to them from the veranda. Zachary toddled toward them and Terrance swooped him up in his arms. Augustus stood leaning against the screen door, his eyes glistening as he looked at the small boy and his father.

"You're out and about early," Augustus said as Emery walked into the kitchen and sat down at the table.

"The sunshine woke me up and I couldn't think of any reason to stay in bed," Emery replied. "To think a few days ago I couldn't even look up at the sky and now I can go outside anytime I want to. It is like I've been transported to a whole new world."

"It's a special place, that's for sure. They know exactly what they are doing by robbing you of the outdoors. Is it true they have a cover that shuts the sky out?"

"Yes, a cover is kept closed a lot of the time. They open it to allow the rain to fill up the water supply, but they keep it closed most of the time."

"It is very calculated, the things they kept from us," Terrance said. "All the things that matter, really. First they take our identity. They take family and belonging. They take pleasures like food and the enjoyment of growing it, preparing it, and partaking of it together. They take nature and connection to place, to the earth, sky, and water. They prevent us from having experiences that might shape us, make us individuals, and bring us fulfillment or joy. They very deliberately limit our existence so that we can be molded to whatever they need."

"When did you begin to question your status, Terrance?" Emery asked.

"I think I always carried the knowledge that I was more, that life was more than what it was inside the wall. I never fought it, though. I'd seen early on what would happen if you put up a fight."

"I am not going to ruin this beautiful day by dredging up all that bad stuff," Terrance said. "The way I look at it, I was one of the lucky ones to get away from the evil of that system, and I'm happy you did too Emery. We can only hope Dixon and lots of others can too. Right now my priority is looking after myself, my wife, my son, and the baby we're expecting. Maybe someday I'll be strong enough to do more."

"Terrance is going to show me how to pull weeds from the garden after breakfast," Emery said.

"Well, isn't that so kind of him," said Valerie with a chuckle. "He loves planting a garden and picking his produce, but he's not real keen on the weeding part. Anyone for another pancake?"

"I'll take another one," Emery replied. "It was very nice of you to make these, Valerie, and that bacon was really tasty."

"I'm sure Terrance mentioned I'm not much of a cook, but who has to be when he gets such pleasure from it? I find plenty else to do without taking the cooking from him."

"Janey did all the cooking," Augustus said. "She used to say I couldn't even boil water, but that wasn't true. I could make myself a cup of tea. I did find it hard after she died, though. First it was a while before I had any desire to eat, and then I realized just how little I knew about the kitchen. I barely knew where the pots and pans were kept, let alone how to cook something in them. I think men these days are better at knowing how things are done in the household."

"I can't complain," Valerie said. "Terrance does his fair share around here."

"That's all I get, my fair share?"

"What did they task you with when you were released?" Emery asked.

"I was trained to work in a shop making machinery parts. I assembled a particular part all day long. As tedious as it was, you couldn't let your mind wander or the whole line would get out of sync. After eight hours of work I saw that line in my dreams."

"Is that where you still work?"

"No, after I left the machine shop I was apprenticed with a cabinetmaker and I build furniture now. I love it. I can take pride in what I create now, unlike when I put out hundreds of components that were lost in the huge machine."

"That's sort of like we are as Less Thans, a tiny part of the big machine," Emery said. "When we escape we become individuals. Tanya said they wouldn't bother to try to find me unless I had been groomed for a special job. When she said special job, do you think that meant the jobs assigned lifelong contracts?"

"Maybe. They usually slot the especially compliant Less Thans in those jobs, figuring they will never try to escape them. But sometimes the ones who do fight are punished in that way. Getting released with a two-year contract is the best situation, I think, although getting the whole system abolished would be even better for the ones caught in it."

"Do you remember a girl named Daisy? She would be a few years younger than you."

"Yes, I think so. A quiet blond girl?"

"Yes. She keeps to herself but stirs up trouble, it seems. She was the one who took her dining test at the same time as I did. She was offered food by an Elite. Both she and the Elite were removed. Daisy was incarcerated. That's how I came to be tasked at the Old Ones' Compound. I replaced her. She's a fighter. I wonder how things will end up for her."

"Let's get out to the garden before the heat of the day. We can't solve everything by worrying about it. The way I see it, if I had the determination to survive, others will too."

§

Emery stood back and looked at the weed-free rows. She had pulled every weed out of the long corn row. She'd cleaned out all the weeds in the beans and hoed the earth on both sides along the three rows. Next she had pulled weeds from the row of peas and weaved the growing vines in through the wire mesh. Terrance had shown her how to check the potato plants for the Colorado beetle. She'd found several mature bugs and some eggs. Then she'd pulled weeds and hoed up the earth, making good mounds around each plant.

Emery pushed the wheelbarrow of weeds to the spot Terrance had told her to dump it. She felt pride in what she had accomplished. Sweat was pouring down her face and she felt a sudden thirst. She would go to the house for a drink and take a small break before tackling the parsnips.

Valerie was just coming down the back stairs into the kitchen with Zachary on her hip. "You look hot, Emery. Why don't you go get your suit on and we'll go for a swim?"

"I told Terrance I would at least get started on the parsnips."

"You can take a swim break. You're free labour, after all. I don't think he'll fire you."

"What does that mean? Isn't what we had on shore last night called *fire*?"

"That's the tricky part of language. One word can mean more than one thing. Fire can also mean to let someone go from a job. It can mean throw something too, like when Zachary fires a toy across the room. You will come to learn these fine points of language."

"I feel like I'll always be backward and stupid because of the way I was brought up. I am embarrassed about what I don't know at my age. But the weird part is that every once in a while I have a memory of something, as if I wasn't always inside the wall. Like the fire last night. It felt as if I'd been beside a fire like it before, but I know I never would have been inside the wall."

"That sounds like how it was for Terrance. He had lots of memories about his first few years living outside the wall, but most of them didn't start to surface until after he was out a while. Maybe you weren't taken as an infant."

"That's what Terrance said.

"I have a friend who is a lawyer. Maybe she would know how to go about getting your records."

"I would not want to draw attention to myself. If someone started asking about my records, they might come looking for me. I can't even imagine what it would be like to get taken back inside the wall after knowing what it's like out here."

"Well, let me just ask her for starters. She might know a way to investigate without alerting the authorities. It won't hurt to ask."

CHAPTER 10

TWO DAYS LATER Emery had the garden completely weed free and had hoed everything, even the packed earth between the rows. She was now swimming below and above the water. She had also sat for a couple of hours each night after dark in front of a fire on the shore. Terrance had made two more delicious suppers, Valerie had made pancakes every morning, and Emery washed the dishes after every meal. She was even getting better at helping to look after Zachary.

This morning she called into Valerie when she heard Zachary awake, offering to get him out of bed to give Valerie the chance to sleep in a bit. As Emery opened his bedroom door, she felt overwhelmed with a feeling of belonging. In such a short time, this house and these people had become hers.

"Emmy," Zac said, reaching his little arms up to Emery as she lifted him from his crib.

"Good morning, sweet boy. Daddy has gone to work and we are going to let Mommy sleep some more. Emmy will change your diaper then take you downstairs for breakfast."

Emery looked out the window above the changing table and could see a steady rain falling. She felt thankful for the moisture the dry earth of the garden would greedily soak up.

Downstairs, Augustus was sitting at the kitchen table in the dim light holding a coffee cup. Emery turned the light on and put Zac in his high chair.

"You startled me, Grandpa. I didn't hear you down here."

"I've been sitting at this table for an hour or more. I'm holding this cup but I haven't even made the coffee. I was fine when I got out of bed, but walking into the kitchen I felt a weakness and sat myself down to try and shake it. It's a dark day with the rain and I'm seeing things in the shadows of this room. You two being here might do the trick, 'cause I haven't been able to do anything but stare into space imagining myself back thirty years. I kept waiting for Janey to walk in."

"Sorry I'm not Janey, but I can make a pot of coffee, and this little guy will liven things up."

"I was right about this place, wasn't I?"

"Yes, you were. I love it here. In the short time I've been here I've learned so much and feel like such a part of everything. It must have been awful when they took you away."

"In the first few hours I thought I would die," Augustus responded, speaking slowly. "I figured I had nothing left to live for if I wasn't here where I belonged. I remember about day three I had decided I'd just stay in my bed and give up and then Janey showed up. I saw her standing right by my bed, although I knew she wasn't really there. She gave me a good strict talking to. The words I heard were so similar to the words I recall her sister saying to her about a month after Tate died.

"Joanna was fifteen years younger than Janey," Augustus continued. "In some ways Joanna was like a daughter to us, a big sister to Tate, and losing him was heartbreaking for her as well, but from the first moment she took over and got us through. She tended to Janey when all she was able to do was get herself to the bathroom. She guided both of us through the days around the funeral. For weeks she made Janey take every morsel of food she ate and each drop of liquid she swallowed. Then one day Joanna got Janey up in the morning, took her out, sat her down on the veranda, and let her have it.

"'You do not get to give up. You are Tate's mother and you will carry him into this world, to keep his memory alive and to call witness to the fact he was here. Would you want him to shrivel up and blow away if he had been the one called to bury you? Are you willing to stop being the woman Gus lives his life with? Do you want him to take the same path you are taking? Is it not selfish of you to decide that he must lose his wife along with his son?'

"Janey listened to her sister that morning and made the choice to keep living. And when I lay in that narrow bed days after getting to the compound, Janey came to me and hurled a similar rebuke. I got myself out of bed that day and put my best foot forward. So tell me why this morning I feel like I need that talking-to again."

"We all need a good talking-to once in a while, Grandpa. Where is Joanna now?"

"Joanna moved away when she got married and it was years before we saw her. Janey and she wrote letters and kept in touch, but when she finally came to visit we realized she had kept her illness a secret. She'd been fighting cancer for several years. We only met her daughter Janelle once when she was about ten. Joanna brought us her graduation picture when she came to visit just months before she died."

Augustus got up and went into the living room and minutes later came back into the kitchen and passed Emery a cardboard-framed picture.

"Joanna just had the one child, like her sister. Her name was Janelle, but Joanna always called her Jane."

"This is the woman in my dreams," Emery declared, her voice faltering and her hand shaking. "Augustus, this is the woman I always see in my head."

§

Daisy heard the metal click of the door at the end of the corridor. She saw movement go by the small barred window in her door but didn't expect the door to open. It had been two days since they had brought food to her. The Keeper guard had left her a bottle of water, and she now only had two or three sips left. Would they simply starve her to death or let her die of thirst then come take her lifeless body out and dispose of it?

And how many days had she been in here? She looked up at the tally marks carved into the wooden window trim. Just ten days. It seemed so much longer ago since she'd been dragged from the Elite dining hall. She barely had the energy to scratch the marks for the first three days. They had given her something to settle her when she'd fought back all the way to the cell area and something more after Vincent had come to her cell. He'd left cursing while rubbing the spot on his arm where she'd bitten him.

Then after the medication wore off she'd fought with words only and refused to repeat the mantra Vincent demanded she say. *I am of no value. I have no importance. I am only what you require me to be.* Not only did she not repeat those lies, she had loudly denied them. *I am of value. I am important. I will be what I want to be.*

After six days of that back-and-forth fight Vincent decided the withdrawal of food would be the only way to gain her compliance. Daisy found irony in the fact they even called it food. It was her defiant action of accepting the food on the table in the dining hall that had gotten her here; that and the audacity of believing herself worthy. They were holding back the lumps of nourishment that with each bite would remind her of her unworthiness. To die refusing this reminder seemed fitting, and she would not give in to their tactic.

§

Valerie walked into the kitchen to see Emery clutching a photograph. Her face was as white as a sheet and her body was trembling. Augustus quickly explained who was in the picture and told Valerie of Emery's reaction to seeing it.

"I had a feeling she was related," Augustus added. "Some power greater than all of us sent her into my room. Joanna told Janey she had the duty to bear witness to Tate. Janey told me I had to go on to bear that same witness and to carry her memory on, and now Emery appears to be the one who bears witness to Joanna and to Janelle."

"Do you really think just because she looks familiar to me that I must be her daughter, and Joanna's granddaughter? Don't you think that is a bit farfetched?"

"No, I do not. I have lived long enough to be certain of one thing: that the things we understand are minute compared to the vastness of the things we don't understand. Can you explain how a tiny flat parsnip seed becomes a parsnip? Can you explain how the clouds form in the sky? Can you explain how our hearts beat and our blood flows through our veins? Humans try such explanations but fall short on really knowing any of it. So why is it not possible that we are pulled by forces much greater than we will ever understand?"

"Is Joanna's husband still alive?" Valerie asked Augustus. "Would he be able to verify Janelle had a daughter and maybe know how Emery got to be placed inside the wall?"

Emery crossed the room and picked up the coffee pot. "I don't know if I want to know what he might be able to tell me. As much as having a past, a mother, and possibly a blood-related grandfather would be wonderful, would knowing I was robbed of that be better than thinking I never had it? You said yourself, Valerie, how hard it was for Terrance to come to terms with that. Maybe just having what I have now and being grateful for it would be less painful than finding out a truth that might include my mother's death."

Augustus held out his cup, letting Emery fill it, and waited a few seconds before speaking. "It is your decision, Emery. I have a phone number for Joanna's husband. I was never fond of the man, possibly because he took Joanna so far away from us, but if you want me to try and contact him I will. Don't rush your decision. Maybe you might even want to wait and talk it over with Terrance. He would understand your feelings."

Emery found Terrance in the garden picking peas and beans for supper. The day had moved quickly, and even amid the activities, Emery could not shake the conflicting feelings she felt after seeing the photograph and being presented with the possibility she was Augustus's niece's daughter. She had waited for a chance to talk to Terrance, hoping he might be able to help her understand what she was feeling.

"How did you react when your father found you?"

"Hello to you too, Emery."

"I might know who my mother is. I might really be related to Augustus. Not to you, I guess, but I might be your Great Aunt Jane's sister's granddaughter. Maybe I wasn't taken as an infant, because I remember her name and I have always seen her face, I think."

"Okay, slow down. You are obviously troubled by this information. How about you help me pick the rest of these peas and beans and we'll sit on the veranda and get them ready and talk about all of this?"

A few minutes later, Emery began shelling the peas while Terrance snapped the beans into the pot sitting between them on the veranda swing.

"I told you I had lots of memories of my parents when I first got to the Establishing Compound," Terrance began. "I had blocked out all my memories of the day they took me from my father. It wasn't until after Dad found me that I remembered more. I remembered waking up that morning to the sound of my father yelling. He was downstairs, telling someone to get out of his house. His loud words frightened me. Then I heard stomping footsteps on the stairs.

"Three men and my father burst through my bedroom door. Two men were holding my father and he was swearing and hollering but at the same time trying to comfort me. I was crying, burying myself under my pile of blankets, thinking they wouldn't see me.

"The biggest guy plucked me out from under the covers and threw me over his shoulder. One man knocked Dad onto the floor and the other one kicked him. I could hear the sounds of my father's pain fading as I was carried outside and put in the van. I was crying but I couldn't fight the strength of the man and the straps he quickly buckled, fastening me into a seat at the back of the van. I was not the only kid in the van, but I was the only one crying. The others were silent, their fight already over I guess. By the time they delivered us, my fight was gone too."

"I keep dreaming of someone running with a child over her shoulder," Emery said. "Now I know it is always the woman in the photograph Augustus showed me today. Do you think I was the child over her shoulder? Was she trying to get away from the people that finally got me?"

"That is quite possible, Emery," Terrance replied. "You probably weren't a newborn when they took you if you have that memory. If your mother was a single parent, maybe she managed to hide you for a couple of years. Do you remember anything else?"

"Fire. I didn't know I even knew what fire was until the other night. The bonfire you made seemed really familiar to me. I knew about marshmallows, although there was no way I should have. I have a memory of being at a fire with the woman I saw in the photograph. My mother and I had campfires, I think. We toasted marshmallows."

"I was troubled at first when my bad memories came, but after I let them sink in I was thankful for them. My father had such guilt about letting me go, and I might have blamed him if I hadn't had the clear memory of how hard he fought to keep them from taking me. The years we were separated were harder for him than they were for me. I was young, and even though I suffered, I adapted to my surroundings."

"Then you think I shouldn't be afraid to let my memories come? What if I find my mother? How do I deal with that?"

"You just do. None of what happened was your fault, and not hers either. I have no idea what her circumstances were, but she clearly tried to take care of you. It was out of her control and out of my father's control.

Laws were put in place causing the suffering and the breakup of families. We were both caught up in those terrible laws. But we survived. My father survived too, and maybe you will find that your mother did as well. The years they robbed from us cannot be reclaimed, but we can make sure they don't take our future."

"Are you two going to bring those peas and beans in to cook?" Valerie asked, opening the screen door. "Everything else will be cooked and you two will still be out here gabbing."

§

Vincent stood at the open door with the guard inches away, as if the thin girl across the room might suddenly knock them both over and bolt through the door.

"The supper trays are coming down the corridor. Are you ready to give in? Surely a couple of days of stomach rumbling have brought you to your senses, number 57. *I am of no value. I am of no value.* Say those words and a tray will be brought in to you."

"My name is Daisy. I am not a number. I am Daisy and I have value."

Vincent turned, stepping out into the corridor. The heavy door shut behind him and the lock clicked.

"She isn't hungry enough yet," Vincent said angrily. "And don't take her any more water."

CHAPTER 11

THE PHONE RANG SIX TIMES before Augustus heard a gruff hello.

"Is this Robert Melvin?"

"Yeah, who's asking?"

"It's Augustus Davidson, and don't even bother pretending you don't know who I am. I didn't expect much from you, but I did expect you'd have the decency to at least acknowledge Janey's death. Didn't really think you'd show up at the funeral after the row we had at Joanna's graveside, but a call or a card wouldn't have killed you."

"Is that what you're calling about after all this time? I thought you were locked up."

"Did you, now? Any chance you were the one who set them on me? I hear there's a finder's fee, and you'd do anything for a dollar."

"What do you want?"

"I want to ask you about Janelle."

"What about her?"

"Well, what can you tell me about her?"

"I can tell you she's a piece of trash. She stood at her mother's grave with her dirty little secret and then expected me to support her and that kid."

"What kid? Did she have a daughter?"

"Oh she did, and thought she could run from the law with her. She got caught, though, after four years of living like a hobo, and the kid went where she should have gone right after she was born. But none of this is any of your business, old man."

The phone line went dead after the loud bang of the receiver being dropped. Augustus sat with the phone still in his hand, trying to take in the information Robert's few words had delivered. Janelle was pregnant at Joanna's funeral, which was fourteen years ago. Janelle had a baby girl and took her from the hospital, keeping her from being taken for four years. Robert had said they had lived like hobos. She had kept on the move, trying to keep her daughter from being taken to the Establishing Compound. But they had taken her. Everything Robert had reluctantly told him made it entirely believable that Emery was Janelle's daughter, Joanna's granddaughter, his great-niece.

Augustus walked outside to where Emery was kneeling on the ground thinning the long row of carrots. He stood a fair distance away, not wanting to startle her but also not exactly sure he was ready to tell her about the phone call. Would it be easier for her to face the future if she knew less about her past? Would having a mother who, by the way Robert had spoken, was still alive be welcome news? It certainly didn't appear she had a grandfather willing and anxious to know her.

It wasn't his place to weigh the pros and cons for Emery. The truth of who she was and what she had lived through belonged to her. She was the only one to decide what she would do with that truth. Keeping it from her was not an option. She had been held prisoner long enough and the freedom she deserved could only be found in the truth.

"Emery, can you stop long enough to come to the veranda? I have some things to tell you."

§

"So how old was my mother when she had me? What month do you think I was born if she was pregnant with me at Joanna's funeral? I'm already or almost fourteen years old. Did my grandfather say where my mother lives? Where does he live?"

"First of all, your grandfather is not a nice man, and I don't think he can be trusted. I know you are anxious to find out more information and have your identity proven for sure, but Robert Melvin is not who we should go to for those facts. He knew I was taken to the compound, and from the way he said it, I think he may have had something to do with them coming for me. He didn't give Janelle any support when she had you, and I wouldn't be surprised if he had something to do with them finding you too. He said Janelle and her baby lived like hobos for four years."

"What is a hobo?" Emery asked.

"A hobo moves from place to place with no home."

"I think I remember that part. In my dreams we are always leaving in a hurry. Sometimes my mother is running. And in my dreams we are usually sleeping outside. Do you think I really remember that? Would I remember things if I was only four when they took me?"

Valerie had stepped out onto the veranda a few minutes before, quietly listening to the interchange between Augustus and Emery. She had heard Augustus's side of the telephone conversation and was not surprised Emery was bursting with questions.

"Terrance was five, and you would be surprised at how much detail he remembers," Valerie said. "His father was astounded by the things Terrance was able to tell him once he started allowing himself to remember. He remembers a lot of things about his mother too, and he was four when she died."

"And fire. I knew about fire," Emery added. "Sometimes the fires in my dreams are under grates and my mother is cooking something on the grate. I don't know how I even know that but since I've been here it all seems clearer. I had no knowledge of such things when I was inside the wall, so my dreams back then didn't make any sense."

"Campsites often have those type of fire pits," Valerie said. "Maybe you and your mother moved around from campsite to campsite, in the warm seasons, anyway. I wonder where you lived in the winter."

"I do remember white fields and fire in a black box."

"She must have taken you to a cabin somewhere. The fire was probably in a wood stove," Valerie said.

Augustus stood up and walked the length of the veranda. "The cabin. When Janelle was a little girl her mother brought her here for her one and only visit. Our neighbour had a team of Belgian horses and gave sleigh rides. Reggie took us on a sleigh ride along his trails to a cabin on the far corner of his property. We got warm and had our lunch there. Janelle loved it. Reggie died a few years ago and Doris went to live with her daughter. The property was sold, but as far as I know the cabin is still standing."

"Do you suppose Janelle came here and stayed in that cabin with Emery?" Augustus asked aloud, but more to himself than to Emery or

Valerie. "Why didn't she bring the baby to us? Janey and I would have welcomed her with open arms."

"There are lots of questions to be answered, that's for sure," Valerie said. "I think we should start by getting my friend to search for Janelle. As a lawyer she can access official records. Maybe she can contact her."

"What if she doesn't want to see me?"

"I can't imagine why she wouldn't," Augustus answered. "From everything you remember and the little bit Robert told me, it seems she fought really hard to keep you."

§

Daisy was almost asleep when she heard the door open. It was getting harder and harder to stay awake, her hunger a weakness she couldn't shake. Her delirium was causing her to see things and she couldn't keep the scenes straight in her head. The jolt of the door closing brought her to her senses. She bolted upright.

"I have food."

The guard—Jonathan, she remembered him being called—was standing in front of her. His face seemed shadowed and possibly she was dreaming.

"I brought you some food," he whispered. "I am going to leave it. Take your time eating it, as your stomach might reject it after this much time. I have set a bottle of water down in the corner. Hide the tray and the bottle under your cot so Vincent will not see them from the window. I will sneak you in another portion in the morning."

Jonathan left as quickly as he'd come, and it wasn't until Daisy put the food to her lips that she actually accepted the reality of him having been there. She scooped a small amount into her mouth, then moved for the water. She had been sure her death was mere days away, but with nourishment and water perhaps her demise was not yet to be.

Why was Jonathan defying orders and bringing her food? Perhaps he could be trusted and would assist her escape. Daisy ate another bite, formulating a plan. If Jonathan continued to bring her food and water and took the evidence of it away each time, Vincent wouldn't know she was being fed and hydrated.

Daisy took a sip of water, afraid that guzzling the entire bottle would, as Jonathan had cautioned, cause her to vomit. Hopefully her starvation wasn't sanctioned by the authorities and Vincent would be afraid that if she actually died in her cell he would be blamed. If that was the case, her declining condition might alarm him and force him to take her to the infirmary, offering up a reason for her decline as something other than his order to withhold any food or water.

Taking another bite, Daisy thought about escape. Getting away from this cell, out of this prison compound, and out from inside the wall might be possible. Imagining herself somewhere else had always been her driving force. But where was that someplace else, and what would her future be there? Fear had always haunted her, but even with such vast uncertainty she knew without a doubt that whatever was in her future, it would be better than the past she'd known and her present circumstance.

§

Terrance stood on the front step of his neighbour's home. On the walk over, it had seemed to him a simple thing to go the Millers and just ask if the cabin on the far end of their property was still standing. The Millers were friendly enough, but their friendliness had so far been nothing more than an occasional wave and a time or two when Bert brought over his tractor with its snow-blower attachment to clean out their driveway after an especially huge snowfall.

Terrance had never really gotten to know Bert Miller or his wife, Mary. How strange would his question about the cabin seem? Would he have to give details about Augustus and Emery if he were to ask if they could go see the cabin? They could just sneak on to the property and make their way back to the cabin without asking.

Terrance realized as he was about to knock that his real fear was exposing the fact that he and Emery had been raised in the Establishing Compound. He was also afraid to divulge the fact that Emery and Augustus had escaped. Terrance was well aware of the fact that since the laws were put in place that built those compounds, neighbours often reported on each other for profit. What could he ask Bert Miller about the cabin without the risk of revealing his reason for asking?

"Hello, Terrance," said Mary Miller when she opened her front door. "Are you looking for Bert?"

"Is he around?"

"Actually, he just left a few minutes ago. Did you need something?"

"Well, I feel a bit foolish coming over to bother you, but I just wanted to settle an argument my cousin and I were having. Not an argument, really, but could you just give me some information that would clear up something for us? He remembers as a kid coming here and going on sleigh rides. The man who lived here before you had a team of horses and gave sleigh rides in the winter. I remember going on them myself. But my cousin remembers going to a cabin at the end of the ride. I don't think I ever did. He is sure there's a cabin on the edge of your property. Is he right?"

"Yes, there is. We didn't even realize it was there when we bought the property. Bert hired a young fellow to cut some logs for the shed he built a couple of years ago and he came upon it."

"So it's still standing?"

"Yes. I haven't been back there, but it's still standing, I know that. You're welcome to go back and have a look. Bert had a road put in to get the lumber out and I think you could drive a truck back there if you wanted to, for the money he spent on the damn thing. It's quite a walk, but you could walk back. Just walk up the hill a ways and you'll see the road. Follow it and I believe you'll come to the old cabin."

"Thank you. We just might do that. Tell Bert I was by in case he sees us trooping up the hill and wonders what we're doing."

"No problem. How's Valerie feeling?"

"Good. She hasn't had a sick day with this one. Maybe that means it's a girl. She was quite sick with Zac."

"Boy or girl, a baby is a blessing. Tell her to come by sometime."

"I will. Thanks again."

CHAPTER 12

VALERIE'S FRIEND ROXANNE got right on the search. She found the story compelling and as it happened had just completed a similar search for a client. That search had uncovered a list of former recruiters who were willing to talk about the time they spent rounding up children for the Establishing Compound. One such recruiter was Elizabeth Forgraves, and Roxanne was minutes away from meeting her at a nearby coffee shop.

Valerie was to join them there. It appeared from the records that the last case Mrs. Forgraves had worked on was the recruitment of a four-year-old girl on a remote road in Ravenville. Valerie did not feel Emery was ready for such a meeting, so she was going to pretend she was the mother of that child, even though the age difference might be evident to the woman. Roxanne was hopeful that Mrs. Forgraves wouldn't right away dismiss Valerie's claim.

Elizabeth Forgraves was sitting in the back booth in the far corner under the large espresso sign, just where she told Roxanne she'd be. She looked up, her face quite expressionless as Roxanne walked toward her.

"Hello, Mrs. Forgraves. I'm Roxanne Jarvis. I hope you haven't been waiting too long. The traffic was worse than I expected."

"No problem, I've only been here a few minutes. Please call me Beth."

"It was so nice of you to agree to meet us, Beth. My client has been looking for answers for some time. She is expecting again and so happy for the gift of another child, but her pain of being separated from her daughter has never lessened."

"I am not sure I can help your client. What did you say your client's name was?"

"Janelle Thompson. It was Janelle Melvin then. She thinks her daughter was given the number 37."

"We didn't number them. We were only told the parent's name and the location where we were to apprehend the child. Do you know exactly where I found her daughter?"

"As I said on the telephone, we believe the child was taken somewhere in Ravenville."

Elizabeth Forgraves fumbled with the pendant around her neck. She was a frail woman, her grey hair dishevelled and unkempt. Her face seemed hollow and her eyes showed a deep sadness. She seemed uncomfortable, her eyes darting around the room. "I could still be prosecuted for divulging any confidential information."

"The information I have is all on public record. Oh, here's Janelle now."

Valerie walked over and slid into the booth beside Roxanne. A somewhat awkward introduction was interrupted when the waitress came over to the table. The three women placed coffee orders, and then sat in uncomfortable silence. Valerie was the first to speak.

"You cannot know how thankful I am that you agreed to see me. I want to say right up front that I don't put the blame for what happened on you. You had a job to do."

"I must say, I wasn't thrilled to get your lawyer's call. I have tried to put you out of my mind. I couldn't even remember what you looked like. I remember your little girl, though."

"Janelle only started trying to find her daughter around the time she figured she would be released. She didn't really know where to start looking, but a friend of hers contacted her when a girl around the right age showed up with her uncle. The girl seems to remember being taken from a farm in Ravenville. Janelle has not approached the girl yet because she wants to make sure she's her daughter before going to her. She hopes you can help her figure that out."

"Your little girl's name was Ann Marie, wasn't it?" Beth Forgraves asked.

Valerie looked at Roxanne quickly before replying. "Yes, Ann Marie. You were the recruiter who took her from me."

Beth Forgraves looked away, her breath becoming more rapid and her tension mounting. She took a deep breath before speaking.

"The word *recruiter* seemed so important at first. I was pretty puffed up having such a title and thrilled to be making the salary that came along with it. I'd also been convinced that the work I was called to do was necessary. Society needed workers willing to keep the wheels turning. People had become so self-absorbed and too proud to do certain jobs. We were shown videos and given indoctrination training and told that the formation of Establishing Compounds was the only way to ensure a reliable work force for the future. We were also lectured about the weaknesses in our society, one of them being single mothers draining the system with their carelessness."

Beth took a long sip of the coffee from the cup the waitress had just placed in front of her.

"I'm sorry. I didn't mean to offend you," Beth said. "I see things so much differently now. We were trained to think that way. At first it sounded archaic; like something from the past. But after a while it made sense. It was our role to find infants born to single mothers and *recruit* them. Then after the Second Same-Sex law was passed we removed those infants from the hospital, sometimes without even informing the parents. That was always difficult, but taking an older child from their home was the worst. We were given a lot of pre-briefing before that task. By the time we went to the homes we were totally convinced it was in the child's best interest."

Beth picked up her coffee and took several more sips before continuing. "But some of the experiences tore me apart. I was becoming less able to conduct that sort of recruitment. And I was beginning to question the morality of it. And then came the morning I was sent to find you."

Valerie looked at the emotion in the woman's shaking frame and downcast expression. She quickly put herself in the headspace of a woman being told about the day her four-year-old daughter had been forcefully removed from her. She wanted details she could later share with Emery, hoping to jog her memory and further prove her identity. But she did not want to say anything that might give her impersonation of Janelle Melvin away.

"Can you tell me about that morning?" Valerie almost whispered. "I have my memories, but I really need to hear it from your side if you don't mind."

Beth took another swig of her coffee. "I quit that very day. I know that doesn't make what I did any less painful for you, but I just want you to know that as I was pulling your little girl out of your arms, I knew what I was doing was evil. I have never quite been able to get your wailing out of my head. Ann Marie went quietly, though, which was almost as haunting."

"How did you find us?"

"We got a call from a man saying he knew where Janelle Melvin was hiding with her little girl. He said his wife's sister lived in a house on a country road near Ravenville. The North Lake Road."

"That bastard," Valerie muttered. "It was my own father who reported me. He got paid, right?"

"I didn't know it was your father. I'm so sorry to be the one to tell you."

"I think I always knew. How much did he get paid?"

"Fifty dollars was the going rate for just reporting a recruit. If the child was actually rounded up, another fifty dollars was paid out."

Valerie's eyes filled with tears, and she did not have to conjure up the emotion causing them. She couldn't even imagine her own father selling Zachary for a hundred dollars.

"I think I'm going to have to process what you are telling me. I was going to ask you about Ann Marie's trip to the compound, but I don't think I can stand to hear any more. As difficult as this is, I am so thankful to know that you stopped recruiting the day you took my little girl. Just knowing another mother didn't have to suffer like I have makes me feel a bit better."

"I wish I could say that's true. Someone else was happy to take my place. I keep my story to myself. I've always been afraid of repercussions and kept a really low profile, but now after meeting you I wish I had the courage to use what I know about that terrible system to help bring about its end."

"I think we all need to work toward that," Roxanne said.

"If you don't mind, I am going to go home now," Beth said. "I wish you all the best, Janelle. I hope you give birth to a healthy child and I hope the girl at your friend's house is Ann Marie. I know you will never get the years back that were stolen from you. Maybe I can meet her someday and tell her how sorry I am and just how hard her mother fought to keep her."

Beth slid out from the booth and quickly left the coffee shop. Valerie switched to the other side of the booth, staring dumbly at Roxanne, trying to fully take in the drama of the interchange. The waitress approached and re-filled their cups.

"Emery. Ann Marie. They didn't even get her name right," Valerie said. "I wonder who messed it up, or when the pronunciation and spelling changed. But Emery is Janelle Melvin's daughter, all right. And it was her own grandfather who turned them in. Augustus said he wasn't to be trusted. I wonder if Janelle knew it was her father who reported her whereabouts. We need to find her. She deserves to have her daughter back."

Valerie drove back to North Lake Road with a heavy heart. She kept imagining having to flee with her infant days after it was born and spend the next four years in hiding. She pictured the horror of having Zachary ripped from her arms and taken away somewhere where she wouldn't see him until he was released into the workforce in his teens. And the nagging fear of the Same-Sex law was foremost on her mind. If this baby was another boy, might he be taken from the hospital?

Walking toward the car, Terrance knew right away his wife was upset. He opened the car door and enfolded Valerie in his arms as she disembarked.

"Are you all right, hon?"

"I knew recruiters took children. I knew you had been taken from your father. But I never really allowed myself to imagine it from a parent's viewpoint. The woman we met told of the wailing and the fight Emery's mother put up. I have been thinking how I would react if someone came to take Zachary. Her own father reported her and told them where she was. We need to have this baby at home."

"Calm down, sweetie. I should have kept you from going. Roxanne could have asked the woman the same questions."

"Did you hear me? We need to have this baby right here. I'm not going to take the chance of going to the hospital. What if this baby is a boy? The woman said she took infants right from the hospital without the parents even knowing. We are not taking that chance."

Emery stepped out on the veranda to hear the last few words before Valerie broke into sobs. Terrance led his wife into the house, but Emery stood still. What had Valerie found out? Was the story the recruiter told so terrible? Flashes of memory filled Emery's head. The crying.

She'd always thought it was the child crying in her dreams, but hearing Valerie's sobs through the screen door, Emery realized it was the woman she always heard in her dreams. The woman's loud and mournful crying filled her memory.

Emery stepped down off the steps. She started walking, not sure where she was headed but somehow knowing the memory of the moment she was taken from her mother's arms was what was guiding her. Down the driveway, past the mailbox, along the shore of the lake. She walked for several minutes before coming to a break in the trees on the other side of the road. She crossed the road and stepped across the ditch. The trees overgrown on either side almost hid the track, but the two ruts of what had once been a driveway were still evident. She began walking in the trail until she reached a clearing.

The car had driven up that morning. A woman had gotten out and walked toward them. Emery was hiding behind her mother's legs. The two women stood talking while she tugged on her mother's legs, trying to tell her she had to pee. The pee had trickled down her leg a few minutes later when the woman was pulling her from her mother's arms. The woman who snatched her ran with her to the open car door. "Mommy, Mommy!" she had screamed and her mother hit and pulled at the woman's back as she was leaning in to fasten Emery's seatbelt. The woman had pushed her mother to the ground, jumped into the driver's seat, and backed up quickly, rocks spraying. Emery had turned her head to see her mother running after the car until she got smaller and smaller, disappearing as the dirt road became smooth and black.

Emery sat on the ground and through the haze of tears gazed up at the sky above. They had been right here. Why hadn't they walked the short distance to the big white house? Augustus would have kept the woman in the car from taking her.

It was quite a few minutes before Emery even considered walking back to the house. A part of her just wanted to stay right in this place. If only just by being here she could return to the very moment she was remembering. If only she could reach out and assure her mother that she was still right here. She would convince her to go to the big white house and let Augustus help them.

Emery imagined the scene again, this time without the red car that had come to take her. She imagined her mother leading her into the woods so she could pee and then them walking up the hill to pick the blueberries hanging off the low bushes. That's why they had walked up the trail. They had carried their sleeping bags and the one bag they always had. The bag that carried her jammies, her silk-bound blanket, and her stuffed tiger. They would fill the yellow can with those blueberries and later sit by the fire and eat them.

§

Augustus was on the veranda when Emery walked into the yard. He stood and started walking toward her. "I was worried about you. We didn't know where you'd gone."

"We were only a little ways from here. Do you know the field where the blueberries grow thick? They still do, by the way. I only picked a handful. Maybe I could take a container later and pick more."

"Blueberries grow all over here, but there is a really good spot that Janey always went to, up on the old Bailey place. Just an overgrown path up to it now. Used to be a farm up there. The Baileys were our closest neighbours growing up."

"That's where we were the morning the woman came to take me. We were so close, Grandpa. You could almost throw a rock from here to there. Why didn't she bring me here?"

"I don't know, dear. I have been asking myself that ever since I found out Janelle and you were so close. There must have been some reason. I guess we won't know until we ask her."

"I wasn't sure before if I wanted to find her. I kept thinking it would be too hard to see her after all this time. But I know now it would just be selfish of me not to at least try to find her. I need to tell her I'm alright. I need to tell her she can come here now. She needs to know she has family and people who love her."

"You are a special kid, Emery. You were raised in a place that tried to take all your compassion and humanity away, and you didn't let it. You are the most caring and thoughtful girl I have ever met. Certainly the greatest young lady I've ever had the pleasure of pretending to be the grandfather of."

"But you really are my great-uncle. I like the name Grandpa better, though. I love you, Grandpa."

"I love you too, Emery."

CHAPTER 13

DAISY FORCED HERSELF TO stay as still and lifeless as she'd been when Vincent entered her cell a few seconds ago. Two sets of hands had lifted her onto the gurney, and she felt the motion as it was wheeled out into the corridor. She shut her eyes tightly and recalled the conversation she had had earlier with Jonathan before he went to alert Vincent of her grave condition.

In minutes, she and Jonathan had devised a plan for her escape, and being moved to the infirmary was the first step. Jonathan would ask to stand watch over her room in the infirmary. He would wait for the opportunity to get her out of the building and hide her until he could get her out of the compound, hopefully before anyone noticed she was missing. For the last five days Jonathan had been sneaking food and water into her. She had feigned increasing weakness and Jonathan had gone to Vincent several times, dramatically playing into Vincent's fear of being blamed for the death of number 57.

Minutes ago, Jonathan had burst into Vincent's office with the hysterical account of number 57's near-death condition. Vincent had immediately instructed orderlies to transport Daisy to the infirmary. Above the noise of the gurney wheels, she could hear Vincent's nervous chatter.

"She was fine yesterday. It must be the flu or something. I don't know how she would catch anything; she's been alone in this cell for sixteen days. I suppose one of us might have brought the germs to her. Bed rest and fluids will fix her I'm sure. Good thing I noticed her condition when I did. It came on so fast."

Daisy squeezed her eyes even tighter, trying not to show any reaction to Vincent's words. Bed rest, as if she had done anything besides lie on that stupid cot in that empty room since they had dumped her there more than two weeks ago. Good thing he noticed. Why was he even bothering to try to convince the men wheeling her through the corridor? They couldn't care less about her condition or his part in it. They were almost as powerless as she was. They were Less Thans who'd been given this job placement after their release.

Vincent began again, pretty much repeating everything he had just said. He was practising, Daisy guessed, making sure he sounded convincing when he actually had to explain to those in charge why number 57 had died.

§

Terrance, in an attempt to make the walk to the cabin seem like an enjoyable outing, had packed a basket full of food. They'd stopped partway in the Millers' wood road to eat their picnic lunch. Valerie stayed home with Zachary, but Augustus assured them he could walk the distance. Emery had mixed feelings about going to the cabin. What if it didn't look familiar? What difference if it did or it didn't? She didn't need the memory of the cabin to convince her she was Janelle Melvin's daughter and her time in hiding had been spent so close to Augustus.

The day was lovely, though, and Emery was determined to enjoy the walk. She had eaten the chicken salad sandwiches and the fruit and cookies, and waited while Terrance and Augustus drank their tea. They talked nonstop, mostly about Augustus's childhood, and Emery allowed her thoughts to simmer. All she really wanted now was to find her mother. Anything she wondered about could be answered by Janelle Melvin, but Terrance thought she should go to the cabin and see if it brought any other memories back, so after the picnic she continued to follow Terrance and Augustus along the wood road.

Emery stopped walking and stared at the cabin in front of her. It was small and the overgrown bushes looked to be swallowing it up. Several of the log supports holding up the moss-covered veranda roof had rotted, causing a precarious dip to one side. Two panes were broken in the six-paned window beside the door, and a ratty lace curtain hung through the opening. A screen door hung from one hinge and the plywood door behind it seemed wedged open enough to allow entrance to raccoons and other animals.

Terrance climbed the one step to the platform and cautiously stepped toward the door. "Let me just make sure the whole thing isn't going to collapse on us before we try to go in."

Nothing about this falling-down cabin looked familiar to Emery, but its condition filled her with sadness. If she and her mother had stayed here, then it was the only home she had ever known. If she went into this cabin now, would that keep her from having memories of it as it was when she had been here as a small child?

"It looks sound enough on the inside," Terrance called out from the open door. "There have been a few creatures in here by the looks of it, but I don't think anything will jump out at us."

Augustus took Emery by the hand. "Are you finding this difficult? You've had a lot to handle in the last few days. It's up to you whether or not you go in, you know."

"I know. It doesn't look familiar to me, Grandpa. Not from the outside anyway."

§

Daisy was hooked up to an IV. She hadn't really expected the attention she was getting and she had already lain here for two days. She thought it would be quicker than this. Jonathan was in every few hours, but there hadn't been an opportunity to sneak Daisy out of the infirmary.

"It seems keeping you alive is a priority," Jonathan whispered. "Vincent has been let go."

"Why do they care if I live or die?"

"Apparently you are to be used as an example to quiet some rebellion going on in the compound. Do you remember the girl who took her dining test with you? She escaped. Took an Old One out of the Old Ones' Compound and disappeared. Two friends of hers were grilled for hours but gave nothing up. The interrogation seems to have brought out a wave of defiance. They released the boy and sent him to the garbage facility with a lifelong contract. They want to show that you have been brought back on side. They plan to parade you around as their poster child for conformity."

"So my escape is not going to be as easy as we thought it would be," Daisy said. "If I do get out of this infirmary, I will need to get as far away as possible."

"Yes, and that is going to be a challenge. I will have to go too, because it won't go well for me if you escape on my watch."

§

Emery sat on the edge of a bench staring at the rusted woodstove, its pipe dislodged and hanging from the cobwebbed ceiling. Her gaze moved slowly around the room, resting on the beam that ran across the ceiling. She stood, moving closer, and then pulled a wooden chair over checking its sturdiness before stepping up on to it.

Ann Marie turned four here today

"My name was Ann Marie. 'Annie, Annie, Annie Marie.' She used to sing to me."

Emery got down and sat on the wooden chair, her hands covering her face, the tears coming quickly.

Terrance crossed the room and put his arm around her. "Valerie told me your real name was Ann Marie. We didn't tell you. I'm not sure why. It seems so mean that you didn't even get called the right name. We can look for your birth records now, and maybe that will help find your mother."

"It will probably give my grandfather's address, and I don't want him contacted. I don't want him to know I am at Augustus's. If my mother had trusted him, she would have gone to him for help or she would have taken me to Janey and Augustus."

"It was Robert Melvin who reported your mother and told them where you were."

"If my legal last name is Melvin, I want it changed. He took me from my mother. He sentenced me to a life as a Less Than. He thought I was nothing, of no value. By making that call he changed who I was supposed to be."

"He has no such power, Emery," Augustus said. "He changed your circumstances for sure, but he has no power over who you are. You are the only one with that power."

"I think I want to keep the name Emery. Is that wrong? My mother called me Ann Marie, but Emery is who I am. Do you think she will understand?"

"Of course she will," answered Terrance. "She will be so happy that you are all right. She won't care what you want to be called."

"Let's go home, "Augustus said.

"Yes, let's," Emery replied. "I need to jump in the lake and get this dust and grime off."

§

Terrance and Valerie sat on the shore of the lake watching Emery swimming out in the deep water. She'd been silent on the walk back and had quickly changed into her bathing suit and gone right to the lake.

"I'm worried that this is too much for her," said Terrance. "I remember how overwhelmed I was when so many things I'd been pushing down started to surface. I felt so guilty, too, although I'm not sure why. I felt in some way I had caused my father's pain. Emery has the added fact that her own grandfather thought her birth was shameful enough to actually take part in her recruitment."

"I know, that must be hard for her to accept. And to think she was so close to this house. Her life could have been so different. Janelle's life could have been too. I wonder where she is and how she is doing. I feel so close to her, probably because I pretended to be her but also just because I'm a mother too. I can't even imagine her agony. I hope she's found some happiness."

"I hope Roxanne can find her."

"If there's anyone who can, it's Roxanne. I think I'll go for a swim too."

"Good, I'll go start making supper," Terrance said.

A while later, Emery and Valerie were towelling off. They had kept their distance swimming back and forth, mindful of the need for the release the exercise was providing.

"I didn't remember the cabin, but I somehow remembered the carving in the beam overhead. I wasn't even surprised when I saw that the name carved there wasn't Emery. It always felt like Emery wasn't my real name. But I want to keep it. I stopped being Ann Marie when that woman put me in her car. I wonder when my name got changed. Did they take the pronunciation a four-year-old had of her own name and record it or did they even bother with my name? They referred to me as number 37. Maybe I said my name and it was repeated and morphed into what it is now. I am proud of it, though. Does that sound stupid?"

"Not at all. You should be very proud of a lot. You survived and didn't let your upbringing strip you of who you are. You are compassionate and brave and helped Augustus get back to his home. You have faced your memories and now are willing to take the next step."

"The next step. I'm not really sure what that is. Finding my mother, I suppose, but that seems like such a small thing when I know the compound is filled with kids just like me. Kids who were taken as babies, and kids who were taken when they were older. Those kids have memories and feel a longing the same as I always did. I don't think I can just live in freedom without thinking about them. Dixon, Sadie, and Daisy deserve freedom too."

The grey clouds burst open and a heavy rain began as Valerie and Emery headed to the house, causing them to pick up the pace and run toward the shelter of the veranda.

§

The room was in total darkness when Jonathan crept in and gently shook Daisy awake.

"It's a nasty night. It's raining heavily. I'm the only guard on duty. My replacement won't be in for two hours. If we get out quickly and get through the east gate without being seen, we could get quite a distance before we are missed. We are going to get soaked, but the darkness and rain might be to our advantage."

CHAPTER 14

DIXON PEELED OFF THE coveralls and threw them in the bin. He had only been here for ten days, but the vile, exhausting routine was already cemented in his mind. The gong rang at five o'clock. He rose from his cot and quickly went to the slot his tray came through. He ate in solitude and then was driven to the garbage facility. For the next six hours he stood and processed waste, pawing through each receptacle, sorting items that held recycling value. The noon gong would go and he had twenty minutes to wash, eat, and return to the line. Six more gruelling hours until another twenty-minute meal break. The next shift was shorter, only five hours of sorting people's disgusting garbage. Then the drive back to barracks, a shower, and sleep.

Eleven days ago they'd pulled him from the sleeping house sometime in the middle of the night. He hadn't even known at that point about Emery escaping with an Old One. They kept asking him where number 37 was. He'd been confused and each time he answered "sleeping house number five," they would strike him. They shook a piece of paper in his face.

"What is this note about? What code did she leave you? What does this mean?"

Once you have tasted flight you will forever walk the earth with your eyes skyward, for there you have been, and there you will always long to return.

He hadn't even seen the note. Where had they found it? He had no idea what it meant. How did they know it was even from Emery?

"Number 45 gave us this note. She was supposed to deliver it to you. She says number 37 had been planning to leave for days. Where was she going?"

For what seemed like hours, Dixon had denied knowing anything about Emery's escape, but the more he protested, the angrier his interrogators got.

"This one needs a lifelong contract. He has the look of defiance in his eyes and has been fraternizing with dissenters."

Dixon had heard about lifelong contracts. They were the dreaded tasking of release. You were housed and kept in servitude doing whatever unfavourable job they needed workers for.

Garbage detail was one of the most disgusting. People no longer had to manage their own waste. Everything that was thrown away came in large receptacles and was sorted at the garbage-retrieval compound. Workers stood at the dumping area and spent hours sorting through the vile, stinking mess of refuse, picking out materials that were sorted into bins for processing. Plastic, metals and glass were the three most profitable.

Dixon stepped under the trickle of lukewarm water, picking up the sliver of soap to rub away the scum of the day. Ten days of a lifetime of this. *Once you have tasted flight*...The words caught in his throat and he allowed the weeping to return.

§

Max had arrived earlier that day with mushrooms and garlic and a job offer for Emery.

"I was wondering if you might want to make some money in the next two weeks before school starts."

School was something Valerie and Terrance had been explaining to Emery. She couldn't even imagine being dropped into school at her age. Apparently kids started when they were five, just a year after she'd been taken. They attended school for ten months of the year and learned to read, write, and work with numbers. She had learned these skills in the four years daily lessons were given, but she was sure her abilities would be inferior to the other kids in the big brick building with the words *Rockport Consolidated School* in large black letters.

"Do I have to go?" Emery asked.

"I don't suppose you have to legally," Terrance replied. "There isn't even a record of you except for the records that say you are a resident of the Establishing Compound. Once someone is released records are provided, but in your case that hasn't been done so it might be tricky to get you enrolled. We just thought you would like to meet kids your age."

"I can't really see how that would be a good thing. What would I have in common with kids raised outside with families? I would seem different, I know that."

So when Max came with his offer, Emery suggested she start to work for him for as long as he needed her and forget about the school thing. It was agreed that Max would pick her up the next day for her first day of work.

"He's getting a damn good worker, I'll tell you that," Augustus said, as he and Terrance sat out on the veranda long after the others had gone to bed.

"That's for sure," Terrance agreed. "My garden has never looked as good. There's not a weed to be seen."

§

The escape had been quite easy. The building had been dark and silent and Daisy had followed Jonathan through the maze of corridors and out the main door. It had indeed been teeming down rain, so running to the gate was of no advantage. They decided instead to move through the compound slowly, mindful of any movement that might risk detection.

"This gate just pulls open," Jonathan said. "I always believed while growing up that the gates were locked and could only be opened by a Keeper or an Enforcer. Once I was tasked as a Keeper I realized how easy it would have been to run away."

"Did you consider it?"

"Always, since the day I was brought here. My sister and I were taken the day after we buried our parents, and the sound of my aunt's crying still rings in my ears."

"You were raised as a Less Than?"

"Yes, but my sister was taken to the other side. Separating us was even more heartless than taking us from our aunt's house. They had to pry Victoria's small hands from my arm."

"Your sister's name is Victoria and she was raised as an Elite?"

"Yes."

"The Elite who offered me food was named Victoria. Did your sister have blue eyes?"

"As blue as the bluest sky."

"Her eyes were a deep blue and the caring and compassion coming from those beautiful eyes touched the core of my being. Because of Victoria's kindness I ended up in the place where I meet her brother and he rescues me. How amazing is that?"

Daisy and Jonathan stopped talking and didn't speak again until they were a distance from the east gate.

"We need to get as far away as possible," Jonathan said. "I was thinking we should find the bus station and buy a ticket to Rockport."

"How do you know all this stuff? I was an infant when they took me. I don't know very much about the outside world. I used to steal books when I was tasked in the Elite library, and I learned some things, but it was all so mysterious to me. But one thing I always knew was I didn't belong inside the wall. Even a caged bird longs for freedom and flutters its wings in its attempt to take to the sky."

It took several minutes to get to the bus station. The bus for Rockport was leaving in fifteen minutes. Jonathan bought the tickets, then went to the vending machine to purchase pop and cheese sticks.

"This isn't the best thing to give you as an introduction to real food, but pop was always a treat for us growing up. On Friday nights Dad always made sure there was pop and snacks for our family movie night."

"What is a movie?"

"It's kind of hard to explain, but you'll find out. Movies are one of the pleasures out here that Less Thans never get to know about. There is so much to discover. I put most of it out of my mind, but once I got released and got the chance to live outside the wall, it came back to me quickly."

"So you live outside the wall?"

"Yes, just a few minutes away from the east gate. I thought of taking you there so we could sleep tonight and leave for somewhere in the morning, but I figured once they find we're missing that will be the first place they look."

"So you were tasked as a Keeper guard when you were released but you are allowed to live outside the wall?"

"Yes, being a Keeper guard in the lockup is a four-year contract. You are paid enough to be able to afford a small apartment and you have more freedom than most. It has risks, though, because Keeper guards are watched very closely. It is all about toeing the line and keeping the system running smoothly so that no one questions it. They need their Keepers and Enforcers to have a vested interest in that. Usually it's the self-serving and hard-hearted Less Thans they choose for this work. I guess in their eyes I fit the bill. Any mistakes or signs of weakness can result in an immediate lifelong assignment, so I went along with everything."

"It was a huge risk for you to bring me food, not to mention helping me escape."

"I guess so, but I could not turn a blind eye to Vincent starving you to death, and I didn't like the plans they had for you once you were taken to the infirmary. I would rather take a lifelong tasking than give up being a caring human being."

Daisy took a swig from the can of pop, coughing and sputtering as she swallowed the carbonated drink. "You liked this stuff?"

"It grows on you."

Hearing the Rockport announcement, Daisy and Jonathan made their way to the bus. Daisy settled into the comfortable seat. This huge metal box on wheels was going to start to move, and Daisy was struggling to stop her body from trembling. Other people were filing onto the bus and did not appear afraid. She could see another similar vehicle pulling out of the station. Apparently people travelled distances this way, so it must be safe.

Daisy closed her eyes and concentrated on the fact that she had finally escaped the life that had caused her so much anguish for so long. She was leaving that all behind her and it was well worth the risk this moving box might hold.

The driver's announcement woke Daisy up from the deep sleep she had fallen into minutes after the bus pulled out of the station. Looking out the window, she could see that it was still dark but the rain had stopped. Life inside the wall ran by routine rather than attention to hands on a clock or digital numbers. She could see the numbers 3:45 lit in red on the dash beside the driver, but she wasn't sure what they represented.

"I don't have a plan," Jonathan mumbled. "Rockport came to mind and I figured it was as good as any place to get away to, but now that we're here I have no idea where we go next. I have a bit of money, but it won't last long if we use it to get a hotel room. We will need money for food too."

Daisy looked over at Jonathan and realized he was as frightened as she was. They had both escaped from a life where decisions were made for them. Being in control was foreign and would take some getting used to. But for now they were safe and free.

"Would it be safe to just sleep outside somewhere?" Daisy asked. "It's not raining anymore and it's warm enough."

"Yeah, I guess so. Sorry I'm not more prepared. I probably should have figured it all out before taking you out of the compound."

"Are you kidding me? You got me out, and that is all that matters. You risked everything to rescue me. We'll figure it all out as we go along. We are not caged birds any longer."

CHAPTER 15

DAISY TURNED OVER, the ground a hard, uncomfortable, but not unbearable bed. At first she hadn't minded it. She'd been exhausted, and once they'd stopped, rest was welcome. They'd walked quite a way before reaching the large brick building and then walking onto the concrete square behind it. In the moonlight she had seen several metal poles and structures that Jonathan said were part of a playground, and the large building was a school. They had walked to the edge of the concrete, finding a roof held up with wooden posts. Jonathan put his jacket down on the grass beside a table of some kind and suggested they sleep the rest of the night under the shelter.

The light caught Daisy's eye when she rolled over. It looked like fire in the sky. As she stared, the sky around the ball of fire rising from behind the far hill illuminated the rolling dark clouds. Light danced and flickered, swallowing the darkness. Daisy had never considered the change that takes place from light to darkness and back to light. The beauty was overwhelming and she gasped, waking Jonathan. He sat up quickly.

"Have you never seen a sunrise before?" he asked.

"No. It is breathtaking. I feel as if I have waited my whole life to see the beauty of it. People see this every day?"

"Yes. Outside the wall, if you get up early enough and the weather is not overcast, you can see the beauty of a sunrise every day. The sun setting also gives an amazing display."

"They have kept this from me, and in doing that have also kept the hope a sunrise brings. Every new day should have such an introduction and not be kept from anyone intentionally by shutting out the sky. I knew the evil of the wall, but this makes it even clearer to me. How can people on the outside stand by and let such evil exist?"

"I wondered that even as a child. I remember being dragged out of my aunt's house. Neighbours gathered, hearing the ruckus, and I was sure they would stop the men who were taking us. I called out to Mr. Roberts, my aunt's next-door neighbour, begging him to stop them, but he stood there silently. Nobody said anything. Mrs. Roberts rushed to my aunt and held her, but nobody stopped the men from taking us. I couldn't understand it. It made me wonder if my aunt had done something wrong and her punishment was us being taken from her."

"Well, I'm not going to forget the sight of my first sunrise. Whatever the future brings, I will keep this memory and use it to give me hope. Nothing on the outside can ever be as terrible as being kept on the inside, away from this beauty."

"That is a good way to look at it. Let's get moving. There could be children swarming this place soon, and I think it would be best if we weren't here. Let's find somewhere to get something to eat."

§

Roxanne dialled the number and waited. She had already called several places, but something about this one seemed right. The information she got was that Janelle Melvin was on staff at the Aurora House Women's Shelter. She hoped as she heard the ringing that whoever answered would allow her to talk to her.

"Aurora House. How can I help you?"

"Hello. My name is Roxanne Jarvis. I am looking to speak to Janelle Melvin."

"Why?"

"I understand she is on staff there. I was hoping to speak to her."

"Why?"

There was something in the tone of that one simple question that alerted Roxanne. Was it fear?

"Are you Janelle?"

There was a pause, and for a second Roxanne was sure the woman on the line was going to hang up.

"Janelle?" Roxanne asked again slowly in an attempt to delay a disconnection.

"Yes."

"Janelle. I am calling for a friend. She is married to Augustus Davidson's great-nephew."

"Augustus Davidson?"

"Yes, he is your uncle, isn't he?"

"Yes."

"Janelle, if you would like to meet and talk rather than speak over the phone I would be more than willing to meet you somewhere."

"What does your friend want?"

"She believes your daughter is living with her. Your uncle Augustus and the girl arrived there a couple of weeks ago."

"What makes her think it's Ann Marie?"

"The girl has memories. And I've spoken to the recruiter who took her from you. The facts seem to add up. Can I meet with you?"

"I don't know."

"Your daughter was taken from you when she was four, right? You were on the North Lake Road?"

"How did you find me?"

"It wasn't your father, if that's what you're worried about."

"Leave me your number and I will call you back."

Roxanne gave her the office number and her cell phone number and immediately after the last digit was spoken the phone went dead.

§

Daisy stared at the heaping plate of food in front of her. Jonathan had ordered, since she had no idea what any of the items listed on the menu were.

"Breakfast is my favourite meal of the day. Wait until you taste eggs, bacon, home fries, and a side of pancakes. And I'll order a pitcher of orange juice so you will be sure to get your fill."

When the two plates of food arrived, Daisy watched as Jonathan shook dollops of some red stuff onto his plate, sprinkled some white particles, and spread something red on what the waitress called toast. Then he picked up a bottle of golden liquid and poured it on his pancake. She followed his lead and went about doing the same thing before taking the tool and picking up the first bite of food.

"It was a reddish-coloured food that your sister offered me at my dining test. It tasted sweet when I took the first bite, but my second bite tasted even better. I licked my lips trying to register the taste as Tonka carried me from the dining hall. I wanted the food, but it was more than that. When your sister turned to me and offered me the food, I saw her kindness. I saw in her eyes the truth of my own value. The first time I failed the test I failed because I got up and walked out, not waiting for the humiliation. The second time I was determined to fail it by taking food, but when your sister spoke to me I knew the real rebellion was to accept and believe that I was deserving. That's what made the Enforcer so angry."

Jonathan picked up the pitcher of juice the waitress had just set on the table. "Would you like some juice, Daisy?"

"How very kind of you. I would love some," Daisy replied.

§

Emery lifted the box onto the tailgate of Max's truck. She had already filled four crates with corn. The corn rows in Terrance's garden were nothing compared with the field of corn on Max's farm. She had been overwhelmed with all the garden plots surrounding the large greenhouse. They had driven by his small house to get right to the fields. Today was an especially busy day, with orders to fill for several stores in Rockport.

"We'll pick the corn first," Max had instructed when they'd arrived two hours ago. "By the time we finish the corn, the dew will be off the other vegetables."

Emery pushed the crate to the front beside the other three. She should be able to fill at least one more. Max had said that there were several varieties of corn planted to ensure a continual harvest. The variety she was picking this morning was called Espresso. Several other varieties were planted and the field of corn would produce well into the fall, Max said.

Summer was certainly a season to love, Emery thought, even though the heat sometimes got to her and bugs seemed to find her quite tasty. Augustus explained the season coming next would be cooler. The leaves on the trees were going to change colour. Winter would follow and the cold weather would likely bring snow. She remembered snow.

White fields were part of her memory of the days they must have been living in the cabin.

And she had always known about snow, first snow being the way to gauge her years inside the wall. She had thought she'd seen ten first snows, which made sense now that she realized she was already four when she was taken to the Establishing Compound. Roxanne was searching for her birth records, and soon she might know her exact birth date. It was the other information she wasn't sure she wanted to know. Would there be a father listed?

"Do you have any kids?" Emery asked as she and Max arrived at the next field, where rows of beans hung heavy.

Max passed her a basket. "No. We wanted them, but then Penny got sick."

"Your wife's name is Penny?"

"It was. She died three years ago."

"I'm sorry."

"Yeah, me too." Max turned away, wiping at his eyes with the sleeve of his shirt. "How about you start picking the yellow beans and I'll start on the green? We can sell whatever we get, and there's a lot here to pick, but I need to be heading to Rockport by noon. It's almost an hour's drive, and the stores like to be stocked before the after-work shoppers come in. What we don't get today we'll pick for our customers tomorrow."

As they picked the beans, Emery and Max were too far from each other to talk. Emery was sorry she'd asked him about kids and his wife. She should be more cautious and not so quick to pry into people's lives. She had so much to learn about the outside world.

"I'm sorry if I sounded angry a while ago, Emery," Max said as they got close enough to speak again. "I find it really hard to talk about Penny. I keep to myself pretty much anyway, but I know that's not always the best thing. This farm was a dream we both had, and the first few years after we bought it were filled with long, hard days of work. We cleared more land, built the house, the sheds, and the greenhouse. Every year we planted more plots, and believe me, we had our fair share of obstacles. But Penny's diagnosis made everything else seem like a walk in the park."

"What does a walk in the park mean?"

"Easy, effortless, enjoyable, I guess. I forget that you haven't been exposed to language and conversation filled with figures of speech."

"A Less Than took Augustus to the park. He got in trouble because Ronda, the manager of the Old Ones' Compound, didn't want Augustus to do anything he would enjoy. Why are people so mean? Did you know my own grandfather was probably the one who sent recruiters after me to take me from my mother?"

"That's hard to believe, isn't it? Your mother must have loved you a lot to hide you as long as she did. It must have been difficult for her."

"That's what I keep thinking. She doesn't even know that I'm okay. Valerie's friend is trying to find her. What was wrong with Penny?"

"Breast cancer. We made the decision for her to have both breasts removed, hoping it would save her. She was so upset thinking she wouldn't be able to nurse a baby, and she worried I would look at her differently or maybe not love her anymore. She was wrong. I loved her more every day for the year and three months we had together after her surgery. The cancer had spread to her lungs and bones."

"I'm so sorry, Max."

"Thank you. Let's get these beans in the truck and then have a snack before we start picking peas."

§

"Emery's mother just called me back," Roxanne said before even saying hello when Valerie answered on the second ring. "She wants to meet me later and talk. I'm meeting her at the fountain in Rockport. Did you want to join us?"

"I don't think I should. I think for the first meeting it would be less intimidating for her if it was just you. She is probably frightened. You can understand if she isn't completely trusting of people. Her own father betrayed her."

"I suppose you're right. I am going to suggest she meet Emery, though, or at least go see Augustus and begin the process."

"Emery is working today but should be home by suppertime. I would want to check with her before springing a surprise visit on her."

"Of course. I don't want to rush either of them."

"Let me know how the meeting goes."

The Rockport fountain was a focal point in the Rockport Community Park. It sat in the middle of a manmade lake and a cobblestone walkway circled it. Benches were situated along the walkway shaded under large weeping willows and maple trees. Roxanne walked to an empty bench and sat to wait, watching for the woman fitting the description Janelle Melvin had given her.

"I will be wearing a red shirt and blue pants. I will be carrying a brown purse over my shoulder. My hair will be pulled back in a braid."

The park was a bustle of activity. The afternoon sun was hot and the breeze warm. Roxanne took a long swig from her water bottle while scanning the several people walking toward her.

§

"I packed us sandwiches to eat on the way," Max said. "This is my busiest delivery day. Tomorrow we'll deliver to the Roadside and we'll take the time to enjoy some of Ruth's good cooking. But today it's store after store. I'm not complaining, though; getting the produce contract with those grocery stores was the big break we needed to get our business off the ground. Penny did the legwork for that. She had a pretty convincing way about her. She sure convinced me real quick that she was the one I wanted to spend my life with. Only got ten years, but some people don't even get that."

"Augustus had fifty five years with his wife, and he still doesn't feel like it was enough. I don't know if my mother and father had any time together. I don't think I want to fall in love. I figure if I don't, it won't hurt as much."

"Good luck with that, Emery. It's not a choice, really. The right person comes along and you don't stand a chance."

"Do you think you will ever fall in love again?"

"Well, I guess I can't say I never will, but if I do she'll have big shoes to fill."

"What does that mean?"

"I've got to stop using dumb sayings when I'm talking to you. Penny did not have big feet, but...oh, never mind. Some of our sayings are pretty stupid when you try to explain them. Here, eat a sandwich. We're about twenty minutes away from the first stop."

§

Roxanne saw Janelle while she was still quite a distance away. She was wearing the clothing described and she could also see a brown purse over the woman's shoulder, but it wasn't those things that caught her attention. Roxanne was taken aback by how much the woman walking toward her looked like Emery. She stood to greet her. "I'm so glad you agreed to meet me, Janelle. Please come and sit."

"I go by Jane, Jane Kimball," the woman said abruptly before sitting down. "I'm surprised you found me by my old name."

It was a few seconds before she spoke again. "I have had other people claim to know things about my daughter. In the first few years it seemed every few months someone would make up a story trying to convince me they had information about Ann Marie. Some people even tried to get me to pay for the information. It is terrible the people who profited or tried to profit from the immoral system that takes children away from their parents. I wasn't very trusting before I had my daughter taken, and the years afterwards didn't make me any less cautious. I'm sorry if I wasn't very friendly when you called. I also have to be suspicious in my line of work. Most women in our shelter are hiding from someone."

"I understand, Jane. I certainly can see why you would be skeptical, and I didn't want to overwhelm you at all. My friend Valerie didn't come with me for that reason. We want to give you time to process what we are telling you. We also want you to help us fill in the blanks for the girl at my friend's house."

"You said her name was Ann Marie?"

"Actually, she goes by Emery, but we think that is only because her name got changed slightly after she was taken. She remembers certain things that lead us to believe she is Ann Marie. She went right to the place in the cabin where her name is carved on the beam."

Ann Marie turned four here today. Tears streamed down Jane's cheeks. "I carved those words. The cabin is still standing?"

"Yes. Emery remembered staying in a cabin, and Augustus thought it might be the one on the property next to his place. They took her there to see it. She didn't remember it when she saw it, but once she got inside she went right to the beam."

"When I was a kid I went to that cabin with Aunt Janey and Uncle Augustus. The week we visited them is my happiest childhood memory. My mother was so different while we were there. She laughed and wasn't scared. I told her we should stay, but she said we couldn't. She went again just a couple of weeks before she died. I wished she'd stayed that time. You said Ann Marie has memories. What else does she remember?"

"The place she was taken from. A long driveway that led to an open field. A red car, picking blueberries. Bonfires and roasting marshmallows."

"Oh my heavens. Ann Marie loved marshmallows."

"She remembers moving from place to place. Is that what you did?"

"Yes. I knew when she was born that she would be taken from me. As soon as I could I left the hospital without telling anyone where we were headed. Not that there was anyone who cared. Ann Marie was born here in Rockport, but I headed to Ravenville. I hoped it would be far enough away. I went from campground to campground in the first two months. It was summer, but as the fall weather got colder I knew we couldn't stay outside much longer. Then I remembered the cabin near my aunt and uncle's house. We spent five winters there."

"How did you manage? Where did you get food, money, firewood, even?"

"The couple who owned the cabin knew I was there and helped me as best they could, and I did things I wasn't proud of. I stole, did some disagreeable, even illegal things. I just did what I had to do."

"Why didn't you go to your aunt and uncle for help?"

"My father is a very bad man. I said my mother was not afraid when we were at my aunt and uncle's. That was only because my father didn't know we were there. She wouldn't stay because she knew if she did he'd go there looking for her. He beat my mother and by that time had already started beating me, and she was afraid he would do something to her sister. I was just a kid, but I knew her fear was real. I had that same fear. No matter how hard it got hiding, moving around, stealing food, and all the rest of it, I wouldn't go to them and put them in danger. But somehow just being nearby gave me some comfort. How did Ann Marie find Augustus?"

"Well, that is a long story, and maybe one she could tell you herself. You want to see her, don't you? I know she is anxious to see you."

"Of course I do. My father doesn't know anything about her, does he?"

"Your uncle called him just to find out if you had a daughter but didn't tell him anything. He doesn't know she's with Augustus, but he knows Augustus is back home. Augustus thinks your father was the one who reported him and had him rounded up and sent to the Old Ones' Compound."

"That would not surprise me. I have nothing to do with him, and I'm not the scared kid I was the last time I saw him, but I still know what he's capable of. I would not see Ann Marie if I thought he would find out about her. I will have to give it some thought. Is she happy?"

"She has suffered. Being kept in that compound is not a good life, but she is strong and determined. She is a really brave and wonderful kid."

"I am so glad."

"I think maybe she takes after her mother."

"Thank you. I don't know about that, but thank you anyway."

"How about I give you Valerie and Terrance's number and when you're ready you can call them?"

"Okay. Will you tell my daughter you met with me?"

"Do you want me to?"

"Yes, you can tell her. Please tell her I am so happy she got away. Can you tell her how sorry I am?"

"I will, but she does not blame you. She will be very glad to see you when you are ready."

Jane rose from the bench. She tucked a stray piece of hair behind her ear, her eyes darting along the walkway in both directions. "I just have to make sure he doesn't know anything. I don't think he even knows where I am, but I need to make sure."

§

Emery was just closing the tailgate of Max's truck when she saw her. *It couldn't be*, she thought, wondering whether or not to run up behind the girl who had just walked by on the sidewalk in front of where the truck was parked. The man walking beside her was taller and older. If she were to run up and speak to her, perhaps the man would be a threat to her. She had already been worrying that it might be risky coming into Rockport so soon after her escape. Had Daisy escaped, or had she been released and her assignment was in Rockport?

Emery was still trying to decide what she should do when Max returned and motioned for her to get in the truck. Daisy and the tall man were almost out of sight. The opportunity to speak to her was disappearing quickly.

Max pulled out of the driveway and headed in the opposite direction, stopping Emery's inner debate. Daisy had been wearing a strange-looking outfit, not even the garb of the last division. The outfit looked like the pajamas Tanya had given her, except Daisy's were a faded blue colour. The tall man had been wearing a uniform of some kind. So many questions plagued Emery on the silent drive back home. Why hadn't she spoken to the girl who had left such a lasting impression on her and had given her the courage to escape? If it had not been for Daisy, Emery would not have been in Rockport delivering vegetables on this beautiful sunny day. If she had spoken to her, what would she have said?

Emery tilted her head, trying her best to see the sky above through the windshield as the truck sped down the highway. The wide-open sky was the very essence of her freedom. She was no longer contained within a space where a cover could be pulled over, preventing her from gazing at the sky above. Next time she came to Rockport, she would keep a look out for Daisy, and if she saw her again, she would go right up to her, regardless of the risk. She would thank Daisy for the fearlessness she had shown on the day of the dining test and for the seed she'd planted that day, giving Emery the push she had needed to find her own bravery.

CHAPTER 16

EMERY HAD BEEN ANXIOUS to get in the lake after her second long day at work. The morning had been spent in the garden picking produce for two stores in Ravenville and the order for the Roadside Diner. They had enjoyed a late lunch at the diner. It had been so nice to see Ruth and Tanya again. The day had been busy and packed with activity, but Emery's mind kept going back to seeing Daisy walking along the sidewalk the day before. She hadn't mentioned it to anyone.

Last evening Valerie had filled her in on Roxanne's meeting with Janelle Melvin. She went by Jane now, Valerie said, and she was very interested in seeing her daughter. Jane was being cautious, though, because of her fear of Robert Melvin. It had been fear that had kept Emery from rushing up to Daisy. There were good reasons for their fear. The Establishing Compound had cemented that fear, and it was not to be taken lightly. Being forced to go back there would be a fate she couldn't even let herself imagine.

Needing time by herself tonight to process her turmoil of thoughts, Emery had come to the lake right after supper and planned to stay in the water as long as she could. Conversation at supper and while cleaning up had been constant and left Emery feeling overwhelmed.

"I knew Joanna had a terrible life with him, but I had no idea he was hurting her," Augustus said. "We should have known. He changed shortly after the wedding. He was all lovey dovey at first, but right away he decided they were moving. It wasn't even the fact that they moved more than an hour's drive away; it was the way he controlled her. Joanna only called Janey when Robert wasn't home. I should have known."

"Roxanne says Jane still seems to be afraid of him," Valerie said. "That is probably why she goes by a different name."

"Joanna wanted to call her Jane when she was born, but Robert wouldn't hear of it. They compromised by naming her Janelle. Janey tried to get Joanna to stay longer that last visit. She was sure there was more going on than Joanna would say. I'm only glad Janey never had to know how bad it really was. We would have helped her and we certainly would have helped Janelle and her baby. And to think she stayed in Reggie's cabin four winters and we didn't even know it. Why didn't Reggie or Doris tell us?"

"DorDor," Emery said, looking up from her supper. "I remember DorDor. Sometimes I would sleep in her big bed under the blanket of pretty squares. And DorDor sang to me."

"Doris and Janey were good friends," Augustus said. "I can't imagine her not telling Janey if she knew it was Joanna's granddaughter she was helping to look after."

"I think Jane asked them to keep it a secret," Valerie added. "She was very sure if her father found out he would report them, and turns out she was right. She was also afraid his violence might hurt you or Janey. Robert Melvin sounds like a monster."

"I might be an old man, but I've got a mind to pay that man a visit and settle the score. First of all for the pain and misery he caused Joanna and Jane and then for reporting Emery and turning the authorities on me."

"Promise me you won't do that, Grandpa."

"I won't go looking for him, but I'll tell you if he has the nerve to come here, he'll get what's coming to him."

"Jane was very clear about making sure Robert Melvin doesn't know anything about Emery before she comes to see her or you Augustus," Valerie said.

"Max said you put in two long days and worked hard, Emery," Terrance said, changing the subject.

"Yeah, I guess. It was fun though," Emery replied.

"He said you were real quiet on the way home yesterday. He felt bad he'd worked you so hard."

"I didn't mind."

§

Emery dove into the still water. The evening air was cool, but the water felt wonderful. Valerie had almost come with her but stayed behind to put Zachary to bed. Emery was happy for the time alone. It worried her that Augustus was so worked up about Robert Melvin. He felt so guilty for not intervening and felt terrible about not knowing Joanna's daughter and granddaughter had been so close by. Knowing that her own grandfather was such a terrible man bothered her, and it was troubling to think that fear of him might keep her mother from coming to see her.

But even with all of this to process, Emery kept coming back to thoughts of seeing Daisy walking along the Rockport sidewalk and her hesitation to run up to speak to her. Would Daisy have known anything about Dixon or Sadie? As happy as she was to distance herself from life inside the wall, she couldn't shake thoughts of her friends being still trapped there. And what about the blue-eyed girl? Daisy probably hadn't seen her again and wouldn't know what her fate had been.

Floating on her back, Emery could see the moon becoming brighter in the darkening sky. No doubt if she stayed much longer someone would come looking for her. Reluctantly, she swam in to the shallow water and stood up. Knowing she could return to these waters tomorrow was comforting. She would figure it all out. She would let this place fill her with the courage she needed to face whatever the future held. Her mother must have believed the same thing when she fled to the fields and lakeshore surrounding Augustus and Janey's house.

Emery wrapped the large striped towel around herself and began the walk up the hill. The night sky was vibrant, stars blinking and the bright moon lighting the path. She stopped, turning for a moment to take in the beauty of the shimmering lake surface. Turning back, Emery saw a shadow at the top of the hill. Valerie was probably coming down to make sure she hadn't drowned. "I'm fine," Emery called out.

There was no response, and as Emery got closer she realized it was not Valerie. The silent figure moving closer toward her seemed dreamlike. Emery felt no fear, just an overwhelming feeling of familiarity and longing.

"Ann Marie."

Emery gasped as the woman passed her a tattered stuffed tiger, its stripes faded, one button eye missing, the other hanging by a thread. Emery clutched the stuffed animal for a few seconds before reaching out to her mother in an emotional embrace.

The next few minutes were a blur of emotion. Both felt there was so much to say but so little that would change where they found themselves at this moment. But being here on this moonlit night in view of the lake and the big white house, a house that meant safety, security, and homecoming to both Emery and Jane offered the reunion both had hoped for.

"How did you get here?" Emery asked.

"I took the bus from Rockport, just like I did the day I took you from the hospital. I got off at the gas station where the highway meets the North Lake Road and I started walking. The day I walked carrying an infant, several cars stopped offering me a drive, but tonight no vehicles passed me. I didn't take a drive that day. I was so afraid someone would know I was hiding my baby and report me. Tonight my fear was different. Even though I am quite sure he doesn't know where I am, I always fight the terror he left me with."

"How did you know I was at the lake?"

"I stood partway up the driveway, trying to find the courage to knock on the door. I heard the splash and when I looked toward the lake I saw you stand up. I will remember that beautiful sight until the day I die."

"Come in the house. You are staying, aren't you? We have so much catching up to do. Augustus will be so pleased to see you. He has been through a lot too. Janey died eight years ago. He was taken to an Old Ones' Compound about two years ago."

"Yes, the lawyer told me that. She thinks my father reported him, and I have no doubt she is right. How did you find Augustus? You didn't know you were related, did you?"

"That is a long story. Come in and tell him you're here. He will be thrilled. Augustus's great-nephew Terrance, his wife, Valerie, and their little boy, Zachary, live here too. They will all be so happy that you came."

Augustus stood up quickly and came right across the room, wrapping his arms around Jane. "You look just like your mother. Oh, I wish Janey was here to see you."

Jane was unable to speak. The tears that had started just before Emery had opened the door were now full-scale sobbing. She felt like the ten-year-old girl who had arrived to the loving welcome of her aunt and uncle so many years ago. She had never felt a welcome so sincere and a place so safe. It had been the longing for this feeling she had battled all those times she had almost walked up the driveway or across the field first with her baby, then her toddler, and finally her little girl. For four years she had stayed close but refused to put her aunt and uncle in danger. Robert Melvin's evil was not to be taken lightly. He was more than capable of the kind of violence that could have put all their lives in danger.

Terrance walked toward Jane and Augustus, reaching out to them both. "Come sit down, Jane. Would you like tea, a cold drink or something? Valerie will be down in a minute. She will be so pleased that you've come."

Augustus guided his niece to the couch and sat down beside her. Emery followed Terrance into the kitchen, offering to help make the tea.

"Are you okay?" Terrance asked.

"I'm fine. She just appeared on the hill when I was walking up from the lake. At first I thought I was imagining her. She has appeared to me so many times. But she kept walking toward me and when I got close enough to almost touch her I knew she was real. She walked all the way from the Fast Gas on the highway."

"Wow. Valerie will be so glad. She was worried that Jane would be too afraid to come see you."

"She said she is quite sure Robert Melvin doesn't know where she is. Do you think we will be all right?"

"Yes. We will all be just fine. Most men like Robert Melvin are basically cowards. They treat their families so terribly because they are messed up and take out their anger on those weaker than themselves. They aren't so brave when light is shed on their abuse. I don't think he'll come looking for a fight, but believe me, if he does he'll find one."

"What if he finds out she's here and that I'm here and just reports us?"

"We'll fight that too, Emery. But tonight we don't have to worry about it. Tonight we just have to welcome your mother and take the time to get to know her. Tonight we just have to be family. What are you holding?"

"It's my tiger. She kept it." Emery turned away, overcome by emotion.

"It's okay, Em," Terrance said, his hand resting on Emery's shoulder. "It's okay."

§

"I had a friend call him asking for me," Jane was explaining to Augustus when Emery and Terrance walked in with the tea. "He said he had no idea where I was. 'She could be dead for all I care,' he said. I hope he does think I'm dead. Janelle Melvin is dead, anyway. I have changed my name to Jane Kimball; not legally but in any way that might give him a way to find me."

"We had no idea how bad things were for your mother and you. We had suspicions about his control over her, but we didn't know he physically hurt you both. I would have stopped him if I'd known."

"That was what Mom was so afraid of. She said she would never forgive herself if he hurt you or Aunt Janey. She knew you would confront him and she was afraid he would kill you. It wasn't the cancer that killed her, Uncle Augustus."

Jane picked up her cup of tea, her shaking hands almost causing the tea to slosh onto her lap.

"What do you mean, Jane?"

Jane took a sip of tea and began speaking, her words as shaky as her hands. "For the first few months after she was diagnosed, he never laid a finger on her. He seemed genuinely worried and was almost kind to her. She'd had surgery and the doctors were hopeful they'd gotten the whole tumour and told her she was cancer free. That seemed to be the announcement he needed to start beating her again. He told the police she'd been weak, stumbled and fell in the dark hitting her head on the fireplace. I stood in fear and listened to his lie and let them take her lifeless body out of the house. He threatened to kill me if I told anyone anything different."

Augustus reached out and held Jane, letting her take the comfort and release the pain she'd held on to so tightly. "That bastard."

"I wanted so badly to come to you and Aunt Janey. I wanted you to meet my baby girl and I so desperately wanted to tell you what had happened to Mom, but I couldn't."

Silence hung in the room for a few seconds before Jane spoke again, her voice rising in its insistence.

"I didn't tell you this for you to do anything about it, Uncle Augustus. At this point it would be my word against his. I do not want anyone confronting him. Promise me you won't."

Terrance poured hot tea into Augustus's cup. "So many terrible things happened in the past, but I think the best we can all do is look to the future. As difficult as it is to accept, the past cannot be changed."

"It makes my blood boil that he could get away with such a thing. Poor Joanna. What a terrible life she must have had with that man—and to think she died by his hand."

"Terrance is right, Uncle Augustus." Jane took another sip of tea, then turned toward Emery. "I have my daughter back after all these years. I am finally back in the house that my mother told me was the place she loved most in the world with my uncle, a man she adored. My father can shrivel up and die in his miserable loneliness. I am done letting him control me in any way. That is the best way I can honour my mother's memory. Ann...I mean, Emery? I will call you Emery, as you have had that name longer than the one I gave you. Sweet Emery, my darling girl. Now, tell me how you found Augustus."

CHAPTER 17

THE FOLLOWING TUESDAY, they pulled into the Dominion Grocery Store parking lot. As if by arrangement, Emery saw Daisy and the same man coming out of the grocery store. Max had barely stopped the truck before Emery jumped out. She was not going to miss this opportunity to speak to Daisy.

"Daisy!" Emery called out across the parking lot. "Daisy, I'm the girl from your dining test. I'm Emery."

Daisy was not wearing the faded pajamas she'd been wearing. Instead, she wore a long, flowing dress that hung loosely and looked much too big for the slight girl walking toward Emery. The man was wearing black pants and a plaid shirt that looked too small. Their expressions showed some concern, and for a second Emery thought the pair was going to turn and run.

"You sat across the table from me. Have you been released, Emery?"

"Sort of. What about you?"

Max walked up behind Emery. "I am going to take this box into the store, Emery. You and your friends can sit in the truck out of sight from anybody who might be around and catch up."

Emery slid in behind the steering wheel, Daisy squeezed into the middle straddling Max's cluttered console, and the man took a seat on the passenger side. It was a couple of seconds before anyone spoke.

"This is Jonathan. Do you remember the girl who offered me food, the blue-eyed girl? Jonathan is her brother. Victoria is her name."

Emery looked over at the man Daisy was introducing. How had Daisy come to be in Rockport with the brother of an Elite?

"Yes, I certainly do remember the blue-eyed girl. I have not forgotten her kindness or your bravery."

"You are probably wondering how Daisy and I met," Jonathan said. "I was not raised as an Elite like Victoria. We were separated after we were taken from our aunt. I was raised as a Less Than, and after my release, I was given the assignment of Keeper guard."

"You don't have to be afraid of that, Emery," Daisy assured. "He helped me escape. He doesn't want to be caught any more than I do. He is no threat to you either. You escaped, right?"

"Yes, but tell me more about your escape. Where did you escape from?"

"I was incarcerated after the dining test. I was punished and scheduled for strict brainwashing before being returned to the compound. Actually, they were probably going to release me with a lifelong contract of some kind unless I convinced them I had learned my lesson and accepted my status."

"But you didn't?"

"No, she did not," Jonathan answered. "She really angered the guy assigned to brainwash her. He decided her punishment needed to include starvation."

"Oh my goodness. That is terrible. As awful as our food was, not having anything to eat would be terrible."

"Jonathan was the Keeper guard assigned to my room. He snuck food and water in to me."

"Wow. And then you helped her escape?"

"Yes. She pretended to be weak and was taken to the infirmary. We waited a couple of days, and then escaped when the opportunity presented itself. They were determined to break Daisy and planned to offer her to the Less Thans as an example of conformity. Your escape riled them up. One poor guy was given the worst lifelong contract possible when he wouldn't give them any information about you."

"Do you know his name or number?"

"Not sure, I just know several people were questioned after you went missing and the guy that always sat with you in the eating house was interrogated."

"Dixon. It must have been Dixon," Emery said, her voice trembling. "What is the worst tasking?"

"Garbage detail," Jonathan answered. "It's long days of sorting garbage, seven days a week for the rest of the Older's life. And from what I hear, their lives are sometimes not very long. A lot of illnesses and disease come from the garbage and the miserable life they are forced to live."

Emery was crying, unable to find the words for the news she'd just received, when Max opened the driver's door. "What's wrong Emery? What have they said to upset you?"

"My friend Dixon has been given a terrible lifelong tasking and it's my fault," Emery said between sobs. "I should have known my friends would suffer if I just took off. How could I have been so thoughtless?"

"It is not your fault, Emery," Daisy said. "You are not to blame for the evil of a system that regards some people as less than human. Do you know what Dixon's last name was? Maybe we can do something to help him. Maybe he has family on the outside that could help us fight for his release?"

"Daisy has the crazy idea that we can do something to put an end to the Establishing Compound," Jonathan said. "With each day we've been out, she's gotten braver and more determined. She stole our clothes in broad daylight off of someone's clothesline. My plan is to keep a really low profile, but Daisy thinks we should do just the opposite."

"Either way, you are not going to be able to do anything right now," Max said. "It will take a while to come up with a strong plan. How about the three of you help me unload the rest of the produce and then we'll go somewhere for lunch. Where are you two staying?"

"We have just been sleeping outside wherever we can find shelter," Daisy answered. "Jonathan's money is almost gone."

"Well, I'll offer you a roof over your heads for now. I can give you some work. Am I right to trust these two, Emery?"

"Yes, for sure. Daisy was a Less Than, a really brave one, and Jonathan helped her escape."

"Well, we'll have to squeeze in the truck and hope we don't get stopped for having more passengers than seatbelts. Are they looking for you two, do you think?"

"Yes, probably. I wouldn't blame you if you don't want to take a chance with us," Jonathan said.

"I'll take the chance," Max stated. "Seems to me if more people took a stand against that damn foolishness, it would have ended long ago."

§

Dixon looked down at his hands. The look of the black sticky streaks running up his bare arms sickened him. He was becoming used to the stink, but the grimy feel that seemed to permeate his whole body was getting more difficult to deal with. Even his nightly shower couldn't seem to take the feel away. And it seemed his head barely hit the pillow before the gong was waking him to begin another day of this disgusting regime.

When he'd seen Sadie that morning, he'd known something major had happened. His first thought was that Emery had been hurt or killed even. Sadie looked so downcast and frightened at the same time. Her words, *"She's gone,"* had done nothing to quiet his panic. The truth was he had been in a panic since returning from his dining test the day before. He had had no idea the test would be so upsetting. He could normally use his humour to lighten any negative effects of the way he was treated.

At first when he was taken into the Elite dining hall, all he could think of was talking to Emery about the grandeur of the place. She had tried to tell him after her test, but he hadn't really listened. The sights overwhelmed him, and then as the trays were carried in, the smells of the steaming dishes of food had completely captured his senses. Tonka had roughly pushed him into the chair and stood back, waiting.

He'd been in a fog. The Elites were speaking loudly to one another, and the atmosphere was festive. He knew he was not a part of it and basically kept his head bowed, trying hard not to respond in any way. He completely blanked out what was going on around him, and it took a few seconds to realize Tonka was talking to him.

Elites were getting up from the table. Loud sounds of chairs being pushed in and dishes being taken from the table echoed in his head. Tonka grabbed his shoulder roughly, repeating his instruction. "Get up, you dolt. I've seen lots of Less Thans zone out and not respond, but none have looked as vacant and stunned as you."

Tonka let out a laugh that seemed to hold volumes of disgust and irritation before directing his next remarks to the Keeper standing inches away. "This Dixon kid is some stupid. Hope the kid they got to keep was smarter than this one. Bigshot banker thought his kid would be exempt from the Second Same-Sex law, the very law he helped to write. Sherwood Dixon thought he was such a bigshot."

"Stop your daydreaming, Dixon." The bellowing voice of the Keeper at the end of the conveyor belt jolted him back to reality. He'd missed a few feet of refuse as it slowly passed by, and he knew inattention would not be tolerated. Daydreaming indeed. What would he dream about?

§

The four enjoyed a delicious meal at the Timberland Restaurant before squeezing back into the cab of Max's truck for the ride to the North Lake Road.

"Daisy, you remember Augustus. He escaped with me. It's his house I live in. I am actually related to him. I am his late wife's sister's grand-daughter. I can't wait to introduce you to Terrance and Valerie. We live on a lake. Terrance was a Less Than. Do either of you swim?"

"When do you think I would have learned to swim? I know what swimming is, though. I snuck books into my sleeping house for years, and that's how I learned most of what I know about the world outside the wall. I used to clean the Elite library. I wasn't supposed to even look at the books, but I figured out a way to get them out. I'd hide a book in the bottom of the garbage bin every day, then stick it in the bushes when I emptied the garbage so I could pick it up later. I learned to walk back with a book tight against my chest and no one ever noticed. Tell me more about Augustus. I loved that man."

"Augustus is special. I got tasked to the Old Ones' Compound to re-place you. I met him on my first day. I'd been curious about the Old Ones for quite a while, so getting to work there was a dream come true. It also made me think more about life on the outside and getting away from life as a Less Than. Seeing your bravery at the dining test made me want it even more. And then I met Augustus and some of the others."

"So how did you break him out?"

"Basically we just walked out the front door. Some changes were com-ing to the compound and we needed to get out when we did."

"Ronda hated Augustus. She hated that we had fun and cared about each other. What was she going to do, drug all the Old Ones who still knew what was going on?"

"Ronda is gone. Lois took over and was going to fill up the compound by basically making every Old One bedridden. She was even worse than Ronda."

"That makes me furious," Daisy said. "We need to bring the wall down and change the system that treats the Old Ones with such disrespect."

"Simmer down there, Daisy," Jonathan said. "You can't just go raging up to the east gate demanding abolition of the entire system. They wouldn't just incarcerate you this time. You would be disposed of, and it wouldn't be the first time they dealt with dissenters that way. We need to figure out a plan."

"Valerie's friend is a lawyer, and she's been digging in to records and the history of the wall. Our compound is the only one still in existence, and there are only a few Old Ones' Compounds being run in connection to the system."

"Really?" Jonathan asked. "I assumed walled compounds were everywhere. We were taught that society could not exist without Less Thans and Elites. We were not allowed to believe anything else was possible. Who keeps ours running when the others have disappeared?"

"I don't know the answer to that. Augustus says the laws came into place over forty years ago. The laws still exist, but only a few people are enforcing them. We need to find out more if we are going to make the changes Daisy talks about."

"You're right about that, and we will," Daisy said. "Change only comes about when someone decides to make it happen. I read about people that did just that. A man named Nelson Mandela sat in prison for twenty-seven years believing he could change South Africa."

"Can you tell me anything more about Dixon?" Emery asked. "Do you know where the garbage facility is he was tasked to?"

"It is the one nearest the wall. It is about an hour's drive in the opposite direction from Rockport. I heard a bit from the Keeper who took him there. Fenwick Mountain Landfill and Processing Compound is what it's called, I think. He took four Less Thans there the day he took your friend."

"This is the lake," Emery announced. "Do you mind stopping, Max?"

"No, not at all. Emery waded right in the first time she saw it," Max said. "Don't worry about getting the seat wet if you want to do the same thing."

§

Dixon pulled the thin blanket up over his shoulders. He'd been given an extra half hour on the floor to make up for the minutes his mind had wandered. Now lying here he could keep processing the words Tonka had said. Dixon was his *last* name, a family name, and his father was a man named Sherwood Dixon. His father was a banker, an Elite, and Dixon had been taken from him. He had an older brother, by what Tonka had said; an older brother who had been left to live outside the wall with the family Dixon hadn't been allowed to have a life with.

Did his family ever think of him? Did his mother, father or brother wonder where he was or how he was doing? Would they feel shame and disgust if they could see him in this vile place? Did they ever think of looking for him? Would there ever come a time he would be free and could look for them? And if he found them, could he ever be a part of Sherwood Dixon's family again?

CHAPTER 18

EMERY PICKED UP POTATOES from the furrows Terrance had dug, dropping them in the small pail. "A family supper," Terrance called it as they set out to the garden to pick the vegetables. John, his wife, Selma, Roxanne, Jane, Max, Daisy, and Jonathan were all joining them for supper. Valerie had cleaned as if she were expecting important guests.

"They are important guests, Emery," Valerie said. "And this is our first family celebration since you and Augustus got here. John has wanted to come to visit Augustus and meet you, and now he gets to meet your mom and your friends at the same time. Terrance is going all out with the menu, so it's the least I can do to have the house clean and tidy."

"I am nervous. Is that dumb?" Emery asked.

"No, not at all, but what are you nervous about?"

"I don't know. I feel like I might be a disappointment to my mother. I don't know things and sometimes I feel stupid. Daisy is so smart. She's read lots of books and knows stuff. John might think I'm an outsider."

"I'm not going to tell you not to be so foolish. Your feelings are real and I understand what you are feeling, but believe me, no one else thinks those things. Your mother is so proud of you. She called Roxanne yesterday to thank her for contacting her. She is thrilled to have you in her life again. John does not think you are an outsider at all. He and Selma are very excited to meet you. I know you think Daisy is so brave and wonderful, but I think you are just as brave. And from what you have told me about Daisy and Jonathan, neither one of them would judge you or criticize you in any way. And Max, of course, is your biggest fan."

"He is awfully good to me. He paid me already for the one week I've worked, and he was very generous. I'm not sure what I need money for. I can give it to you guys."

"Are you kidding me? You help so much around here that we should be paying you. Save your money. Believe me, it can come in handy.

Augustus wants to ask Jane to move in here. How do you feel about that?"

"How do *you* feel about it? Doesn't she live at the house she works in?"

"She does right now, but I think she is considering giving up that job and finding one in Ravenville. I think she wants to live near or with you."

"Really? I hadn't even let myself think about that happening. I would hate to leave the lake, but we can't just all move in here with you guys."

"Like Augustus says, this is a big house. There's lots of room for everyone. Zachary would sure miss you if you moved somewhere else."

Emery picked up the pail of new potatoes and followed Terrance to the corn row.

"What would you think of Jane living here?"

"I would think it was great."

"You don't wish Augustus and I had never shown up? You don't wish it was just you, Valerie, and Zachary living here?"

"Not at all. It was never our house anyway. It was my grandfather's family home, and Uncle Augustus and Aunt Janey kept it the home I was lucky enough to find when I needed it so much. I don't feel any entitlement to it. No more than you or Jane have. And Valerie is more than happy to have you all in our lives."

"I really want my mother to move here. We have so much catching up to do."

"I don't get to see my dad and Selma enough, but I'm still very thankful I have what I have."

"I know. I keep thinking about Dixon. He is trapped in a lifelong contract with no say in his future. I can't help blaming myself for his fate."

"I feel really sorry for the guy too, but it's not your fault."

"But I have to try to do something. Daisy has some ideas and I am willing to go along with her plans, but the first thing I want to do is see if Roxanne can find out anything about Dixon's background. I want to find out if he has a family who could try to fight for his reassignment. Did he ever tell you anything about his past?"

"I don't think so. I was so oblivious to things back then. I really believed we all just belonged there. Even with my vague memories of being taken, I somehow accepted the fate of everyone around me. I never asked Dixon if he remembered anything about his past. What about you? Did he tell you anything?"

"No. He was always funny, hardly ever serious about anything, and acted like nothing bothered him."

"We all had our coping strategies. Let's hope Roxanne can find out some information about him.

§

When Daisy got out of Max's truck, Emery noticed she wasn't wearing the loose-fitting dress from the day before. Jonathan was wearing a shirt she'd remembered seeing Max wear. Outfitting Jonathan wouldn't be hard for Max, but Emery wondered if Daisy was wearing Penny's clothes.

"This house is beautiful," Daisy stated enthusiastically. "When Augustus talked about his home, I always tried to picture what it would look like, and it is even nicer than I imagined."

"We like it," Augustus declared while reaching out to enfold Daisy in his arms. "It is so good to see you, Daisy. It seems like a lifetime since we had our afternoons together. I hope you are ready to lose a game of checkers to me later."

"You look wonderful, Augustus. I am so happy you got to come back to your beloved home. It looks even better than you described it to me. It's a mansion."

"It is to me," replied Augustus. "I'm thrilled I get to welcome you to it. Now introduce me to your friend. I understand this young man helped you escape."

"This is Jonathan. Jonathan, this is the famous Augustus."

Terrance stepped out onto the back veranda just as two more vehicles pulled up into the yard. John and Selma got out of one as Roxanne and Jane stepped out of the other. "Everybody's here, and everything is ready. Come on in."

For the next few minutes the dining room was a loud, busy bustle of activity, introduction, and conversation. Looking around it reminded Emery of the dining test but without the Keepers, the Enforcer, and the heavy, frightening feelings. These people belonged to her and she was welcome and wanted at this table. She brushed a tear from her cheek and passed the plate of chicken to John.

"This meal is amazing," Jane said. "Does he cook like this all the time, Valerie?"

"Pretty much. Not usually this much food, though."

"And all these vegetables are from your garden, son?" John asked.

"Everything except the brussels sprouts. Max grew those."

"I've never been a fan of brussels sprouts," Selma remarked, "but these are delicious."

"So you have three employees now, Max," Roxanne said. "That must make things a lot easier."

"For sure. I used to get people now and then when I couldn't keep up, but it looks like Daisy and Jonathan are going to stay for a while, and Emery is keen to keep working, so I'm all set. I'm even thinking of expanding a bit in the spring. I'd like to start selling produce packs to individual families."

The conversation went back and forth, covering a wide range of topics. Sporadically Zachary would capture everyone's attention with a word or behaviour too cute to ignore. It wasn't until dessert that a quiet seemed to take over the satiated crowd and the conversation took a more serious tone.

"Roxanne, I need you to try to find out something about someone's past," Emery stated. "How do you go about doing that?"

"Well, I start with birth records. Do you know the person's last name?"

Emery shuffled in her seat. It hadn't been until she spoke a moment ago that she realized the tension and worry she'd been holding in. Even in the midst of this enjoyable meal surrounded by friends and family, a part of her was deeply haunted by thoughts of Dixon suffering in what could be a lifelong exile. "I don't know his last name."

"You know what, Emery," Jonathan said, "I think Dixon might be his last name. The day the other Keeper guard took Dixon to Fenwick Mountain, there was a buzz of gossip about one of the Less Thans, and once I started thinking about it, it came to me it might have been your friend they were talking about. One of the other guys said something about who the Less Than was—something about his father being Sherwood Dixon."

"Sherwood Dixon?" Augustus said. "He was one of the businessmen who came up with the whole Establishing Compound concept. He was a nasty piece of work. He had his finger in lots of pies, and most of them illegal, from what I've heard. His empire crashed awhile back, I think. There was talk of his death being no accident. One rumour was he was murdered, another that he took his own life."

"Really?" Roxanne asked. "That certainly gives me somewhere to start. Should be lots on public record. How did a son of his get raised as a Less Than?"

"There was a lot of underhandedness and backstabbing going on," John said. "It was such a terrible time, with so much greed and treachery disguised as positive political action. A lot of people fell for the rhetoric. Some still believe in the system, but not many, as evidenced by the fact there is only one compound left. But that seems to be making the few still benefiting from it more determined to hold on, and possibly more dangerous for those who oppose it."

Daisy had gotten up from the table during the discussion. She hadn't left the room, but had been pacing, her back to everyone. She turned now and her face held a serious expression, her voice loud as she spoke, grabbing everyone's attention.

"I don't care how determined or dangerous they are. I have every intention of making sure every person inside that wall sees the light of day and finds a different life as soon as possible. Seems to me getting your friend released is where we need to start, Emery. Are you with me?"

"I sure am, Daisy. I think the time for being quiet is over. Maybe Dixon has family that will stand with us and make some noise."

CHAPTER 19

FRASER DANIEL DIXON was born to Mary and Sherwood Dixon in Rockport sixteen years ago. He was a second son, their first boy, Kyle Sherwood Dixon, born fifteen years earlier. Records showed the father's death and stated the mother's whereabouts as unknown. Kyle Dixon lived in Rockport and was the owner of a small gallery, bookstore, and cafe. Published as Ky Dixon, he was also an author with some notoriety.

This was the information Roxanne called with the day before, giving Emery and Daisy what they needed to know to find Ky Dixon, with the hope he might be willing to start a campaign to free his brother. Max pulled his truck up to the parking meter in front of Phoenix Gallery, Books and Edibles.

Daisy hopped right out and Emery followed her. Max decided he would wait outside, letting the girls go in alone to introduce themselves and present their case to Ky Dixon.

"We're looking for Ky Dixon," Daisy said to the woman behind the counter.

"He's in the back. Who can I say is looking for him?"

"We are his brother's friends," Emery answered.

Ky Dixon walked out of the back room, his tall frame moving slowly. He took the glasses that were resting on top of his head and put them on before stopping a few feet away, taking in the details of the girls. He had been skeptical when Julie said friends of his brother were asking for him. He'd quickly done the math figuring out how old his brother would be, and at least the two standing in front of him were in that age range. He extended his hand.

"I'm Ky Dixon. What can I do for you?"

"Your brother is a very good friend of mine," Emery said, aware that her voice cracked as she said it. She wanted this man to think she was strong and in control, but she was on the verge of crying like a little kid.

"Let's go sit down. Can I get Julie to get you something? A coffee or cold drink?"

"We're fine," Daisy said. "We didn't come for refreshments. We came to tell you your brother needs help."

"Okay, no refreshments, but come sit down anyway. You'll have to excuse my confusion. I haven't known anything about my brother since he was taken as a baby, and I was only fifteen at the time. How do I know your friend is Fraser?"

Daisy and Emery followed Ky to a corner booth and sat down across from him.

Emery started talking first. "Your voice sounds just like his. He is tall like you, but his hair is dark and his eyes are much darker than yours too. I've always just known him as Dixon. He is really funny and kind. He does not deserve what has happened to him."

"And what exactly has happened to him?"

"It's my fault. After I took Augustus from the Old Ones' Compound, they took him from his sleeping house. They kept asking him about my escape and accused him of covering for me. They released him. He'd had his dining test. His tasking is a lifelong one. Dixon is at the garbage facility."

"Slow down. You have a name, I assume."

"Emery."

"Slow down, Emery. I don't have any idea what you're talking about. First start by telling me what makes you think this Dixon guy is my brother."

"We're sure he is," Daisy said. "Your father was Sherwood Dixon, right? You had a baby brother who was taken and put in the Establishing Compound, didn't you?"

"Yes, that's how the story goes. I'm not always real keen on claiming my father, but yes, my birth records state it's Sherwood Dixon. He wasn't much of a father, though, so my little brother didn't miss out on much in that regard. I take it you two girls were raised in the Establishing Compound."

"Yes, we were branded with the status of Less Than, just like your brother was," Daisy said. "Whether you liked your father or not, I assume you had a better upbringing than that. Don't figure you were treated like you were the lowest scum of society."

"No, I guess not, although around here, being known as Sherwood Dixon's son isn't much better. 'Pond scum' was one of the nicest names I've heard him called. And I won't tell you some of the nasty ones."

"We can hear all about your hard life some other time," Daisy said. "We're here to ask you to help us find and free your brother. We also want some support for getting a movement started to take the walls down of the one remaining compound and put an end to the system that took your brother in the first place."

"You're a feisty one, aren't you? What makes you think I'd be interested in getting mixed up in that mess?"

"Let's just focus on Dixon, or Fraser, as you call him," Emery interrupted. "In case you don't know, a lifelong tasking at a garbage facility is the worst life imaginable. He basically works from sunup to sundown sorting through garbage. He never gets outside, never breathes fresh air or feels the sun or the rain. He has no human contact except for the person standing on the line beside him. He will never have a girlfriend, a wife, or a family of any kind. He will grow old and die inside the confines of that wretched place. He was sentenced to that life just because he was my friend. We need to do something to get him out. If you won't do that as his brother, just help us as a compassionate human being."

"You two make quite a pair. One of you all fight and fire, the other one all heart and poetry. How could I help but get on board?"

"I don't even know what poetry is. Are you going to help us?" Emery asked.

"Yes, I'll help you. Not sure exactly what I can do, but I'll help."

At that point, Max walked in through the door and over to the booth. He extended his hand to Ky Dixon before sitting down beside him.

"I take it the girls have given you their pitch. Now let's the four of us put our heads together and figure out where we start. That poor kid shouldn't have to stay another day longer in that hellhole. Who do you know in this city with any clout, Ky?"

A half an hour later the group moved into Ky's office and Stephanie Gilford walked in to join them. After Max had asked who Ky might know with some ability to help, he had messaged a friend who happened to be a reporter at the *Rockport Daily Herald*.

"I tried to get Ky to let me do an exposé on the Establishing Compound system when his first novel came out three years ago," Stephanie Gilford began. "He denied the story mirrored his own life and the fictional baby stolen from the cradle in the mansion was his brother, but anyone with half a brain knew differently."

"Don't belittle yourself, Steph, you have more than half a brain," Ky said. "Just seemed like it would be a publicity stunt at the time, but these two girls have convinced me there is more at stake than just plugging some piece of fiction. I never really let myself think too deeply about what my brother and the other kids dropped into that system are put through. I can't quite believe they still have the authority to decide what jobs they take and if certain people get lifelong contracts doing the most disagreeable jobs. Apparently that's what's happened to Fraser."

"That's where we should probably start then," Stephanie said, turning toward Daisy and Emery. "Tell me everything you know."

After writing all the details Daisy and Emery could tell her, Stephanie set down her notepad.

"I am going to start by writing a story specifically about the practice of assigning young men and women to lifelong jobs. Most people believe that in a free society a person should be able to make their own choices and follow the path they decide to take. Two- or three-year taskings seem reasonable to many people, but lifelong contracts might be something else entirely. Add to that the idea that the lifelong contracts are the most disagreeable jobs and there are no requirements to make the working conditions in such places humane and tolerable. It is a form of sanctioned slavery, and I think most people are unaware such things are going on."

"That seems a good place to start," Max said. "Then I think we need to really dig into who is profiting the most from such practices and who is operating the walled compound you girls came from. How is it the other ones have folded but this one is still going strong?"

"I think you're right, Max," Ky said. "Some greedy bastards are running the show, but I would suggest we take it slow."

"We have no time to take it slow," Daisy interjected. "Kids are kept prisoner in that terrible place. Even those being raised as Elites are not getting the life they deserve. They keep the cover over that side too. It is not right that someone gets to completely decide what kids are allowed to think and what their lives will be. Not to mention they've been taken from their true families."

"I hear what you're saying, Daisy, but I saw what happened to my father when he began to question and oppose the ones who put the system in place."

"Did he have second thoughts when they took Dixon, I mean Fraser?" Emery asked.

"Well, that would make him sound much more caring than he was. Basically, he had second thoughts when my mother made his life a living hell. I don't know what he thought her reaction to having her infant ripped from her arms would be. Trying to placate her, he went about trying to fight Fraser's recruitment. It was a shock to him when they took Fraser, and I don't think he understood at first that it was a deliberate action to put him in his place. Anyway, what I'm saying is that the people in charge are not a nice bunch. They don't fool around with subversion. We need to make real sure we know exactly what we're up against. They are not going to roll over and play dead."

"Where should we start?" Emery asked.

"Follow the money," Max said.

"Exactly," Ky said. "I know which upstanding businessmen have the dirtiest hands. The thing is, we have to have some firm facts before we go after anyone. We need to know as much as we can find out about the power behind the wall before we can start to chip away at it."

"Where do we begin to learn what we need to know?" Emery asked.

"Let me do some digging," Stephanie said. "How about I write my first article? We could all meet back here tomorrow and I'll let you see it before I give it to my editor. I'll also let you know what I've found out by then."

"I didn't expect I'd be signing up for a mission when I got out of bed this morning," Ky said.

"Well, at least you got to do what you wanted to when you got out of bed," Daisy said. "Think about your brother, with no choice at all in his day or in any days until we get him out of there."

"All right, all right, you've got me on your side, Daisy. Now can I at least get Julie to bag you up some of our famous cinnamon buns? It's okay if we still enjoy our food, isn't it?"

Ky closed his office door and allowed the emotion he'd been carefully containing to erupt.

"I am such a chickenshit coward. Those two have more courage and fight than I've ever had, and they were raised without a voice or any of the advantages I was given. I let on I'm so cool, so unaffected by my past. Scared shitless is what I've been since the day they took Fraser and my life blew up. My father went missing and my mother was put in a hospital, but instead of facing any of it, I just pretended like none of it happened."

"What hospital was your mother put in?"

"They called it a hospital, but it was a senior's home. She was only forty-five but she'd aged overnight and they had her on so much medication she was barely functioning."

"Is she still living?"

"I don't even know. After they found Dad's body I went to live with his friend Harrison, and I got the message loud and clear that it would be better if I didn't ask any questions."

"Harrison Crawford?"

"Yes."

"Wasn't his death suspicious last year?"

"Oh yeah, for sure. Most of the men who created the Establishing system have died. Only a few are left to benefit from the millions of dollars it has generated. The empire has crumbled but those few are hanging on to the remnants of it."

"How was the money made?"

"It is a huge network of contract payoffs. The whole concept of the Less Than recruitment was to provide cheap labour to companies that paid a kickback fee. They also built several senior care homes that were connected to the individual compounds. They took assets and the income of the residents and basically eliminated the labour costs in those facilities by having Less Thans work there."

"What do you know about the lifelong jobs the girls were talking about? The garbage one sounds terrible."

"Garbage facilities, manufacturing plants, factory farms, and food-processing plants are the main ones. Finding workers for these disagreeable jobs was the primary motivation for creating the system. They were my father's idea, which makes the fact that Fraser is trapped in one even worse."

"Why did they raise Elites in the compounds?"

"They wanted to program a generation who would support their vision and go along with their deals."

"The whole thing sounds insidious and farfetched."

"Stranger than fiction. I had a lot more written about it in the first draft of my first novel, but I wrote most of it out. I was just as afraid then as I was when I was fifteen."

"Don't be so hard on yourself, Ky. You were just a kid."

"I'm not a kid anymore. If those girls can stand up for what's right, it's time I did the same. I need to rescue my little brother and maybe I can even find Mom."

§

Emery was already swimming a distance away when Daisy waded out to her waist. This was the third time she'd waded out this deep, but the other two times she had walked back to shore without making herself get completely wet. Both times she'd felt like a coward, a big baby, too afraid to immerse herself in the lake. She was determined not to leave the water this afternoon without dunking herself at least.

Emery had taught herself to swim and gave Daisy the same advice Augustus had given her. *Just get your face wet* seemed easy enough. It didn't seem like such a big deal, but she hadn't been able to do it yet. She was normally not afraid of anything. Or at least, that was the impression she tried really hard to give everyone. Jonathan had been fooled at first but lately was beginning to see just how vulnerable she really was.

"I don't remember a thing," she'd admitted to Jonathan, opening a floodgate of emotion she hadn't even realized she'd been desperately holding back amid all the talk of people's past. "I made my name up. It came from the first book I stole. *The Great Gatsby*. I didn't even bother to read the book, but I claimed the name Daisy Buchannan. Until then I'd only been called number 57."

"Well, at least you can read," Jonathan said, letting his own emotion show. "It wasn't until just a few years ago they started giving instruction on reading, writing, and arithmetic to the Less Thans. At first it was part of the plan to keep them completely illiterate. It certainly limited our job choices, after two- and three-year contracts were finished."

"I can teach you," Daisy said.

"Do you think there is any point now?"

"Of course there is. There is always value in learning new things."

Daisy thought of that sentiment as she ran her hands along the surface of the water. *There is always value in learning new things.* Why swimming seemed to be one of those things she wasn't sure, but reminding herself of those words was motivation enough to get her to drop into the water. Standing back up she sputtered a bit, realizing it hadn't been as terrifying as she had imagined, so she dropped herself again. When she came back up she could see Jonathan and Max cresting the hill.

Daisy was anxious to tell Jonathan about their meeting with Ky. She wasn't sure what she had expected of him, but at least he hadn't refused to help them, and having his friend write an article about lifelong contracts seemed a reasonable place to start. They had discussed the next steps on the way back to North Lake Road.

"Augustus will probably know who the businessmen Ky was referring to are. He knows more about the history of the laws and policies that created the Establishing Compound than he has shared with me," Emery said. "I think he hasn't told me more, thinking it would upset me."

"I wonder just how many people are involved in keeping the Establishing system running," Emery asked.

"I think it is very interesting that just one walled compound remains," Daisy said. "There aren't as many Less Thans and Elites as I thought there were. Did you know there are only three full sleeping houses on the Less Than side? I didn't know until Jonathan told me. I thought they were all still full and that the infant and toddler buildings still had Less Thans in them. They don't. From the sounds of things, recruitment stopped a while ago."

"That's interesting," Max said. "If the population is low and the recruitment has stopped, maybe it won't be as hard as we think to end it completely."

"Someone still profits from the taskings," Daisy said. "They probably don't want their access to cheap labour to dry up. And the lifelong contracts, of course. Maybe hitting that first is the best way to go after all. I must admit I was a bit disappointed when all we got today was a newspaper article."

"Don't underestimate the power of public opinion," Max said. "If you want a cause to take hold, informing people is the first step."

"What about the Elite side, Daisy?" Emery asked, still digesting what Daisy had said about the empty sleeping houses. "Any idea how many of them are still inside the wall?"

"Not really, but I don't think there are infants and young children on that side either."

§

"I would call what you were doing almost swimming," Emery said as she and Daisy walked up the hill toward the house. Max and Jonathan were still on the shore gathering some wood for the bonfire they planned on lighting after supper.

"Well, I went under, anyway. I see what you mean about the floating part when you're under water. I'll keep trying."

"I was really surprised at first when you said about there being no babies and little kids inside the wall, but the more I think about it the more sense it makes. Nobody I knew was tasked in the building that used to house the babies. It had been a while since I'd seen younger kids outside anytime. I think I just thought they were being kept inside. I knew there weren't as many Less Thans eating in our eating house as there used to be. I wonder what the population really is."

"If it's small, it won't be as hard to relocate the Less Thans, and it will be easier to find all the families they came from," Daisy added.

"Do you know if you were an infant or an older child when you were recruited?"

"I know absolutely nothing. That probably means I was an infant. But I have nowhere to start to look for my true family. I borrowed my name from F. Scott Fitzgerald."

"Who?"

"I'll tell you later."

"Where's my baby? Where's my baby? Someone has stolen the baby."

Meredith parked her cleaning cart and pulled open the door. The agitated hollering and desperate plea for her baby was a daily occurrence with number 2456, and one Meredith would do her best to quiet before Lois heard it.

"Her dose is obviously not strong enough," Lois had said two days ago when Mary had been in such a state that not even Meredith's usual charade of finding and passing something that served as a baby to her would settle her hollering. It had taken the doctor and a hypodermic needle to quiet her in that instance.

"Mary, the baby is right here." Meredith wadded up a towel and passed it to Mary in a manner one would pass a small infant. The woman quieted immediately.

"My sweet boy. You had your mama in quite a state."

The woman cuddled and kissed the pseudo infant, cooing and singing, rocking her child into an imagined sleep state. This would keep number 2456 settled for a while.

The same scenario always put number 2456 into the throes of uncontrollable panic. The baby would be missing, her conjured cradle empty. Perhaps Lois was right and a heavier medication would relieve Mary Dixon's turmoil. But as Meredith watched Mary lovingly cradling the wadded-up towel, she wondered if even drugs could quiet this woman's demons.

CHAPTER 20

Lifelong Contracts Keep Workers Trapped in Misery

Stephanie's research had uncovered five garbage, eight manufacturing, and four food-processing facilities where Less Thans were currently employed under lifelong contracts. The article shed light on the jobs being done and the life of at least one thousand released Less Thans being forced to live in compounds set up to provide free labour under the most despicable conditions.

"What do you think, Daisy? Have I shown the scope of the problem?"

"There are one thousand people trapped in lifelong contracts? From what we figure, that is a lot more than the number still left inside the wall."

"It's definitely the place to start kicking up a fuss, but the powers that be aren't going to turn over one thousand captive workers without a fight," Ky said. "People have no idea such a thing goes on right in our midst. The shit is going to hit the fan, so to speak."

"That sounds disgusting," Emery said.

"Will your editor publish it?" Max asked.

"He wasn't too keen at first," Stephanie replied. "But then I presented the fact that some of those workers are as young as twelve, and some have been in servitude for thirty years. And of course there's the compelling fact that Sherwood Dixon's son is among them. The name Sherwood Dixon still carries some weight when it comes to something being newsworthy. My editor is as interested in making money as the next person. He figures the story might sell newspapers."

"Oh, the old man's name sold newspapers, all right."

"What about your mother, Ky? Is she still living?" Emery asked.

"As far as I know. She was institutionalized after Fraser was taken and my father died. I went to live with a family friend and was never told where she was. I lost a brother, mother, and father pretty much all at once.

"It seems to me you need a family as much as Dixon does," Emery said.

After leaving Ky's place Max and the girls delivered the orders they'd brought into Rockport before driving to meet Jane for lunch.

"I've been thinking about the offer Augustus made me," Jane said a few minutes into the meal. "I would have to give up my job at the shelter, but it might be time for me to do that anyway. Getting so involved in other people's misery takes a toll, especially when I've been juggling my own. Now that I have you back in my life, Emery, I feel like maybe it's time I live a lighter, less complicated life. I could probably get a job in Ravenville."

Max took a bite of his food before speaking. "I know it might seem like I am offering jobs to anyone who comes along, but I was thinking the other day I really need a bookkeeper and office manager to run what has become quite a going concern. Might that be something you could do, Jane?"

"I was just finishing my first year of business college when I got pregnant with Ann Marie—I mean, Emery. I have a basic idea of bookkeeping. I could try."

"That would work, Mom. And Valerie is going to need some help once the new baby comes. I can't think of a better thing than having you living with us. I know Augustus would be thrilled. He still feels so badly about not knowing we were so close. He's slowing down, too. I have noticed a difference in the last few weeks. He needs as much family around as possible. I feel sorry for Ky. He has nobody. He lets on he's fine with that, but I don't think that's how he really feels."

"You'd take in all the strays, wouldn't you?" Jane said.

"What is a stray?" Emery asked.

"Any poor little animal with no home. Like me," Jane said, her voice faltering. "I'm definitely a stray. I should be providing a home for you, not the other way around."

"There are going to be lots of strays if we get the wall opened up and the lifelong contract people released," Daisy said. "We need a plan for that. We need to try to find the families who lost them and people who might we willing to take them in if their families are not found. Even Augustus's house isn't that big. We need to know exactly what we're up against."

"You're right, Daisy," Max said. "Let's see what happens after the article comes out."

"I have a network of social services I've had to access for the women and kids that have come through the shelter," Jane said. "I can speak to some of those people. We need to get the records and names so we can start looking for families."

"We don't need to do it overnight," Max cautioned. "We will figure it out."

"I just need to get Dixon out and find out how Sadie is doing. There is room at Augustus's house for them for a while, anyway."

§

Augustus leaned on the cane, waiting for the strength he needed to make it the rest of the way up the hill. He'd found the cane in the upstairs hall and it had immediately brought back the memory of his father using the hand-carved cane he'd fashioned from a piece of maple. He'd carved the face with a long flowing beard. The knob, which looked to be a comical hat atop the head, was worn and smooth. His own father had used the cane for many years and had been a younger man than Augustus was now when he'd first needed the stability the cane provided. Augustus was four years older than his father had been when he died.

Now an old man barely able to walk his beloved wood road. Where have the years gone? Augustus thought as he started his shuffle again. But this was a trek he didn't plan on giving up anytime soon.

"Mind if I come along with you?" Terrance asked.

"Not at all. But I'm slow moving. You might get tired of waiting for me."

"I don't mind walking slowly at all. It's a beautiful day and it seems to me a stroll is the best way to take in this beauty. I suppose you've seen a lot of changes in this landscape over the years."

"Yes and no. We had a few more cleared fields when I was a boy, and some of these trees have gotten bigger, but for the most part the place is the same as it's always been. Still the best place on earth as far as I'm concerned."

"We're pretty fond of it too. Valerie and I are thrilled to be able to raise our family here. It is so kind of you to let us stay."

"You're kidding, right? You are my brother's grandson and his name-sake. This place is as much yours as it is mine."

"Do you think Jane will move here?"

"I hope so. She's family too, even if she's a branch off another tree. Lots of room for us all, I figure."

"For sure," Terrance said. "I know Emery would be happy to have her mother living here. You don't think Robert Melvin will come nosing around, do you?"

"Part of me wishes he would. I promised Emery I wouldn't go looking for a fight, but believe me, if he steps on this property he'll get what's coming to him."

"I hear you, Gus. I just hope he doesn't come near. We don't need the kind of trouble his type would bring us. And there's no bringing your niece back."

"I know all about that, Terrance. There's no bringing back the ones we've lost. Did your father ever tell you about my boy Tate?"

"Yes, and as a matter of fact, that's part of the reason I caught up with you this morning. Valerie and I have been thinking, if you don't mind, and if the baby is a boy, we would like to name him Tate."

Augustus stopped and shakily leaned on the cane. He took a deep breath before speaking. "Another Tate Davidson. I'd be real pleased, Terrance, real pleased. And where more fitting to ask me than right here, the place he loved so dearly. I'm going to die a pretty happy old man."

"Don't be talking about dying. We want you around a good long time so both our boys get to know you."

"I don't know about that. I think my days might be numbered, and I think the number could be fairly small. I've lived a good life, and it might be just about time for me to head on home to see Janey and my boy."

"Don't let Emery hear you talking like that. I don't think she'd think she's had you long enough."

"We don't get the choice sometimes, Terrance."

§

Jonathan was heading back to the greenhouse when Max's truck pulled into the yard. He'd been picking squash all morning and so far had covered ten pallets with the harvest. Once they sat a while in the sun, he would start bagging them up.

"How'd you make out?" Jonathan called across the yard.

"It's going in tomorrow's paper," Daisy answered. "We'll see what happens after that. It's a start, they keep telling me."

"I know if you had your way you'd be ramming a backhoe into the wall and knocking it down, then leading the people out."

"I know you're making fun of me, but yes, something like that," Daisy said.

"Jane is going to start working here, Jonathan," Max said. "She's pretty sure she can get us on the straight and narrow and maybe this place can run like a real business. I'm ready to have a boss again. How I've kept everything together without Penny is beyond me. I suppose having so many around might force me to slop the house out a bit too. I don't have to tell you and Daisy that it needs a good cleaning."

"You're sure you're ready for that, Max?" Emery asked.

"Yes, I think I am. Your mother is going to need a car so you and she can get back and forth every day. Tomorrow I'll go see what I can find for her. Do you suppose she knows how to drive?"

"I don't know. I don't know much more about her than you do. Thank you, by the way. I really appreciate everything you are doing for me, Jonathan and Daisy, and Mom."

"I wouldn't do it if I didn't want to. Now let's stop yapping and go bag up the squash. These vegetables don't sell themselves, you know."

§

Jane emptied the dresser drawers, laying the clothes out on the narrow bed in her small room. She could probably pack all her belongings in the medium-sized suitcase Lori was lending her. She certainly didn't have much to show for the thirty-three years she'd lived. Most people by the time they were her age had a home, possessions, and a life. She would have no trouble moving her belongings into a bedroom at Uncle Augustus's home.

At least she would be with her daughter. She had a job and a future. No more running and hiding. She was returning to her safe and secure place. She could leave this place and the fear behind.

Max had mentioned her buying a car. Luckily Robert Melvin had taught her something worthwhile. He'd taught her to drive two months before she'd turned sixteen. For some reason, he thought his daughter should be able to drive him around as soon as she was of legal age. Not that Robert Melvin followed many laws.

She'd gotten her licence on the first try, and even though she'd never had a car when living on her own, she had always kept her licence up to date. She even had a few dollars saved that might be enough to purchase a half-decent used car.

§

Victoria looked carefully at each house. It was the second time the driver had slowly made his way up Winchester Street. She was sure at least it was the right street. They had tried to interest her in other options when her release was approved, but all she could think of was finding her aunt's house on Winchester Street in Rockport.

Once she was there she would decide what she would do with her freedom. As an Elite, she had several options, but for now a reunion with her aunt Janet was foremost on her mind. And then maybe the possibility of finding Jonathan. She wondered what options he had been given.

"It's the red one, I think."

"I'll park the car, Miss Victoria, and wait. Unless you want me to go up the walk with you."

"No, thanks. You can wait in the car."

Her time spent in re-training after being removed from the dining hall was a bit of a blur. She deliberately blocked out Tennyson's rebuke and the days that followed. The same kind of videos she'd seen all her life and the similar simulations were repeated over and over, stressing the fact that she was superior in every manner to a Less Than.

During it all she used the same strategy she'd relied on since her first day in the Elite Compound to counter that message. Every time a negative statement was made about a Less Than, she would bring up a memory of Jonathan and quickly dismiss the lesson the exercise was trying to impart. She would never believe her brother should be treated any differently than her, and the way she was being trained to act would never be who she was. Their parents had taught them about love and compassion and that would always be the way she would treat others. She hoped Jonathan had been able to keep the same conviction after his indoctrination.

The best she could hope for as she waited for the re-training to be complete was that she be allowed to go to her aunt's house and begin her search for Jonathan. She would display compliance and contrition if it resulted in the chance to begin her release in the same place she and her beloved brother had been separated. Hopefully her aunt would be there waiting.

Victoria rang the bell, her whole body shaking. Would she even know Aunt Janet after fifteen years? And would Aunt Janet know her?

"Victoria." The grey-haired woman embraced the girl at her door and opened it wider, motioning for her to enter. "I have waited for this day. Not that I've deserved it. Can you forgive me?"

After a few emotional minutes, Victoria walked back to the car, took out her one suitcase, and told the driver he could leave. She stood a moment, remembering the scene on this sidewalk so many years ago. She could almost hear the echo of her cries and Jonathan's comforting words. He had kept reassuring her everything would be all right. As wonderful as being here and being welcomed by her aunt was, things would not be all right until Jonathan was here too.

CHAPTER 21

VALERIE FINISHED putting the sheets on the bed in one of the small rooms on the third floor. Jane had chosen this one instead of the larger one she'd been offered.

"I don't have many possessions, and I love the view of the lake from this one," Jane said when she arrived a few minutes ago. Valerie had offered to make up the bed while Emery took her mother to the lake. With the cooler evenings and early mornings, swimming would come to an end soon, and Emery was taking advantage of every opportunity to get in the water. She was now swimming as if she'd been born knowing how.

Valerie set the pillow sham on top of the bedspread and turned to look out the window. It really was an amazing view, and the house seemed even more a home to her than it had when they'd first arrived. It was so hard to imagine the life Emery and Daisy had had inside the wall. She wouldn't blame either one of them for putting it completely out of their mind and concentrating on the future, letting go of the past. But instead, both Emery and Daisy were determined to free those still confined within the wall.

It felt somewhat selfish, but Valerie couldn't help but hope that life here would not be put in jeopardy by the actions being taken to put an end to the Establishing Compound and the terrible practice of lifelong contracts. Perhaps her worry was just brought on by hormones and the vulnerability of the third trimester. She couldn't seem to control her emotions or her anxiety. Had she been this fragile when she was carrying Zachary?

§

"Well, it made the paper," Augustus announced, walking though the kitchen door holding the morning paper. "Front page, no less. It will be pretty hard for people to miss."

Terrance passed Zachary to his wife and sat down beside Augustus so he could see the article. "Ky Dixon just called. He said he and the reporter who wrote the article were on their way here to see Emery. I called Max, and he, Jonathan, and Daisy are coming over to hear what they have to tell us. Apparently, even before the article was published her digging uncovered some startling information. Ky said it was a hornet's nest and Daisy would be all over it."

"Maybe I should call Roxanne too," Valerie added. "A lawyer's perspective might come in handy. This isn't going to be easy, you know."

"That's a good idea," Terrance said. "Looks as if this might not be a quiet Saturday after all. I better plan on feeding this crew too."

Emery and Jane walked into the kitchen. "What crew?" Emery asked.

"We're going to have a houseful," Augustus said. "Your friend's brother, the reporter, Max, Daisy, and Jonathan are all coming over. And that lawyer friend of Valerie's. I'm going to take my walk in a few minutes and get some quiet time before the crowd shows up. I'm all for stirring things up. I certainly hope when the dust settles all the poor folks caged up in the compound can be given a better life. But I'm an old man. I don't know what good I'll be to the cause. But I'm behind you, that's for sure."

Emery walked over and hugged Augustus. "Are you kidding me, Grandpa? You are the most rebellious guy I know. Remember how you could rile Ronda up just by laying on the charm and refusing to let her get to you? Your charm and your stubbornness are exactly what we need fighting beside us."

"I don't know about that, my darling. But what I do know is, you and Daisy have exactly what it takes to make a difference in the lives of each of the people caught up in that terrible system. And furthermore, I believe the time is right. I'd hate to see many more days go by before those poor people are given the chance to stand in the open air, look up at the vast sky above, and know the incredible gift freedom and choice are in our lives. You gave that back to me, Emery, and I will always be grateful until I take my last breath."

"Well, I'm going upstairs and getting this wet bathing suit off," Jane said. "When I come down, just tell me what I can do to help you, Terrance. Don't think for one minute I'm not going to pull my weight around here."

"What does *pull your weight* mean?" Emery asked.

"It means she's my sous-chef today, anyway," Terrance replied. "If we are going into battle, it won't be on empty stomachs."

§

Stephanie plopped the folder down on the kitchen table. Terrance and Jane hovered nearby, caught up in preparing, cooking, and baking a feast, judging by the smells already wafting through the room. Augustus had gone for his walk and Zachary down for a nap, but all the others, including Roxanne, were seated around the table waiting for what Stephanie had to tell them.

"I have an unbelievable amount of information in this folder. My source has provided records, documents, and more than enough to give us a place to start."

"Your source?" Max asked.

"Last night, just as I was leaving the newsroom, a woman arrived asking to speak to the person who'd been nosing around at Fenwick. My editor directed her to me. She came loaded down with more than fifty documents detailing just about every aspect of the entire Establishing Compound system. She is not willing to come forward or have her name divulged, but what she brought me certainly seems credible."

"The woman's friend was an office worker within the compound. There is a paper trail for all the dirty dealings that make the fat cats all their money," Ky added. "Her friend had been accumulating proof for several years and was about to blow the whistle. Someone got wind of it and the friend is now a lifelong employee of the Fenwick Sewerage facility. They confiscated all her files, but she had left duplicates with her friend."

"This woman had been too afraid to come forward until she got wind of me asking questions the other day," Stephanie said. "It took a bit of convincing for her to let me copy the documents."

"The network is even more impressive than I imagined. And pretty nasty too. It seems the powers in control will go to great lengths to keep it running smoothly," Ky said. "I've always had my suspicions, but in one of the documents Sherwood Dixon is referred to as a casualty, a sacrifice for the greater good. And my mother is in the Old Ones' Compound nearest the compound you guys were in. She is registered as number 2456.

"Oh my goodness, Ky," Terrance said "I remember her. She was the one who had such desperate outbursts. She was always frantically trying to find her missing baby."

"She was the woman Tabitha was told to take from the courtyard to see the doctor," Emery added. "The poor woman. That breaks my heart."

"It breaks mine too, and makes my blood boil at the same time," Ky said.

"The whole system is being run by about twenty Enforcers and attendants. They answer to the men in charge of the profit-making enterprises the Less Thans are raised to keep running. The Elite population is quite small too, compared to forty years ago when they filled that side so they could turn out a large group of people who would back up the system to serve their own interests. There is a lot here to sift through. I haven't made sense of it all yet."

"She has birth and recruitment records too," Ky said.

Daisy looked quickly toward Jonathan, who reached out to take her hand. The room went silent, somehow sensing the gravity of that announcement. She got up quickly, almost knocking her chair over, then rushed out, letting the screen door slam behind her. Jonathan got up to follow her.

"Daisy isn't her real name. Are there names listed?" Emery asked.

"No names, just numbers," Stephanie answered.

"Her number was 57. Is there anything there about number 57?" Emery asked.

Jonathan reached Daisy outside. "It's okay, Daisy," he said, wrapping his arms around her and trying to steady her shaking body.

"I don't know what I want to find out," she asked between sobs. "Do I want siblings and parents who have grieved for me, or do I want to have been taken from a single mother unable to fight for me, or a father not allowed to keep me? Or how about being completely orphaned? Is that what I want? How about I was left at a fire station or on the steps of a hospital? I made myself up. There is no such person as Daisy Buchanan. Do I want to know who I really am? Do I want to know the real story?"

Emery walked out onto the veranda. She waited until Daisy's crying stopped and gestured for her to sit on the porch swing. She passed her a piece of paper. Daisy clutched it for a few seconds before scanning it to find the information it could provide.

Number 57: Two-year-old female, father deceased, mother severely injured in automobile accident, recruitment carried out at Whitecliff Regional Hospital, status assigned: Less Than.

"We have some lunch ready," Terrance said, stepping out onto the veranda. "Do you feel like having some, Daisy?"

"Sure," Daisy answered. She walked back into the kitchen and tossed the paper onto the table in front of Stephanie.

Max looked up at Daisy and Emery. This bombardment of facts had to be difficult to hear. Part of him wished they'd left well enough alone. He knew how easy that was to do. Keep yourself busy enough and you can keep yourself from feeling the unpleasant stuff. Plant more vegetables and keep on keeping on.

"Augustus should be back down by now," Emery said, breaking Max's train of thought. "I'm going to go up the wood road to meet him."

"Want me to come with you?" Max asked.

"No. That's okay. Enjoy your lunch. We'll be right down. Leave us some."

At each turn in the road, Emery expected to see Augustus walking toward her. The breeze that had been cooler first thing this morning had died down and the sun was warm. Augustus would be thirsty in this heat. She should have grabbed some water to take to him.

A squirrel scurried across the trail, startling Emery and causing her to stop for a moment. She listened to the silence. Something kept her from hollering out to Augustus. The silence somehow seemed sacred. She thought of Ranger bounding up the trail. *I'm going to talk to Grandpa about getting another dog.*

Emery was almost to the top of the hill before a feeling of foreboding grabbed her. Her breathing accelerated a bit and she sped up turning onto the trail that led to the park. The name she called out came as a hoarse whisper. "Augustus."

She saw the bright red plaid of his shirt first. It seemed out of place against the earth tones of the forest floor. He didn't move as she called out his name again, moving toward the still and prostrate figure lying on the ground, his face fully looking toward the sky. She knew before kneeling there would be no breath.

Tears came but no sound accompanied them. She felt a plethora of emotion, but no sadness. Augustus had made the trek, and almost as if he'd chosen to, he'd lain down beside Tate, gazed up into the sky, and took his leave. Emery wanted to simply lie beside him, allowing him this resting place. She could not yet leave his side to go for the others, and her heart broke to think of them lifting him from this place.

"I will return to my woods and there I will die."

Jane was the first one to get to them. She'd became alarmed when Emery and Augustus had not returned after everyone had eaten and the lunch dishes were done and put away. She had led the trail of people hiking up the hill to find what was keeping Emery and Augustus so long.

"I couldn't leave him," Emery said as her mother knelt down beside her. "I couldn't leave him."

Max drove his truck up quite close to where Emery had found Augustus. Max, Ky, and Terrance lifted Augustus and laid him on the blanket Valerie had spread out on the floor of the box.

"I'm going to ride down with him," Emery said.

Daisy got into the box and sat beside Emery. "We both will. Max will drive slowly, Emery. He will be fine."

When they got down to the house, the coroner's car was there. Emery held on to Augustus's hand before getting out from beside him.

"It's only your body leaving, Grandpa. You are still up in the park with Tate. You will always be there. And I will always be here to make sure no one forgets him or you."

§

Emery had been in the lake for a long time before Valerie swam out to talk to her. She'd been vaguely aware of the bustle of activity in the yard. Several cars had come and gone. Ky and Stephanie had left. Max and Jonathan had driven away, coming back a while later. John and Selma had arrived. The Millers had come over. How had word of Augustus's death spread so quickly?

"Are you okay, Em?" Valerie asked.

"I don't know what I am. Part of me knows he is at peace. He went exactly the way he wanted to go. I feel happy that I played a part in getting him back home so he could do that. I keep thinking of him dying in the small, stark room in the compound compared to seeing him on the forest floor. He was looking up at the sky when he passed, and I am so happy for that. But how do I go on without him? This is his home, not mine. How can we be here without him?"

"I know. But think about it from his point of view. He brought you here. He embraced us when he found us here. He invited your mother back here. He saw us all being here as a gift he could give. Would he want any of us to reject his gift?"

"No, he wouldn't. But it is too much. I don't know how I'll get through any of it without Augustus to help me. I want to take up the fight to get Dixon released. I want to work toward ending the system and freeing the Less Thans and the Elites. But how will I ever find the strength I'll need without Augustus?"

Emery began swimming toward the shore. She began sobbing as she stood to leave the lake. Valerie rushed to her side as Emery collapsed.

Jane stood waiting for the sobbing to quiet before walking up and sitting down beside Valerie and Emery.

"Terrance has some supper ready if you think you can eat, Emery," Jane said.

"Let's go up and try, Emery," Valerie said. "You don't have to do it all today, and you don't have to do any of it alone. We are all here for you. We're here for each other."

They made their way back up to the house and inside. Emery sat down at the kitchen table. She could tell that Daisy had been crying. Of course she wasn't the only one suffering this loss.

"I wanted to leave him there," Emery said. "Part of me wanted to just walk away and not disturb him. I felt so calm, but when I started swimming I realized how angry I was. I felt angry at him for leaving me, for choosing Tate and leaving me alone. I just got him. I never had a grandpa, and it wasn't long enough."

Terrance set a plate of food down in front of Emery. "Funny, Augustus and I had a talk yesterday about just that; not having someone long enough. When I think of that talk now it seems to me he knew the end was near for him. He said we don't get the choice sometimes. I don't think he chose to leave us, but I do think he chose the place. I think he knew his time was coming."

"I loved him too," Daisy said. "Part of me was so jealous of you, Emery, because you got to be the one to bring him home and you got to be the one to call him Grandpa."

Emery stood up and walked over to Daisy. She leaned down and attempted to hug her. Daisy stood up to better receive the embrace. "You gave me the courage, Daisy. He loved you too. He was as much your Grandpa as mine and I know he'd be thrilled for you to call him that. He was so happy you got to come here."

"He was one of a kind, that's for sure," Jonathan said. "There's going to be lots of tears in the next few days."

"We'll give him a good send off and then we'll do what he would want us to do, which is get on with living," Terrance said. "He gave us a perfect example of someone who did just that."

CHAPTER 22

THE NEXT WEEK WAS A TREADMILL of funeral arrangements, the funeral, and the coming to terms with Augustus really being gone. With all this, Emery was somewhat oblivious to the firestorm brewing since the release of the newspaper article. She'd heard talk of the protests that had been held outside the facilities Stephanie had revealed in her article and was aware that there were petitions being passed around calling for the Establishing Compound to close.

"Look at this," Terrance said, passing the morning newspaper to Emery.

Three Hundred Gather Outside Fenwick Mountain Landfill

"I wonder if Dixon even knows people are protesting," Emery said.

Daisy and Jonathan walked into the kitchen. "There's another protest today," Daisy said. "Max is coming with us. Your mom and Terrance are going too. Are you coming, Emery? It's supposed to be even bigger than yesterday's."

"The newspaper says the police are prepared to disperse further protests," Emery said. "It says they were not prepared yesterday but future protestors can expect to be challenged. The authorities will maintain a perimeter and protestors will not be allowed on the property."

"That doesn't matter. We have to increase the numbers and keep up the protest. People are taking notice."

"Ky and Stephanie are meeting us there," Jonathan added. "She is going to have a camera crew and Ky is going to demand that he be allowed to see his brother."

"He doesn't think they are just going to let Dixon out to talk to him, do they?" Emery asked. "I hope all this attention isn't making things harder for him or putting him in danger. We know how they sometimes handle trouble. Look at what they tried to do to you, Daisy."

"That was an act of one person, and no one even knew I was in there. I had no one to fight for me. Dixon has family, someone willing to go out on a limb for him."

"How do you even know sayings like that?" Emery asked. "Augustus explained that one to me a few weeks ago. He had said he should have gone *out on a limb* for Joanna. Limbs break. Branches can only hold so much weight. I hope we're not rocking the boat for Dixon."

"See, you're catching on to all the foolish ways we talk," Terrance said. "Boats and trees and taking risks. It seems to me it is about time we all do that. I saw my share of how things were handled in the compound. But I'm not telling you those horror stories right now. We need to stay optimistic and work together. The ball is rolling, and there won't be any stopping it."

"I am going," Emery answered loudly. "In the last few days all I've wanted to do was stay right here. Part of me thinks if I stay here I'll always have Augustus with me. But I know I can't keep the rest of the world out just by staying here, and staying here won't protect me from the evil out there. They came right into the yard and took Augustus. I had so much fight in me before Augustus died, and I worried it was gone, but I keep thinking about Dixon. I am going, if for no other reason than the hope that they will let Ky speak to him and maybe I will get a glimpse of him. And maybe he will get a glimpse of me and at least he will know we are trying to free him."

Valerie walked into the kitchen. "The middle of a protest is no place for a pregnant woman in her last trimester, but I will be with you in spirit. Terrance is picking John and Selma up to go as well. This whole thing has been blown wide open. Roxanne has several clients petitioning to have their children released from the Establishing Compound. People are finally stepping up to put an end to it."

"I've got lunches packed," Terrance added. "I don't figure there's anywhere close by the Fenwick facility to buy food."

"We're not going on a picnic," Daisy said. "Do you think the people inside get decent food?"

"I don't know, Daisy," Terrance replied. "But it won't hurt to have some nourishment to keep our strength up."

"Just humour him, Daisy," Valerie said. "Feeding others is what Terrance does."

"Nothing wrong with that," Max said as he walked through the kitchen door. "I put a few hampers of apples in the trunk of Jane's car. We can eat them, Daisy, or you can pass them out for people to eat or throw at the barricades. There are already hundreds of people gathering outside the Fenwick Mountain facility, as well as protests beginning at the other facilities mentioned in Stephanie's article, and crowds gathering outside the Establishing Compound. News crews from all over the country are gathering as well. Change is coming."

§

Even with all the talk on the drive about yesterday's protest, Emery was overwhelmed by the throngs of people she could see in the distance as they approached the Fenwick Mountain Landfill. Vehicles lined the road, and it was obvious they wouldn't be driving much closer. One lane of the narrow road was congested with people walking from their parked vehicles. Signs and banners were waving above the heads of the crowd. *Free the Garbage Pickers*, one sign said, bringing tears to Emery's eyes.

"They're people, not garbage pickers," Emery said. "What a stupid sign."

"We know that, Em," Max said. "It's just a sign. It won't matter what the signs say once they close the facility down. Each person trapped within those walls will get the justice they deserve."

Jane pulled the car into a gap in the line of vehicles. "We'll park here and walk to get closer. Stephanie said her news crew was going to try to get right up to the main entrance with Ky, hoping to get someone out to speak to them."

The noise level got louder and the crowd thicker as they walked. The chant Emery could hear above the cacophony held the words "garbage pickers." She wondered if Dixon could hear the chant from inside. Was he standing at the conveyor belt, processing garbage with the echo of the protests outside? Did he imagine her being in the crowd? Was he hopeful and optimistic or was this throng just making life inside more difficult?

"Free my friend Dixon," Emery began in a whisper, then with increasing volume. "Free my friend Dixon."

§

Dixon sensed the tension long before he'd gotten on the line this morning. The short drive from the barracks to the facility had been blocked by a crowd that had apparently slept there all night. The driver cursed as he weaved slowly through the tents and sprawled bodies on the ground.

"I should just run over a couple of protesters. That would wake them up and get them moving. It's likely to get worse when the sun comes up. The word is that some mucky-muck is looking to spring his brother. Wouldn't want to be that kid. Chances are the bosses will give him the exact opposite of what his bigshot brother and the news crew coming with him are asking for. Can't think they'll just let the Dixon kid traipse out of here to freedom. They're starting to sweat bullets, though, I'll tell you. Maybe you losers will get sprung because of this mess after all. I know I'd be happy with a better assignment. You idiots stink!"

§

"We're not going to get anywhere near the entrance," Daisy said, interrupting Emery's chant. "Let's find a spot to sit and maybe just one of us can worm our way through the crowd."

"You're not going anywhere by yourself, Daisy," Jonathan said. "Do you see that line of police? They won't hesitate to round up whoever they can get their hands on if the crowd gets unruly. I'm not letting you in the middle of that."

"What are we here for if it's not to make a fuss?" Daisy asked.

"This is a fuss already, Daisy," Max said. "These crowds can't be ignored. I think Jonathan is right. We are making a difference just by being here. You don't need to get yourself rounded up and thrown back inside the wall. We need you out here with us."

Daisy grumbled and sat down. "Fine, I'll stay put for now."

The hot afternoon sun was quieting the crowd somewhat. There had been a few flare-ups, and Emery was aware of the mounting tension. Terrance passed out food to several people. Selma had scouted out the closest porta-potty, which apparently had been provided by a local businessman. Returning from her last trip to it, she'd said the atmosphere was somewhat like a carnival.

"What is a carnival?" Emery asked.

"A fair, a celebration of some special occasion," Selma replied. "That probably doesn't help much. The people seem quite festive, upbeat, and good-humoured. Even the police seem pretty calm right now. They just separated the crowd to let the news crew up to the entrance and didn't try to prevent protesters from following them."

"Is anyone coming with me?" Emery asked.

Emery, Daisy, and Jonathan zigzagged through the crowd, getting within a few feet of where Stephanie and Ky were standing. A cameraman and a woman holding a microphone were talking to Ky, but the noise of the crowd prevented Emery from hearing what was being said.

"I'm going closer," Emery said. "I want Ky to see me so if he gets to talk to Dixon he can tell him I'm here."

Daisy took Emery's hand and pushed through the crowd. "Free Fraser Dixon, Free Fraser Dixon!" Daisy began to chant as loudly as she could.

Ky Dixon turned his head toward them and smiled.

"He saw us," Daisy said before yelling her chant again. Several people around them joined in. "Free Fraser Dixon. Free Fraser Dixon."

The metal door opened and a large man stepped out, walking toward Ky, Stephanie, and the film crew. He grabbed Ky's arm, pulling him toward the building. With his other arm he reached out to block anyone else from following them. The door opened and the big man led Ky into the building, the door snapping shut behind them. Emery rushed to Stephanie's side.

"What if they don't let him back out?" Emery cried.

"We have just broadcasted him entering the building," Stephanie said. "It is being covered live on all the news outlets. They aren't going to keep him in there. We just need to stand our ground and wait, Emery. Let's keep up the chant."

§

Dixon had been taken from his station and led into a small office. He'd been pushed roughly through the door and told to sit before the door closed behind him and he heard the click of the lock. He rose to his feet and looked out the small barred window. For the first time he could see the front step of the building he'd been coming to for weeks. He had always been ushered through the underground entrance in the shadows of early morning and taken out the same way in the evening darkness.

He was surprised by the landscaped grounds still evident even with the huge crowd of protesters. The front had no doubt been designed to make the facility look attractive and pleasant and not reflect the misery and grimness on the inside. The small window was also providing him the first glimpse of daylight and the outside world he'd had since they'd brought him here. His eyes blurred with tears as he tried to focus on the sights he was seeing. He wiped his eyes and focused.

Emery. Were his eyes playing tricks on him or could he really see Emery standing between a man holding a large camera and a woman holding a microphone with the letters *CRC News*?

§

"We are speaking to Emery Davidson, a friend of the young man whose release is now being negotiated by his brother, local business owner and author Kyle Dixon, son of the late Sherwood Dixon. Emery, can you tell us how you know Fraser Dixon?"

Emery had almost refused when just seconds ago the reporter had asked her for an interview. Her first fear was being recognized by someone who could return her to the Establishing Compound. Then she thought quickly of Robert Melvin. He wouldn't have any idea what she looked like and her name would not be a clue to him. She would say her last name was Davidson. She muttered a quick request to Augustus under her breath, asking for him to give her the courage she needed before giving her consent.

"I only knew him as Dixon. We have been friends all our lives. We were both taken from our families and raised in the Establishing Compound. His placement at this facility was my fault. He was punished when I escaped."

§

Dixon sat back down quickly when he heard the office door being unlocked. Two men he had never seen before stepped into the small room. The older of the two sat behind the desk and motioned for the other to sit.

"Well, you've caused quite a ruckus, Mr. Dixon."

Dixon looked up at the man speaking and quickly realized he was not referring to him.

"I suppose now with all this news coverage you think I'll just hand your brother over and let you two walk out the front door."

"I can't really see what choice you have. These crowds have gathered in part as a protest to free my brother, but we both know it's gotten much bigger than that. Your facility and the deplorable conditions your workers are trapped in have been exposed, and just letting one worker go is not going to be enough."

"That is not up to me. I am only the manager here. I don't recruit the workers and I only maintain a system that people with a lot more power than me have put in place. Now, I have brothers, Mr. Dixon, and I do sympathize with you."

Ky turned to Dixon and extended his hand. "Hello. I am Kyle. I'm your big brother. I'm sorry it took me so long to come for you."

Tears were streaming down Ky's cheeks, and Dixon fumbled with words to reply to his emotion. What do you say to a person you didn't even know existed—no problem? It's okay? Don't worry about it? Nice to meet you? Please get me the hell out of here?

"Do you know Emery? I think I saw her outside in that crowd."

"Yes. Emery is out there. She's the one who came to find me to tell me you were in here."

Now Dixon was crying too. He had gotten so good at keeping his despair at bay, only letting the late-night hours provide any release. Could it be possible this nightmare was coming to an end?

"I think we are between a rock and a hard place here, Mr. Dixon."

"That might be your take on it, but neither you nor I caused the rock or the hard place. I don't see you have much choice about what happens next. You can't keep me in here much longer without the crowd getting riled up. If I walk through the door with my little brother, it will go a long way toward working this mess out. Your superiors are going to have to face up to what is going on here. Even if they don't release all the workers right away, they are going to have to show willingness to improve the working conditions before these protests stop. Now that people know about lifelong contracts, they are soon going to be a thing of the past."

"I haven't spoken to my supervisors yet. I don't expect they'll drive up and confront this crowd. From what I know, most of them want to keep as far away from this as they can. It might surprise you who the people are who run this place. They're not stepping in anytime soon to expose themselves."

"So doesn't it seem that it's up to you whether or not I get to leave with my brother this afternoon? Surely you can see it's the right thing to do."

"My staff is a bit afraid that letting one worker go might cause the others to rise up."

Dixon began to tremble, thinking of the workers he'd stood silently beside for weeks. He hadn't had any contact with them, didn't know their names, had barely had a second to look at any of them. The main methods of insuring compliance were the anonymity and constant toil. If the line stopped and the workers were given a chance to interact, what would the result be? Did any of them have the energy to fight, to speak up for themselves and for each other?

"Hit the main breaker and tell them the power is out," Dixon said. "Tell them break time will be longer and supper meal will be served early. Then transport them back to the barracks as if everything was normal and leave them in their quarters until you can figure out the best plan. I don't think any of them are strong enough to put up much of a fight just yet if it's your staff's safety you're worried about. Gradually give them back their dignity and maybe things will go peacefully."

"Do you think you could get the protest to disperse if we promised to do what your brother just suggested?"

"I can try," Ky answered. "If Fraser and I walk out of here the chances are better to do that than if I walk out alone or don't come out at all.

"My name is Fraser?"

§

Max and Terrance made their way to where Emery, Daisy, and Jonathan were standing. Word that Ky had been taken into the building and that a friend of Dixon's had been interviewed for live TV had spread through the crowd.

"He's been inside for over an hour," Daisy said.

"The door is opening," someone hollered.

The same large man who had taken Ky in now stood in the doorway. Looking worried that the crowd might swarm him, he stepped back and pushed Ky and Fraser onto the granite steps. The metal door clanged shut. Loud cheers resounded. Someone handed Ky a megaphone and he raised it to his mouth in an attempt to quiet the cheering. The camera-man moved closer, ready to film the exit and document the interchange.

"My brother, Fraser Dixon, is being released from this facility. His lifelong contract ends today. Production within these walls has been temporarily halted and workers will be transported back to their bar-racks shortly. Please allow the vehicles to move without interference. Negotiations for humane working conditions have been promised. Management is asking for an end to this protest to allow for these negoti-ations to unfold in a peaceful manner."

Ky waited for the loud outcry to quiet before continuing.

"I would not be asking for this if I did not believe in the possibility of these negotiations. I will be the first to call for the protests to resume if I do not see the negotiations proceeding and if lifelong contracts are not quickly abolished and workers bound by these contracts released. Now, please allow my brother and me to leave the premises unencumbered. We have many years to make up for. Please give us some privacy and respect my brother's need to come to terms with the ordeal he has been through. Thank you."

Ky lowered the megaphone. Stephanie squeezed through the crowd to get to the steps. The cameraman was close behind her, and she motioned for him to back away. She walked up and embraced Ky. Hand in hand, they walked down the stairs, Dixon close behind them. Emery stood frozen, wanting so badly to rush to Dixon.

The crowd cheered as Ky, Stephanie, and Dixon wove slowly through. Emery stood in place, knowing she wouldn't follow them. What could she possibly say to her friend to make up for the misery simply knowing her had caused him?

"Aren't you going to go talk to him?" Daisy asked.

"No. I am going to do what Ky asked. Give him his privacy and the time he needs to process what he's been through."

"It's not your fault, you know," Daisy said. "You didn't send him here and you had no part in creating the evil system that has the power to run such a place as this. I'm sure he doesn't blame you and would be happy to see that you are all right."

"Not today," Emery said, abruptly walking in the opposite direction. "Let's find the others and go home."

§

Fraser slid into the back seat of Stephanie's car. Walking through the huge crowd, he had continually scanned the faces, looking for Emery. In the seconds of realization that he was being let out the door with his brother, he had imagined her waiting at the front of the crowd. He so badly wanted to reassure her that he wasn't blaming her. He'd been so proud of the courage she'd shown by escaping. Sadie had seemed so angry, but he'd never felt that anger; only regret that he hadn't had the courage to do the same. He hadn't even had the courage to fail the dining test. Tonka had been right about him. Dimwitted and useless. Why would Emery want to greet a loser like him?

§

The first glimpse of his face flashed so quickly on the screen Victoria wasn't even sure it was him, but as the camera focused on the girl being interviewed, she could see Jonathan standing directly behind. She had always wondered if she'd recognize her brother all these years later, but she was sure it was him. It was the same face she'd kept so close in her memory; he'd just gotten older and taller. Her heart beat rapidly as she called her aunt to come see.

"It's Jonathan on the news," Victoria hollered. "Come see him, Aunt Janet. Quick, come see him."

The cameraman had scanned the crowd before returning to the people surrounding the girl. Jonathan had taken the hand of the girl standing beside him and moved closer to the girl who had been interviewed, who seemed overcome with emotion. The crowd erupted and the camera zeroed in on the front door of the Fenwick facility.

"He's okay, Aunt Janet, and he's on the outside. I need to find him."

§

The waters of the lake were getting colder, and Emery dreaded the day she was unable to make herself run in. The leaves on the trees were quickly showing the colour Augustus had described to her. She had been so sure she'd see those colours with Augustus. She was sure he would be with her as the leaves fell and the bare branches waited for the first snow. She was sure ice covering Flossie's pond would be something they would witness together.

Emery dove under, wondering for a split second if she had the will to resurface. She was filled with sadness, fear, hopelessness, guilt, and regret. This glorious place that seemed so full of promise only spoke of defeat right now. The joy she took from gliding through this water seemed hollow and vacant.

Emery poked her head up and saw her mother walking down the hill toward her. She was not wearing a bathing suit but was carrying two of the folding lawn chairs from off the veranda. Jane set them down on the sand when she got to the shoreline and began carrying some firewood from the pile Terrance kept supplied for bonfires.

"I'm building a fire, Em. It's been a crazy few weeks, and we need some alone time. Some alone time with some sticky, gooey roasted marshmallows."

Emery left the water, wrapping herself in the warmth of her towel and allowing the comfort and release her mother was offering.

§

Ky held a pile of folded clothes and a large towel.

"Take your time. There's lots of hot water. I think my clothes will fit you for now. We can shop for some of your own tomorrow. Stephanie's gone out for Chinese. We'll eat when you get out of the shower."

"Chinese?" Fraser asked.

"Chinese food. Oh, I suppose you've never had it before."

"Are our parents alive?" Fraser asked. This question had been on the tip of his tongue on the drive, but he'd been unable to give voice to it. He hadn't actually uttered a word on the way to Ky's place but had let the constant chatter of Stephanie and the occasional reply from Ky fill the time and space of the strange journey. He'd been overwhelmed by the sights, not even being able to process all that moved quickly by him.

"Our mother is, but I haven't seen her for a very long time. She is in the Old Ones' Compound near the Establishing Compound you grew up in. I don't think she has her faculties. She won't know us, but we'll go see her as soon as possible. We'll get her out of that place. Right now the compound doesn't allow visitors, but things are about to change there too."

Fraser took the clothes from his brother without saying anything more. He was anxious to get the grimy uniform off. It had become a familiar odour to him, but he was sure his brother could smell the rank garbage and was being too polite to comment on it.

"Can I throw these coveralls away?" Fraser asked.

"Yes, of course you can. I'll get you a garbage bag to put them in."

"A garbage bag..." Fraser's voice trailed off as he entered the bathroom and shut the door. Some garbage bags were easier to slit open than others. Each exposed bag held its own secrets. Its own vile rotting contents that had to be pawed through. Would the bag he stuffed his disgusting garments into be opened and processed by someone he had worked beside, or would there indeed be negotiations freeing the workers who had shared his misery?

Fraser stripped naked, leaving his soiled garments in a pile on the floor. He stepped into the white porcelain tub. He turned the tap far over to the red side, stepped under the shower spout, and let the hot water flow over him. No tears came, only a deep feeling of relief and gratitude.

CHAPTER 23

THE DAY BACK AT WORK was a welcome distraction for Emery. The gardens were pretty much all harvested. Jonathan was circling one of the large plots on the tractor finishing up the final ploughing, turning the empty vines of the squash patch into the earth to break down and decompose, enriching the ground for next year's planting. Emery was pulling the rows of corn stalks and bundling them.

"Hard to believe people will pay good money for corn stalks and bales of straw," Max said as he hopped out of the cab of his truck. He grabbed some of the bundled stalks, loading them in the back. "If people want to deck out their back porches and lawns with such things, who am I to argue? We've got a good crop of pumpkins this year, too."

Daisy and Jane were a field over picking the last of that pumpkin crop.

"Did you want to come to Rockport with me this afternoon?" Max asked.

"I could, I suppose, unless you want me to keep working here."

"Thought we might swing by Ky's place after our deliveries."

Emery had not said anything to anyone about Dixon in the week that had passed. There had been non-stop news about the Fenwick Mountain Landfill. The workers had all been released to other jobs after a spokesman for the Landfill had announced the abolition of lifelong contracts. Private contractors were taking over the management of the garbage disposal facility and big changes were already taking place in the other businesses.

Twenty families had come forward demanding the release of their relatives, which was pressuring the closing of the compound. Daisy had met with Roxanne and Stephanie, and all she could talk about were the plans being made to relocate the residents of the Establishing Compound. It looked as if it was really going to happen.

Emery was interested but couldn't bring herself to join in when the others got caught up in the details. She had made herself go to the protest because of Dixon, who she guessed she should probably start thinking of as Fraser. But until going to work this morning she hadn't left home since returning that day. She'd spent her free moments walking up the wood road, as it was now too late for swimming. There had even been frost covering the ground this morning and the leaves had started falling.

"Well, what do you think, Emery?" Max asked.

"I don't know," Emery answered.

"I am sure he would like to see you, Em."

"What makes you think that?"

"Put yourself in his place. Think about how you might feel if it had happened the other way around. Would you be blaming him if he'd been the one to escape and you'd been punished for knowing him?"

"No, I guess not."

"Wouldn't you be anxious to see someone who had cared enough to find a way to free you?"

"Yeah, I guess so."

"I know so. You'd want your friend to come see you. There has been enough suffering. And you did not cause Fraser's imprisonment. Don't you think they took enough away from the two of you? Are you going to let them take any more? People are being freed because of your courage, Emery. It's time you let yourself off the hook. Think of what Augustus would say."

"Augustus told me one time that suffering can make us soft or hard, open or closed. He said soft isn't weak and open isn't a bad way to be. He said we have a choice of what we do when we lose someone or something that we love."

"Exactly. I was a long time learning that lesson after Penny died. You helped me learn it, you know."

"What did I do?"

"You got me to face up to how closed I had become. You brought a lot into my life. Daisy and Jonathan and your mother. Your mother is a pretty special woman, you know. I'm really happy to have you both in my life. Real happy. Is that soft enough for you?"

Max turned away with the armload of stalks he was carrying. The break in his voice alerted Emery to something she'd just begun to notice. It was beginning to occur to her that her mother got all choked up when she talked about Max too.

"Is there something going on between you and Mom?"

"Maybe. What would you think if there was?"

"Oh my goodness. I just finally realized that Daisy and Jonathan were a couple and now you and Mom. And what about Ky and Stephanie? They seem pretty lovey-dovey."

"What can I say? And that's not the reason I think you should go see Fraser. You guys have been good friends for a long time. I bet he's just waiting for you to come see him. I expect he's had lots of adjusting to do in these last few days. Think about how hard it was for you at first, and you weren't living under the conditions he was."

"Okay, I'll go into Rockport with you and I'll go see Fraser. Now let me get the rest of these stalks picked and bundled."

§

"You don't have to worry about getting a job right away, Fraser," Ky said. "You can help out in the cafe for a while and decide what you want to do."

"Living a regular life and being a regular person is exactly what I want to do, and getting a job is part of that. The guy at the grocery store said I could start today doing some sweeping, bringing the carts in, and stocking shelves. Not a dream job, but believe me, after digging through garbage all day it sounds perfect."

"Was he okay with the fact you don't have a social security number? Ms. Jarvis has filed to get your birth records so she can get all your paperwork, but it will probably take a few weeks. It's shocking how they just wiped out the existence of the recruits they took. What a mess it's going to be to straighten out the identities of all those poor kids still stuck inside the wall."

"The guy said he'd pay me under the table until my records come. I don't know what that means exactly, but I start work this morning."

§

Emery was carrying the last bundle of corn stalks to the display by the front door of the store when she looked in the large plate-glass window and saw him with his back to her. She quickly, without second-guessing herself, knocked on the glass. The smile that spread over her friend's face erased all the trepidation she'd felt on the drive to Rockport.

"Nice apron, Dix," Emery said as they embraced.

"Yeah, you should have seen what I had to wear on my last job."

"I did see it."

"And I see you're not wearing Establishing Compound clothes anymore. I've got blue jeans too," Fraser said, lifting his Laidlaw Grocers apron. "They're Ky's actually, but they fit me. Lot of changes, eh?"

"I'm so sorry you got sent to Fenwick, Dixon."

"It wasn't your fault, Em, and by the way my name is Fraser. Come to find out Dixon was my last name. What about you? Did you find out who you really were?"

"Yes, as a matter of fact my real name is Ann Marie, but I decided to keep Emery, and I go by the last name Davidson now. The man I escaped with from the Old Ones' Compound gave me his last name. I wasn't keen on claiming my own. My real grandfather turned me in. They took me from my mother when I was four."

"They took me when I was born. Apparently my father died shortly afterwards and my mother was just steps away from me most of my life. I haven't been able to go see her yet. It is nice having a brother, though. What about you. Any siblings?"

"Not yet, but who knows. It seems my mother might have another shot at a family. So, you're working here?"

"Yeah, just started today. Got to carry my weight."

"I see you're catching on to the crazy way they talk out here. How can you carry your own weight?"

"It is crazy, isn't it, but believe me, no matter how weird it is out here, I will never take the freedom for granted. I really thought I was stuck in that hellhole for the rest of my life. Thank you, by the way. Ky said you hunted him down and wouldn't take no for an answer."

"Daisy and I did. Do you remember Daisy? She's the girl who failed her dining test the day I took mine. She and Jonathan escaped from the infirmary inside the wall. I saw them here in Rockport one day. There is just so much to tell you."

"Well, you don't have to tell me everything right now. I better get back to work. Does Ky know where you live?"

"Yes."

"Good, we'll come visit. We'll get caught up then."

"Good. Any idea where Sadie is? I've been worried about her."

"I don't know. I don't think they sent her to Fenwick. I never saw her if they did."

"They're going to release everyone inside the wall soon. Maybe we can help her find her family when that happens."

"Maybe we can. I'll see you real soon, Emery."

She smiled as she walked back to the truck, with one quick look over her shoulder to the young man wheeling the line of shopping carts back toward the store.

"Well, I guess we don't have to stop at Ky's place now, do we?" Max asked as he walked toward Emery.

"No, I guess not," Emery answered.

"I found this hanging on the bulletin board just inside the door," Max said, passing Emery a sheet of paper. A blurry photograph taken from a television screen had been cropped, enlarged, and photocopied. The words under the photo were *Looking for my brother. Please contact 483-368-2395.* "Look at the face circled. It's Jonathan, don't you think?" Max added.

"That's outside the steps at Fenwick. That's my arm, I think. Oh, it's Jonathan all right. Victoria must be looking for him."

§

Emery's heart raced a bit when they drove into the yard and saw several vehicles. There hadn't been this much activity since the day Augustus died. A couple of worrisome thoughts came to mind before she went to the possibility that Valerie might be having the baby. She jumped from Max's truck and bounded toward the back door.

Valerie was standing at the sink and did not appear to be in labour.

Roxanne, Daisy, Jane, and three people Emery did not know were seated around the kitchen table.

"Come sit down, Em," Jane said. "We're working out some final plans. Roxanne just got word that they are closing the Establishing Compound one week from tomorrow. We need to contact all the families who have inquired about relatives that may be inside. The plan is to register the families and try to match as many residents to families as they are released. We also have to have accommodations for the kids we can't find family for right away. Valerie suggested we bring four or five of them here. We've found several other temporary placements.

"It's really happening, Emery," Daisy said. "A lot of families have come forward. Some of the kids will be old enough to look after themselves if we just provide housing for them until they can find jobs. It's really happening. All those kids will soon be free."

Emery began shaking. She felt a panic rising up from her feet to the top of her head. Something felt so intrusive, so threatening, and she couldn't begin to describe the fear she felt. She ran from the room, bounding up the stairs two at a time as if a vicious animal were at her heels.

The narrow door pulled hard before creaking open just wide enough for Emery to squeeze through out onto the uneven floor of the small balcony attached near the very top of the peaked roof. Worry that it wouldn't hold her weight seemed needless as she pictured herself being able to fly upward if it collapsed. Fly upward like Augustus had done in his dream before he had taken flight permanently, when he chose to lie on the forest floor and gaze at the sky.

Sobs were racking Emery's body when her mother poked her head out the door's opening, touching her daughter's arm but not speaking.

What if leading them here takes this all away? Emery thought. *What if they come to get us, to get us all? They came right into the yard and took Augustus away. They shut him up so he couldn't see the sky, so he couldn't fly, so he couldn't get to where Tate waited for him, so he couldn't bear witness to the fact that Janey and Tate had lived. What if they take it all away?*

Terrance arrived beside Jane and put one foot onto the balcony floor. He too touched Emery's arm, attempting to pull her back into the attic room. "It's okay, Emery. It's okay."

Emery heard Terrance's voice. She felt the gentle tug on her arm and knew she couldn't pull away from it. She put a hand on the shaky railing, knowing if she were to try to move from the range of Terrance's touch, the wobbly railing might let go. Her fear of falling swallowed her confidence in flying. There was no flight unless, as Augustus had explained, it was in manmade aviation vehicles. The flight of dreams was in the mind, in the spirit, but not in reality. If not flight, would the fall take away the pain she was feeling, the deep and frightening pain of facing what was coming without Augustus here to guide her?

"Come inside, Em," Terrance pleaded.

Emery turned toward his voice and saw an even stronger plea in her mother's eyes. She took hold of the door jamb and squeezed back through the narrow opening of the small door.

The conversation around the table was loud and engaged and no one seemed to notice Emery re-enter the kitchen. She walked right past them, her mother following closely behind. Terrance embraced Valerie while at the same time lifting Zachary from the floor. The small family joined Emery and Jane on the veranda.

"We're in this together, Emery," Terrance said. "You don't think I'd stand by and do anything I thought would put my family in danger. The power behind the wall has collapsed. Several people have even been arrested. The mayor of Rockport has resigned. Public opinion has switched from compliance to rage. Roxanne has already filed a class-action lawsuit representing ten families whose children were taken from them. The most shocking news is that Trip McDonald, the owner of a string of hotels and possibly the richest man in this county, has been charged with the murders of Sherwood Dixon and Harrison Crawford. McDonald was thought to be a shoe-in for federal government. He has pulled the wool over people's eyes for years, convincing them he was a philanthropist and a force for social change. He was the brains behind the whole system and has made millions of dollars from it."

"Do you want to know something really comical?" Jane said. "My father called Roxanne yesterday having heard about the class-action suit, with a long, heartfelt story about his granddaughter being snatched out of his arms."

"What did she say to him?"

"The words she used shouldn't be said in front of Zachary," Valerie said. "Zac is repeating everything we say these days, and him casually calling a stranger what Roxanne called your grandfather would be embarrassing."

Daisy walked out onto the veranda. "Emery, I didn't get a chance to tell you, we found a man who claims to be Sadie's father. She has a brother and a sister who can't wait to meet her. The records we have say she hasn't been released yet. Isn't it wonderful that Sadie has a family?"

"Speaking of family," Emery said, taking the paper from her pocket and unfolding it, "Max found this on a bulletin board at Laidlaw Grocers. We figure it's Victoria looking for Jonathan."

Daisy looked closely at the blurry picture. "It's Jonathan in the picture, all right. Victoria must have seen him on the news and taken a picture of the TV screen. He will be thrilled. I'm going right in to call him and give him her number."

The door closed before Emery spoke. "I hope Daisy finds some family through all this."

"Roxanne says that next week's release has been widely announced on television, radio, and social media. She expects crowds of people will show up looking for family members. Maybe there will be someone looking for Daisy."

"If not, she's got us, you know," Terrance said. "We're a mixed-up bunch and there is always room for one more. I hope she already knows that."

"I'm sure she does," Jane said.

"What about the Old Ones?" Emery said. "We got Dixon out and shut down Fenwick, the Establishing Compound is being closed and all that other stuff Terrance said is great, but what about the Old Ones? Augustus was lucky enough to escape, but the others are still in there. And as long as Lois and people like her run the compound, all the Old Ones are just numbers. Vera, Thomas, Vivie, Doris, Dixon's mother Mary, Evelyn, Stanley, and George. They're being forgotten in all this while we celebrate the other victories. We need to do something to free the Old Ones."

"You're right, Emery," Terrance said. "How about you and I go there tomorrow and see if they'll let us in? The upset to the system may have already brought about changes in the compound. If they won't let us in, maybe we can get Stephanie to take a news crew there. It worked last time."

CHAPTER 24

AFTER A RESTLESS NIGHT Emery was up, dressed, and waiting in Terrance's car. How had she gotten so caught up in everything and not given any thought to the people she'd cared for during her short time in the Old Ones' Compound? She had been so wrapped up in her newfound freedom and the euphoria of finding a home and family she'd completely forgotten about the sad and lonely lives of the ones they left behind. And while mourning Augustus she'd disregarded the most important lesson he'd taught her: You must bear witness to those who came before you. Who was bearing witness to the Old Ones made invisible by numbers and an uncaring system that hid them away until they died?

It had been Lois's plan to have every resident bedridden and unresponsive. *"Just put the pillow over my head and hold it till I stop breathing, the day you see that I can't. It's bad enough in this terrible place, but when I can't even get myself around, I don't want to be here."* What state would they find Vivie in if they let them inside this morning?

Walking up to the front door Emery thought of the times she'd followed Rigley up these steps. Would the code she remembered open the front door? If not, would the intercom bring someone to open the door for her and Terrance? Would they be allowed to go inside?

Before they reached the top step the metal door opened, and surprisingly it was Meredith standing in the doorway.

"Emery. It's so good to see you. Come in. You didn't bring Augustus with you. I can understand why he might not want to come back here. It's a different place, though, I can tell you. All the former staff is gone. I have my own office and the title 'Resident Coordinator,' no less. Come in so we can catch up. I assume you and Augustus didn't get caught? There was a big kerfuffle when you left, let me tell you. Lots going on, isn't there? I hear the Establishing Compound is shutting down. You're Terrance aren't you? Worked here for a bit, didn't you?"

Emery and Terrance followed Meredith into a small office. Listening to Meredith's chatter was doing nothing to calm the turmoil in Emery's head and the dread knowing that when her talking stopped she would have to tell her that Augustus was dead. But at least it seemed as if Lois must be gone.

"Yes," Terrance replied, the first break in Meredith's dialogue. "Augustus was my great-uncle."

"Was?" Meredith replied, turning her head toward Emery, who was leaning against the wall.

"He died, Meredith. But he got home first and died up in the woods he loved so much."

Meredith crossed the room and enfolded Emery in her arms. "Oh, I'm so sorry, but so glad he didn't die in here. A few folks passed shortly after Lois began her regiment of heavy medication. I am so glad he escaped before all that."

"Is Vivie still alive?" Emery asked frantically. "She wasn't one of them, was she?"

"No, God love her. As soon as Dr. Dickinson returned and stopped the medication she rallied and seems better than ever. I'll take you to her in a few minutes. But first let me catch you up. You remember Norman and Tabitha? Norman is the manager and Tabitha is in charge of the kitchen. We serve real food now. You won't even know the place."

Emery listened as Meredith rattled off all the changes. Emery was interested, of course, but all she really cared about was seeing Vivie and the others she hoped had survived Lois's time as manager.

"You remember Mary, of course? Her sons are coming to take her home later today. I am so happy for her. Dr. Dickinson thinks that once she gets settled in a home with family around, the quality of her life and her mental state will improve greatly. That's what all these folks need, family, which is why in my new role I have implemented a program where families adopt an Old One. You were my inspiration for that, Emery."

"Do you mind if I go see Vivie?"

"No, go ahead. I'll take Terrance for a tour while you go see her. She's in room 34. That's all we number now, the rooms, not the people."

Emery noticed many changes on her walk from Meredith's office to the hall where room 34 was. She would take her time later and really take in the qualities she could already see making this a welcoming facility, not the stark institution it had been.

Vivie turned her head as Emery walked in, and her smile was everything Emery had hoped for.

"Top of the morning to you. Unless these old eyes are failing me, it's sweet Emery I see. I'm not dreaming, am I?"

"No, you are not, Vivie. You look wide awake and amazing to me."

"A sight for sore eyes, my husband used to say."

After a lovely visit with Vivie, Emery found Thomas sitting out in the courtyard.

"They're feeding us real food," Thomas declared. "That Tabitha is a wonder. The first thing she did was get rid of those ghastly tubes. We sit at tables now and have real food served to us. We even get to request our favourites now and again. Now, the Irish stew isn't quite as good as my Marion used to make, but it's a damn sight better than that lumpy slop they used to feed us."

Walking into the activity room, Emery could see several residents and staff engaged in various activities. There was laughter and conversation. Emery walked over and sat beside Winona.

"Vera's gone," Winona said. "I'm quite sure they overmedicated some of the folks, Vera being one. Thank God Dr. Dickinson came and put a stop to that. But unfortunately it was too late for some of them. None of us know our time, but it's a sin is what it is. How is that old codger, Augustus? He got out just in time. Hope he got a chance to go back to that house he was always talking about."

"He did, Winona, he sure did."

Emery walked back into Meredith's office. Walking past Augustus's old room was emotional, but she felt such joy knowing she'd played a part in getting him out. She felt no need to go into that room and realized just how badly she wanted to get back home. Now that she knew the Old Ones were being cared for properly, she could prepare herself for the day next week when the Establishing Compound gate opened. She would do whatever she needed to do to help with that. Right now she was anxious to tell Daisy about all the changes.

"We're getting a new name," Meredith said. "The sign has been ordered and is being erected next month. You should come for the unveiling of the Augustus Davidson Senior's Care Home. A fitting name, don't you think?"

§

On Fraser's first visit Emery wasted no time showing him all the highlights of the property and had even led him up the track and into the field where she'd been recruited. She'd tried so hard to keep her emotions under wraps, but when Fraser gave in to his emotion, they'd stood for a long time, crying and hugging and eventually laughing uncontrollably before finally reaching a calm and comfortable balance of both.

"Do you remember how hard the three of us would laugh and how quickly we had to pull ourselves together when a Keeper would approach?" Fraser asked. "Sadie was always better at stopping than we were. It's a wonder we weren't thrown in the tank."

"Terrance told me a friend of his died in the tank," Emery said. "The tank was actually a hole dug in the ground with a concrete cover."

"Really? I always thought it was a made-up thing, a lie the Keepers just used to scare us."

"No, it was real. Terrance said his friend Ryan was always breaking the rules, always getting in trouble, and that Tonka especially hated him. He threw Ryan in the tank one day when he laughed at Tonka. Tonka grabbed Ryan and shook him. Ryan fought back and was dragged to the tank."

"And he died?"

"Tonka left him there for four days. When the cover was lifted Ryan was dead. He'd run out of air, Terrance said."

"That is terrible. And obviously Tonka didn't get in trouble."

"Tonka lied and said that Ryan had escaped. They covered up the hatch, leaving Ryan's body where it was. Terrance doesn't think they dug another, but just kept using the tank as a threat." "How can someone be so evil and heartless?"

Fraser asked. "When I was at Fenwick I would look at the drivers who transported me and the staff who ran the line and wonder if they were evil. Most of them weren't, you know; they were just doing their jobs. But once in a while there'd be one you knew right away was enjoying the power they had over another human being."

"And what about the men who started the whole Establishing system, and the men who sanctioned the rounding up of Old Ones?" Emery asked. "What kind of evil is that?"

"I think there is greed and then there is pure evil that is driven by something even worse than greed. My own father was one of those evil men. What does that say about me?"

"Augustus once told me he believed some people allow the hurt and fear in their lives to calcify, to harden and crush all the good. A heart of stone, he called it. He said not many were born that way but far too many ended up in that condition."

"Ky and I found a really nice home for Mom close to the cafe. There are only five residents, and the lady who runs it is amazing. Mom has already made huge improvements. She's a tough woman, that's for sure, after all she's been through. It makes me so angry. It could have been so different."

"That's what I keep thinking when my hatred for my grandfather creeps into my thoughts. I push it right out, remembering that Augustus said we have a choice in what we do with hurt. It's the only choice we ever truly have in life."

"It sounds like Augustus was a very wise man."

"The wisest," Emery answered as she began walking back to the big white house.

§

"As if this day wasn't going to be exciting enough," Terrance said when Emery came downstairs for breakfast. "Valerie's labour has begun. We've called the midwife and Valerie is trying to rest before it gets worse. Selma and Dad are coming to take Zachary for the night. I won't be going to the wall, of course, and with any luck and mercy the baby will have come by the time you guys get back."

A few minutes later, the kitchen was full and noisy. Emery wondered how in the world Valerie was getting any rest upstairs. Selma and John were busy getting Zachary's things packed while Terrance finished feeding him his breakfast. Jane was taking her fifth batch of muffins out of the oven and packing food to take to the wall. Max, Jonathan, and Daisy had arrived.

"Mom, are you hoping to feed everyone there?"

"Not a chance I'd be able to do that, but at least I can offer the volunteers a bite to eat. Roxanne has about twenty people lined up to register and process the kids and families. Then there's the bus drivers. Four buses are going to be on site. We're still not entirely sure of the numbers we'll be dealing with. But they have told us that there is no one under the age of eight."

"Victoria and Aunt Janet are going to be there to help," Jonathan said.

"I thought you might have stayed the night at your sister's," Terrance said. "You must have had a lot of catching up to do."

"We both realized in the first few minutes no amount of catching up was going to make up for the years we've spent apart. As for staying, we were both really happy to see each other but exhausted and overwhelmed by the reunion. We don't have to rush anything. We have our futures together, and right now that's all that matters. And I felt so bad for my aunt. She has blamed herself for not fighting harder to keep us. She wants to be there today for the other families who probably feel the same way."

Two hours later Emery got out of Max's truck and made her way through the crowd to where Stephanie and Roxanne were sitting at a table from which two lines of anxious people snaked. Emery came closer to hear the conversation taking place between a man and Roxanne.

"Your daughter's friend has just arrived, Mr. Hamilton. She will be able to tell you whatever you need to know about Sadie, as they were in the same house growing up. I am sure she would be willing to stay with you and point your daughter out when she comes through the gate."

The tall man turned toward Emery and she was immediately confronted with the same steely stare she'd seen on Sadie's face so many times. The brown eyes and thick brow set in the same determined manner sent shivers down Emery's back. Sadie had always appeared stoic and unflustered, immovable, always giving the impression she was unaffected by emotion or sentimentality. Emery noticed that same resolve in the man standing before her but could see the single tear that had just dropped onto his cheek telling something else entirely.

"Your daughter was my best friend and she is amazing. She is strong and fearless. She made the best of the life we were given and never gave in to self-pity or anger. She never got caught up in wanting more, but I know she will be overjoyed that you are here to receive her."

Roxanne had risen from her place at the table and was standing beside Emery, leaning in to speak into her ear. "Did Daisy come with you?" she asked.

"No, she's coming right behind me though. Jonathan borrowed Mom's car and was picking his sister and aunt up. Did you hear he found his sister?"

"Yes, Valerie told me last night. Speaking of Val, is there a baby yet?"

"No, but Terrance said he would text Max right away when it comes. Why were you looking for Daisy?"

"I think her mother is here. Remember in the records it said she was recruited from Whitecliff Regional hospital, after her mother had been severely injured in an accident?"

Roxanne pointed and it took a second for Emery to see who it was she was pointing to. Several feet away Emery saw a blond woman in a wheelchair. The woman with her began pushing the wheelchair toward them.

"She has been here all night, her friend told us," Roxanne said. "She is frantic to find her daughter. Her daughter's name is Lily, she told me, and she described everything just the way the records state. Her husband died and she was paralysed in the accident. She'd been unconscious for three days and when she finally woke, her misery and suffering were compounded by the fact her two-year-old daughter had been taken. She was years recovering physically and emotionally from the trauma. She's a fighter, I'll tell you. She and her friend camped out so that she would be sure to be here when the gate opens. She is afraid, however, that given her daughter's age she might have already been released and be God knows where by now. I didn't tell her about Daisy."

"She just picked the wrong flower," Emery cried. "She chose her own name from a book she stole from the library. Maybe part of her knew she had the name of a flower and *Daisy* seemed so right. I am going to stay with Mr. Hamilton so I can point out Sadie to him, but I want to be with Daisy when you introduce her to her mother."

"We'll just take our time and do justice to all the reunions, Emery," Roxanne said. "This is more amazing than I thought possible when we began this fight. Maybe good does prevail over evil."

At that moment the loud cry of a woman echoed above the cacophony of the crowd and for a split second everyone went silent. The woman rushed toward the first child to walk out through the gate.

"Hilary!"

The mother and child clutched hands and danced in a circle with an audible swish, even though the possibility of hearing it with all the noise around seemed unlikely. The sound of joy, of relief, of victory, and of something being put right was what the crowd could hear.

Daisy pushed up beside Emery, having rushed in to see the reunion. "This is what matters in all we did," Daisy said. "It was for little girls like this we fought the fight and took the risks we took. It was for the children, for the mothers and the fathers, for the families. We did this for Hilary."

"For Hilary, for Sadie, for all the lifelong contract workers, for Vivie and Thomas and the other Old Ones and for *you*," Emery said, hugging her friend quickly before taking her arm and leading her through the crowd.

Epilogue

I am now an Old One, having seen ninety-five first snows. I have been a young Ann Marie with no last name; number 38; Emery, Emery Davidson, and then Emery Davidson Dixon. I have birthed six children and had the privilege of being present each day they walked this earth and have not felt the pain of burying them too soon.

I have lived all my years of freedom within the walls of this large white house on whose wide veranda I now sit; this house that welcomed me so long ago. I have watched all those with whom I have shared this home grow and age; Fraser, our children, Valerie and Terrance, Zachary, Tate, and Gus, always feeling there was room for at least one more.

I have buried Augustus, my mother, and my dear Max, and have stood at the graves of Terrance and Valerie, encircled in the love of their three precious boys. I have been graced with one sister and one brother and those who were as siblings to me, my darling Daisy, Sadie, Jonathan, and Victoria.

In my years I have seen evil and greed, blemishes to the world and the society of decent people; some as vile as the time of recruitment and establishing, and some less. I walked to freedom and watched as others walked to freedom from within the walls that contained me for ten first snows.

The day the east gate opened, as the cover peeled back and faces gazed toward the sky, is a day etched deeply in my mind and spirit. I hear their words as if the bevy of voices were recorded and I with just a push of a button can call up the sound. In all I've lived I've been most thankful for that moment and have not forgotten their joy.

I have been loved and have loved and I have borne witness to those who walked before me. I only hope those I leave behind will do me the same honour.

Tears fill my eyes as I look skyward.

Acknowledgements

To bear witness to those who came before; I acknowledge our beloved son Zachary, my dear parents and also our dear friend Paul who understood to his core the value of the great outdoors.

Thanks to Terrilee Bulger and Acorn Press. Thanks again to Penelope Jackson who embraced this book and guided me in her gentle, intuitive manner. Thanks Matt Reid for the great cover. Thanks to Cassandra Aragonez for designing the book's interior. As always thanks to Burton, Meg, Cody, Emma, Paige, Chapin, Brianne, Anthony, Skyler, Bella, Caleb and Jenna.

SUSAN WHITE

Susan White's previous books include *The Year Mrs. Montague Cried,* winner of the Ann Connor Brimer Excellence in Children's Literature award and *The Memory Chair,* a Hackmatack book pick and a shortlisted title for the Ann Connor Brimer. Two of her novels, *Headliner* and *Fear of Drowning* were shortlisted for the New Brunswick Book Award Mrs. Dunster's Fiction prize. When the *Hill Came Down* was released in July 2020. White finished a teaching career in 2009 devoting her time and energy to her writing. *Skyward* is White's tenth novel. She lives on the family farm on the Kingston Peninsula, New Brunswick with her husband Burton.